turnpike flameout

Also by Eric Dezenhall

Shakedown Beach

Jackie Disaster

Money Wanders

Nail 'Em! Confronting High-Profile Attacks on Celebrities and Businesses

turnpike flameout

Eric Dezenhall

Thomas Dunne Books
St. Martin's Minotaur ☨ New York

THOMAS DUNNE BOOKS.
An imprint of St. Martin's Press.

www.minotaurbooks.com

Library of Congress Cataloging-in-Publication Data

Dezenhall, Eric.
    Turnpike flameout : a novel / Eric Dezenhall.—1st ed.
        p. cm.
    ISBN 0-312-34061-3
    EAN 978-0-312-34061-2
    1. Survival after airplane accidents, shipwrecks, etc.—Fiction. 2. Public rela-tions consultants—Fiction. 3. Organized crime—Fiction. 4. Missing persons—Fiction. 5. Rock musicians—Fiction. 6. New Jersey—Fiction. I. Title.

PS3604.E94T87 2006
813'.6—dc22

                                                                            2005050402

First Edition: January 2006

10   9   8   7   6   5   4   3   2   1

For my sister, Susan

With appreciation for my friend
Budd Schulberg, the gold standard

Author's Note

I write fiction about archetypes—mob bosses, scheming tycoons, corrupt politicians, decadent rock stars. This inevitably inspires speculation about who these characters are based upon. For the record, the archetypes and plotlines in *Turnpike Flameout* are *not* based on actual people or events, just the kind of lunacy that saturates the news these days.

We live in an age in which it's no longer possible to be funny. There is nothing you can imagine, no matter how ludicrous, that will not promptly be enacted before your very eyes, probably by someone very well known.

—TOM WOLFE

book one

MEGA BOY

In the superstar world the most corrosive virus is permission.
—TINA BROWN

Prologue—Impale the Children

"Shamelessness is the lubricant of damage control."

I'm the pollster you hire when you can't win on the merits. My clients don't have merits. Case in point: The borough of Hopkins Pond, New Jersey, just fired me because I couldn't persuade their community to demand more hazardous waste burial at the KinderTots Day Care playground. They also stiffed me on eighty-three grand in polling fees. Had I done my job right, the logic goes, mommies and daddies would be clamoring for jagged, blood-caked syringes from Lenape Hospital to be entombed on the playground where their urchins played duck-duck-goose every day.

While I'm not responsible for the defeated bill that would have boosted the dumping of nasties in Hopkins Pond, I am responsible for my career choice. I am a rare breed of pollster: unlike the cavalcade of academicians and smartass pundits who make their livings passing judgment on how those of us in the line of fire screwed up, I am hired to actually impact the direction of events that are already heading south.

When you've got a case that has no merits, the trick is to speak with force about things you know nothing about. Shamelessness is the lubricant of damage control. My latest feat was getting a priapic nimrod elected to the United States Senate by creating a campaign for his effete *opponent* that riled New Jersey voters. I conjured up thirty-second TV spots ostensibly supporting our blueblood adversary (I showed the poor bastard playing squash) using slogans such as STRENGTH THROUGH PANACHE and LEADERSHIP WITH ÉLAN. As one Camden bricklayer said in a focus group, "I dunno what it means, but I can't stand that guy's ass."

Sometimes, as in the campaign to impale preschoolers with contaminated hypodermics, nothing works, even if it's damned brilliant. The work I did this summer for the rocker Turnpike Bobby Chin was spectacular (forgive my swagger), but it ended in abject disaster. As depressed as I am about his immolation, I feel compelled to confess to how I almost pulled it off even if I'll be accused of spinning. Which is what I do.

I used to pride myself on my lack of shame, but after a quarter-century in the spin racket, I've come to feel as if a balloon payment of compunction is due. After enduring the occupational hazards of a renegade pollster—my debacles have been showcased at Princeton, my successes go unsigned—I had the good fortune to begin slowing down. I had no remaining fuse for getting fired, blamed, and stiffed on invoices; traveling to the outhouses of America on prop planes; subsisting on vending-machine cuisine; cloaking my improvisational hucksterism in the chin-scratching respectability of "public opinion research"; and enduring media exposés placed by enemies that inevitably contained footnotes about my gangland lineage.

These days, I took only cases that I either believed in, or paid very well. Still, getting rooked for eighty-three grand was a problem because I had subcontractors to pay.

Raised in Atlantic City, I had lived in the Washington D.C. area for sixteen years after graduating from college. I knew I had to leave Washington when more and more of the advertisements in the real estate section of the *Post* described homes for sale as being "just minutes from the White House." As if you'd have to get there REAL

FAST. This grandiose posturing sent me over the edge, the way a couple that's been married for twenty years finally decide to get divorced because they hate the way each other chew. I had worked in President Reagan's White House when I was in my twenties, and did not need to be reminded that my proximity to the big time was in the distant past.

The main reason why I moved my wife, Edie, and our kids back to South Jersey a few years ago was because Edie's dad had hip replacement surgery, and hadn't healed as quickly as we would have hoped. Edie wanted to be near her parents as they aged. I, having lost my parents as a little boy only to be raised on the lam by my grandfather the mobster, understood the need to nest. We moved into a cottage on the grounds of my in-laws' farm in Cowtown, about forty miles inland. My business, Jonah Price Eastman & Associates (the "associates" were a laptop and cell phone), could be operated from anywhere. I began to teach a course in Postmodern Deceit at Rowan University a few days a week during the school year, taking on the occasional corporate assignment or speech, and enjoying—more than I ever imagined— raising my family.

As a compulsion, I compile my Big Theories on life, which I record in a diary that will probably be worth nothing someday. Nevertheless, I share them with my students when the opportunity presents itself, which I always make sure that it does.

I came up with my Big Theory on terrorism while watching TV at a bar overlooking the Margate beach: *Terrorism works because everybody needs it to work.* The terrorists need to terrorize, the public needs a vessel in which to pour its free-floating anxieties, and the news media need to fill a geometrically expanding universe of time and space with something.

Since the blockbuster of September 11, 2001, the Armageddon industry had been predicting that the next big U.S. terrorist strike would come via private aircraft on an important date at a significant place. So it was that two F/A-18 Hornet jets from Maguire Air Force Base in South Jersey were commanded aloft when a Gulfstream V approached the twin Liberty Place towers in Center City, Philadelphia. The very spectacle of stray jets and twin towers in the city of our nation's founding swung the lens of the global media to the Pine Barrens—those haunted woodlands and birthplace of the Jersey Devil comprising one-fourth of our state—where the aircraft appeared to be heading on a jubilant Independence Day about two hours before the evening news.

I was on the beach with my children, Ricky, seven, and Lily, five. I liked to watch them play in the water, but I rarely went in. Not one of life's big enjoyers, I preferred playing scout. Chief Brody in *Jaws*. As the kids attempted to bury each other in the wet sand, I read a special edition of *Philly!* magazine, which ran a feature on the "Top 100 Philadelphia Bar Mitzvahs." (According to the feature, Jared Shandelman of Ardmore "won" with his parents' rental of Veterans Stadium—*and* the entire offensive line of the Philadelphia Eagles—for his affair. The giant Torah scroll unraveling from the goalposts was a nice touch, I thought.)

Lily emerged from a sandy hole she had dug for herself and announced, "God needs me to have a Coke or some-ping." Never a man to provoke the Old Testament, the three of us walked toward the indoor-outdoor bar to fulfill the Almighty's will.

As we approached the bar, I noticed a crowd slowly migrating toward a television that was suspended from one of those fake palm trees indigenous to the Jersey Shore habitat. As I ordered our sodas, KBRO-TV in Philadelphia broke in with the wobbly footage of the Gulfstream V tickling the towers of Liberty Place. The aircraft vanished behind one tower.

God, no.

But there was no sound. A primal groan of relief could be heard around the bar as the plane emerged from the shadow in between the buildings, and whispered across the Delaware River into South Jersey. The news talent, a fossilized local hack named Al Just, Lord of the Furrowed Brow: "We must take pains to underscore that at the present time, we have no evidence that, in fact, we are confronting . . . an act of terrorism on America's birthday."

Bless Al's heart. He had managed to inject the flashpoint words into the region's bloodstream: EVIDENCE. FACT. TERRORISM. AMERICA.

"Is it the bad people again?" Lily asked. A 9/11 reference.

"Nobody knows yet," I said, self-satisfied with deliberation.

"I just know it's the bad people," Lily decided. Ricky studied me for cues of affirmation, having long ago accepted that the Drama Queen would reach the most hysterical conclusion available. I winked at him.

Within minutes, the Liberty Place vaudeville had bounced from local KBRO to global Fox News and CNN. By the time we finished our drinks, Fox News had secured data from the tail number of the aircraft. The plane did not, in all likelihood, belong to a terrorist. In fact, it was entirely possible that something even more culturally seismic was happening:

The plane belonged to a celebrity, and a cranberry farmer in Tabernacle had called KBRO to report an engine flameout, then a fireball in the Pine Barrens.

Over the Edge

"He's a guy who . . . had a little moment."

I took the kids back to the beach house we rented for the summer and continued watching the news. Whenever something huge happens in the news, I take it personally. Edie thinks that I have a latent delusion that I'm somehow involved. She may be on to something.

I was sweating. Even though the house had air conditioning, it wasn't on. Why? Here's why: Edie's and my greatest marital issue is climate control. I'm always hot, she's always cold. The resolution: We are both always uncomfortable.

"If I ever cheat on you, Ede, it won't be for sex," I said.

"What will it be for?" Edie asked from the kitchen counter, where she was stirring a pot of tortellini.

"Air conditioning. I'll just meet some chick at a motel and blast the window unit. Fully clothed. All I want from a woman is Freon."

"How long are you going to watch that sewage?" The only thing Edie hated more than air conditioning was celebrity news. I had married the last earth mother, who wanted a happy home, not a star on the Hollywood Walk of Fame. I thanked God for Edie regularly because while most women would have made the socially appropriate claim to have shared her land-based ambitions, an increasing number secretly defined happiness as a photo spread in *InStyle* magazine. The husband in this scenario was Hugh Jackman.

"Until they find a body charred beyond recognition," I answered. Helicopters were filming search crews milling about like ants. The gratuitously circling helicopters were accompanied by authoritative statements about how the helicopters were, in fact, circling. I watched this in the same spirit that I used to stare at photos of grotesquely deformed tribespersons from Botswana in a library book despite, or perhaps because, doing so gave me nightmares.

"Can't stand not being in the middle of the action, huh, danger boy?" Edie inquired.

"Doesn't look like I could do much at this point," I said as uniformed men picked up pieces of airplane debris on the screen. "God, it's hard to believe . . . Turnpike Bobby Chin—lunchmeat."

"Why do you care?"

"Edie, I worked with him once a hundred years ago. He's Mega Boy."

"He's *not* Mega Boy, he's a guy who . . . had a little moment." Edie appeared royal when she said this. Tall, slim, and doe-eyed, she was not a child of excessive privilege, but had an innate caste that was especially intriguing because she was one-quarter Lenape Indian.

Prior to his second coming in rock and roll, Turnpike Bobby Chin, the music world's maestro of self-destruction, had been a 1970s television child actor who had portrayed a kid superhero called Mega Boy. Raised in Brigantine, just north of Atlantic City, the only child of a Chinese father and Wonder Bread–white mother, Bobby was allegedly born in the kitchen of Skinny D'Amato's 500 Club, where his mother was a dancer or something. Mega Boy dealt with schoolyard injustices in the coolest way: He beat the crap out of his tormentors with his martial arts skills, usually in front of a girl he liked. My young life's ambition in a nutshell.

For a fleeting moment Bobby had become Jersey's second-favorite rocker after Springsteen. Turnpike Bobby's last album, *Turnpike Immortal,* had hit triple platinum two decades ago, displacing Ronald Reagan's second inauguration to the number-two story in the *South Jersey Probe.* Bobby, like Sinatra, defied gravity and had a comeback during the 1980s that was bigger than his first incarnation as a mini-thespian. Just prior to his rebirth, he had added the prefix "Turnpike" to his name to underscore that he was no longer the adorable urchin with the dusty brown bowl haircut.

Turnpike Bobby Chin, circa 1984, was a big-haired, leopard-skin-wearing, lip-glossed pop rocker who had a jones for setting musical instruments ablaze. After he lit up a young woman in his Terre Haute audience (she barely survived), venues attempted to ban the pyrotechnic element of Bobby's show. Bobby objected, citing his freedom to protest in the manner of his choosing, which caused the arena people to capitulate, lest the ACLU start riding them. No one was ever quite clear about what Bobby's arson was protesting in support of or against.

"He's an icon," I argued with Edie. "You can't take that away from him."

"No, *you* can't take that away from him. I just did. There's a twisted little part of you that's awed by these Hollywood cretins."

"Now that's not true."

It was totally true.

Edie vanished upstairs in response to the pleas of an unidentified child whose wet bathing suit was reportedly "caught in the crack." I'd remain here to mourn Turnpike Bobby who was "probably grated on impact like parmesan," according to a jaunty airline safety pundit.

As I watched the helicopters circling above Turnpike Bobby's wreckage like vultures, I thought of something my grandfather Mickey told me in the late 1980s.

"Things usually end up going where they're headed," Mickey griped, knowing full well the Feds, dressed up like tourists, were looking down on us from the roof of the Sea Froth Condominium on Buffalo Avenue. Nominally the bell captain of the Golden Prospect Hotel and Casino, my grandfather hadn't been under FBI surveillance because of his luggage-handling skills.

Mickey liberated this little pearl as we sat on a bench watching a man we recognized as one of his casino's cabaret crooners—who was hauling ass *in reverse*—spill over the steel railing where the Boardwalk ended in Ventnor. Mickey's remark didn't make sense to me at first, to be honest, but it did today, as I considered the tragedy of Turnpike Bobby unfolding on the television screen before me.

The rollerblading lounge singer had worn wraparound sunglasses and radio earphones, kissing off the existence of his surroundings. Mickey and I, of course, had an advantage over the Flying Schmuck because we had lived "down the shore" for much of our lives, and knew where the Boardwalk ended. Who knew where the rollerblader hailed from originally? There was something beautiful about the guy's spastic flight. It was justice encapsulated, the world working how it was supposed to work.

"So there you go, Jonah," Mickey said as the singer flew through the air, his medieval footwear scraping the clouds and his hands flailing about as he wrestled with the great metaphysical questions.

I thought about asking Mickey why he hadn't warned the man, but he had already addressed the outcome's inevitability. He clearly understood something that I had not. At the time, I wrote it off to my grandfather's long-standing contempt for entertainers—he discouraged me from befriending them in the strongest terms—but now I wondered if perhaps there wasn't some deeper wisdom at work.

———

A s the TV blared the hushed cadences of macabre sensation, my cell phone rang to the tune of "Born to Run": "Yo," I said.

"It's me, the practitioner. Are you watching this?" the dogged but feminine voice asked. Cindi Handler, the Delaware Valley's most relentless public relations "practitioner." Cindi overused this term to ridicule the Public Relations Society of America's futile crusade to have its dues-paying members taken seriously as professionals.

"Yes."

"I may need you," Cindi said, agitated. She was always agitated.

"Need me for what?"

"I was hired to handle the PR for Bobby's homecoming event, if you can believe that."

"You did a hell of a job, Cin."

"Fuck off, Jonah. I meant that I was handling the PR for Bobby's greatest-hits concert he was going to do in A.C. tomorrow."

"Well, kiddo, it's force majeure. Fame's a killer. What can you do?"

"I can't explain now."

"What's to explain, Cin? It is what it is."

"Are you home tonight?"

Awesomest Hits

"He's played out, Jonah."

I didn't have much experience with show business. Nevertheless, my years with major politicians eventually taught me how catastrophic success could be a lethal riddle. It was one you had to see close up in order to to appreciate the physics of its devastation, like Atlantic City herself. At a distance, when the summer sun melted like cherry Italian water ice over Kansas, my hometown drew you in like Miss America. Close up in the daylight, however, you could see the sores around her mouth, and you couldn't imagine what had attracted you in the first place. Then you'd see her again at night and conjure up the femme fatale you so badly needed her to be.

Atlantic City was doing its nightly neon dessert melt to the north. Edie and I bathed the kids. Afterward, I read to them from a book about outer space. "When a star collapses and dies, it turns into a black hole. A black hole sucks in everything around it. Nothing can escape, not even light."

Bad selection, Jonah.

"Daddy, will I get sucked into a black hole?"

"No. There are no black holes around here, Lil."

My strategic response was to give Lily so much scientific detail (totally made up) that she became bored and fell asleep. Ricky, pre-dictably, went down without a fight.

Edie and I shared the porch hammock and read, occasionally putting ourselves in danger of a mean spill. When you have little kids, you need to exploit the most trivial opportunities to be close even if it's uncomfortable.

Cindi drove in from Cherry Hill. Her attire was a modified flower child getup: hoop earrings, linen shirt and matching pants that gave off a martial arts vibe, sandals, and a turquoise necklace. She gave Edie a kiss, I made an eighth-grade–level remark about lesbianism, and Cindi and I proceeded to the concrete seawall.

Out of morbid curiosity and celebrity titillation, I wanted to hear more about Cindi's adventures with Turnpike Bobby. I had gotten her the initial gig with him years ago after he hired me to do a few public opinion surveys at the height of his popularity. Cindi had managed to keep his account at varying levels over all these years, which was bet-ter than I had done. My interest was tempered by my fear of getting drawn into another megalomaniacal vortex because I considered my-self retired from the dickhead client business. But with Bobby dead, what could she possibly need from me?

Cindi was on a perpetual diet. She was a tall, big-boned girl who had to work very hard to uphold the "big-boned" characterization versus the one that stalked her: heavy. She was not heavy, but that was due to her noble struggle. She felt, perhaps rightly, that if she eased up on her regimen, she'd turn into a Saint Bernard.

"I need to make a shitload of money and get out of flackery once and for all," Cindi began. Retirement was our favorite discussion topic. "Did you ever think about doing pro bono work?"

"What's in it for me?"

"You're a reprobate."

"Actually, I'm thinking of starting a hedge fund," I said.

"Really, Jonah?"

"Yeah. I need new hedges. Care to contribute to my fund?"

"Asshole," Cindi concluded. "What is a hedge fund, anyway?"

"No clue. There's a whole world out there filled with opportunities I don't understand and technologies I can't operate. It's like looking at *Playboy* magazine when you're fifteen—lotsa cool stuff to see, but you're on your own."

"Is the world getting more complicated, or are we getting stupider?"

"We're getting stupider."

"That's what I thought. Speaking of stupid, last week, I met with Bobby in L.A.," Cindi said, her bare heels gripping the concrete seawall. "I've been handling his East Coast public appearances."

"But he hadn't done anything in years," I said.

"He didn't think he had to, but he still wanted the crowds."

"I'm not clear on what Bobby was going to do in A.C."

"His third 'greatest hits' album is coming out."

"The guy has only done two albums. I thought one of those was a greatest hits collection."

"It was, Jonah. But this new one is called *Awesomest Hits*. All the same songs inserted in a different order."

"Clever."

"He was going to record a live performance in A.C. to launch *Awesomest Hits*."

"What could his people want from you now?"

"I don't know."

"Do you think he's going to fire you from beyond the grave?"

"When we met, he said he needed to do something big."

"An original album would have been nice."

"He's played out, Jonah. He didn't want to record. He just wanted to boink virgins."

"What does that mean?"

"They get delivered to him."

"You're serious? I don't want to know. Did he want anything else from you?"

"He wanted 1984. *Turnpike Immortal* sold nineteen million copies. For a week, it was outselling Springsteen's *Born in the U.S.A.* He never let anybody forget about that week."

I remembered this. There had been some controversy because the sales tally hadn't come from *Billboard,* the prestigious clearinghouse, but from a third-tier music roster called *Hits-o-Freakin'-Rama.*

"What else did you have going for him in Jersey?"

"Coordinate his live performance. Meet with some kissass sculptor who was going to unveil a statue of him on the Boardwalk."

"I'm sorry, I just don't know what kind of advice I can give you."

Cindi, the Bravado Queen, looked pale and said nothing. Did she feel guilty about Bobby's death? Did she know something she wasn't telling me? I was too tired to press.

By the time I returned to the house, Edie and the kids were asleep. I tossed aside an old *Philly!* magazine (that month's feature was the "Top 100 Bentley-Driving Gynecologists") and flicked on the news. Helicopter-mounted cameras were now filming the tops of charred trees as voiceovers made obligatory comparisons to the plane crash of John F. Kennedy Jr. a few years ago. A field beside the trees had been blasted so badly that our TV screen appeared to be showing footage of a moon landing. Turnpike Bobby, in death, would manage one more bout of resentment of Springsteen because one of The Boss's ditties being played along with the broadcast framed the whole drama better than any hack pollster could: *"This New Jersey in the morning like a lunar landscape."*

The Sneer of Defiance

"Do you know who I am?"

KBRO-TV, the region's most aggressive broadcast investigative unit, announced the discovery of two charred bodies in "shredded embers" in the Pinelands. While the talent, Al Just, took pains to note that the bodies had not been identified, he performed the Information Age's equivalent of a coroner's certification by blasting onto the screen using a machine-gun fire effect the faces of other famous musicians killed in plane crashes: Aaliyah. Stevie Ray Vaughan. Ricky Nelson. John Denver. Buddy Holly. Ritchie Valens. The Big Bopper. Buddy Clark. Ozzy Osbourne guitarist Randy Rhoades. Otis Redding. Jim Croce. Jim "Gentleman" Reeves. The Lynryrd Skynyrd bandmates Ronnie Van Zant, Steve Gaines, and Cassie Gaines. Glenn Miller.

Yes, Al, a veritable aviation/musical holocaust was upon us.

KBRO then displayed footage of Bobby Chin throughout the years, beginning with his childhood publicity photo from *Mega Boy,* featuring his trademark puppy-dog–style head tilt, with a broad and dimpled smile that begged you to say *Awwww.* Al Just went on to somberly contrast the childhood photo with Bobby's most famous adult shot. The grown-up picture, taken in the early 1980s, was essentially the inverse of the childhood version: at a concert at JFK stadium in Philly, Turnpike Bobby held his head vertically. His massive hair resembled a volcano of tar. The dimpled smile of his boyhood had been replaced with a defiant sneer, which sparked eruptions from the crowd. Just closed his report by citing a rhetorical question that had once been posed by Bobby's most pernicious journalistic stalker, Derek Plush of *Major Player* magazine: "The enduring mystery of Turnpike Bobby Chin's life is what the hell he has to be defiant about. After all, he gets everything he wants."

Many in the Delaware Valley were outraged by Just's snarky broadcast. His disrespect of an icon who had been killed "tragically" (as opposed to *merrily?*) prompted calls for his resignation. He didn't resign, he just apologized "if my words were interpreted as being insensitive." Translation: Blow me.

Impromptu vigils were held at different locations around the region. A group of Pineys—native dwellers of the South Jersey woods—placed flowers near the scene of the crash. A small group of city workers in South Philly sang Turnpike Bobby songs outside a music store on South Street. A guitarist strummed tunes from *Turnpike Immortal* on a gingerbread street in Haddonfield. MTV and VH1 dove deep into their morgues to recover the Turnpike Bobby Chin music videos that helped to launch the medium in the early 1980s. The TV shorts brought back memories of an era that I had forgotten—the pastel clothing, the confused hair, the gratuitously pouty lips as a proxy for sex appeal, and the dogma that Ronald Reagan was coming to get you.

I stuck with VH1 for a moment. The network was broadcasting a hastily cobbled together rockumentary called *The Awesomest Ride of Turnpike Bobby Chin*. A segment was winding down on Bobby's early career, memorialized by the slow camera zoom on a black-and-white photo of hemorrhagingly adorable Mega Boy, its focus culminating on his eyes. The ominous voiceover intoned, "BUT THE BOY SU-

PERHERO WAS ABOUT TO ENCOUNTER KRYPTO-
NITE . . ."

The next segment briefly covered Bobby's celebrity diaspora after
the cancellation of *Mega Boy*—stills of Bobby as a gangly teenager of
indiscriminate ethnicity and sexuality, early flirtations with rock music, anemic guest appearances on Bob Hope holiday specials, and the
final indignity: going to school with OTHER KIDS.

Finally, the broadcast arrived at Bobby at his fleeting pinnacle in
the early 1980s. The vehicle for conveying the madcap, decadent nature of Bobby's heyday was an awkwardly told shaggy dog story by
other staples of that era, David Lee Roth of Van Halen, Rick James of
"Super Freak" fame, and Ozzy Osbourne of Black Sabbath.

The interview was shot in 1984, according to the on-screen super.
Roth was the central narrator, all but gargling the camera and relegating
James and Osbourne to uncharacteristic wallflower status. Roth's hair
burgeoned like one of those lamps they sell in Spencer Gifts, where you
stick clear plastic wires in a central nucleus and they light up in ever-
shifting colors, like hair plugs. Despite the puffiness of Roth's Reagan-
era hair, his scalp belied an intangible promise of erosion that he
attempted to compensate for with a gaudy display of tongue.

As the story goes, Bobby, David Lee, Ozzy, and Rick were in Las
Vegas. They were waiting in Ceasar's Palace for Bobby, who had
slipped into the lobby bathroom, but did not come out.

Rick James, his dreadlocks swaying to the crosstalk, got in a dope-
hazed line or two, the essence of which was, "I don't know what the
!@#%* wuz goin' on."

This was apparently very funny because Roth, Osbourne, and a
youthful Bobby, who were sitting on a fuzzy white sofa recounting
the memory, howled. Osbourne, in a fit of narcissism, injected his
own recent feat: "It was around the time I got onstage and bit off the
head of a bat."

Roth could barely speak at this point, he was laughing so hard. "So it's, like, ten hours after Bobby vanished. . . . I figure the Libyans got him or something. . . . I go downstairs to pick up my limo, and a purple Caddy convertible—big 1950s fins—comes careening into the hotel's circular driveway. This B. B. King look-alike is driving the Caddy. . . . He's wearing a canary-yellow leisure suit . . . yellow hat with a big feather . . . I look . . . I look in the backseat of the car, and there's Bobby . . . eyes wide open like a zombie . . . wearing a Napoleon hat . . . leaning real stiff out the window . . . his tongue hanging out of his mouth. I think they're gonna stop, but they just keep tearing around the circular drive at fifty miles an hour . . . and this B. B. King double's yellin' 'Weeeee doggie!', the feather in his hat blowin' like crazy."

"Where did the guy take you, Bobby?" the off-camera interviewer asked.

Bobby was struggling to catch his laughing breath. "I have no [expletive deleted] clue . . . I don't remember any of it. All I know is that when I woke up in my hotel room, all my body hair was gone, my ass had been painted silver, I was wearing these huge granny panties with sand in 'em, my knees were scraped raw, and I had iguana bites all over my neck and ears. It was, like, the day that time lost."

Ozzy stuck his face back into the camera's range, adding, "It was around the time I got onstage and bit the head off a bat!"

It was Saturday, three days after the July 4 crash in the pines, and one of those beach days when the sand was so hot, it made me shed my belief that wearing little beach slippers was gay. Ricky and Lily made me carry them from the steps to the beach down to the water.

Ricky believed that the purpose of the beach was to load one's body weight in wet sand onto one's head. I didn't stop this. Lily, on the other hand, believed the purpose of the waves was to knock her down. She, like her father, saw malice where there was only nature. It was all very personal. Lily also liked to eavesdrop on the discussions of others. Today she was particularly captivated by a group of young professional women standing shin-deep in the Atlantic.

My cell phone rang, and I felt that sphincter-spasm one gets when one recognizes the phone number of a hostile party.

My favorite deadbeat technique consists of the client dragging his feet for months on payment so that six months later he can express outrage that you want to be paid for an intangible consulting service that no one even remembers. It's akin to the feeling you get when a two-hundred-dollar dinner charge shows up on your American Express bill a month after you had the meal; you're thinking, "I don't even remember what I ate, why should I have to pay for it?" This is what was happening now with the town council of Hopkins Pond, which was still smarting over the failure of my polling campaign to make the community feel better about puncturing children with discarded syringes. The mayor of Hopkins Pond, my erstwhile client, had been screening the hell out of my calls, and not taking them.

Here goes: "Good morning, Hank," I said. I owed Hank money. About twenty grand. Hank ran the focus group facility that I had used to conduct my Hopkins Pond interviews. In order to pay Hank, I needed to first be paid by my client.

"Hey again, Jonah. You know what this is about, I guess. Heard anything?"

"The last time I talked to Hopkins Pond, they were still contesting my invoice. I keep haranguing them, but I'm not getting anything. I'm hurting, too, Hank."

"Any estimate on time?"

How does never sound?

"No, no estimate. I just don't know."

"Would you call me when you hear something?"

"Of course."

"Because we really need the funds in order to process all our receivables and payroll and what not."

And now poor Hank was doing what those who have been cornholed do in these situations: believing that in the absence of progress, keeping me on the phone and using as many words as possible to describe his predicament would somehow hasten payment.

"I understand. I'm in the same boat, Hank."

"Because we've got these bills and all—"

I felt like stapling my eyelids to my feet.

"I understand, Hank."

"Because—"

I pushed the "End" button, hoping Hank would assume that my mobile phone had routinely lost its connection in the shifting winds of the beach.

A fter ten minutes of surveillance work on the young women standing in the surf, Lily approached me wearing a quizzical expression. Actually, she appeared a bit frightened.

"What is it, Lil?"

"Daddy, see those ladies over there?" *There* was pronounced *day-o.*

"Yes."

"They said they saw a vagina on a log."

"What?"

"They said they saw a vagina on a log."

"I don't understand what that means." I bit my lip because Lily doesn't like being laughed at. She took her eavesdropping very seriously.

"They saw it in New York and said it was funny."

"Are you sure that's what they said?"

"I'm not making it up, Daddy, I promise. They went to New York to play and saw a vagina on a log. How could there be one on a log without the rest of the person?"

I thought for a minute. New York. Play. Vagina on a log. Epiphany: "Lily, is it possible that they said they went to a play in New York called *The Vagina Monologues* that they thought was funny?"

"No, they saw one on a log."

Then, having lost interest in my pedestrian clarification, she fell into the shelly sand next to her brother, and proceeded to cover her auburn hair with seaweed.

"You're shitting me!" a South Philly type shrieked to a crew of friends standing a few yards behind me. Whatever was shitting the guy, it smacked of big news.

I slowly inched back toward them. "That nut job survived that crash?" South Philly said. One of his friends who was wearing radio headphones said, "Yeah, just came over the news."

About thirty miles northwest of Atlantic City, a Wisconsin camper resembling a capsized aircraft carrier screamed as she washed her hands in the Mullica River, which ran through the Pine Barrens. She thought she saw some kind of animal move in the thicket beside her. Her husband ran toward her, and noticed human hands reaching out from the brush. As the woman tried to catch her breath, her husband, a retired beat cop from Appleton, made his way over toward the object wielding a walking stick. He was momentarily startled to see the prunelike, gasping face of a wiry, middle-aged, diluted Asian man, his shoulder-length hair mimicking tentacles.

"My heavens, are you okay?" the woman asked.

After taking a deep breath, the ostensibly shaken filth-covered man said, "Do you know who I am?"

Plushian Roulette

"His stunts have gotten more audacious as his career has declined."

Evidently, such is the arrogance of the celebrity that he believes the public will be fooled by stunts that are so monumentally idiotic that a Hollywood screenwriter would be fired for even suggesting such a plot. I didn't know what Turnpike Bobby Chin was up to with his crash and resurrection, but it was clear that nobody was buying it. Virtually every news report I ran across suggested desperation as a motive. *Major Player*'s Derek Plush, who had savaged Bobby with impunity for years, initially tied himself up in rhetorical pretzels to give Bobby the benefit of the doubt: "Whatever this turns out to be, one thing is for certain: Mixed in with relief at Turnpike Bobby Chin's survival are very difficult questions about what could possibly have happened between the fireball in the Pine Barrens and the tides of the Mullica River."

I really felt sorry for Cindi. In order to control the PR damage, she would first need to understand whatever fraud Bobby was attempting to perpetrate, not to mention the mechanics of its implementation. I envisioned only a disaster that did not appear to be motivated by any strategy besides a celebration of media-age nihilism.

I did have another educated assumption: Every media circus had its clowns, and Derek Plush would likely play the fool in the Shakespearean sense as Bobby's circus came to town. The Shakespearean jester was unique in that he was a buffoon and a genius at the same time; you laughed at him during the play only to realize after the curtain closed that he was the smartest guy in the ensemble.

Plush had a fully equipped television studio in his Spruce Street townhouse. Even though *Major Player* magazine was based in New York, Plush's stranglehold on the celebrity-industrial-scandal complex was so far-reaching that the magazine allowed him to work out of his Philadelphia home, which had been retrofitted with a studio and satellite apparatus in the mid-1990s during the O. J. Simpson trial. The broadcast news media believed that a celebrity scandal story without a mordant sound bite from Plush was like a bagel without a hole. So, rather than making Plush studio-hop, they would just schedule satellite time for him to pop frantically into American living rooms without shedding his slippers.

Bald, bullet-headed, and bitchy, Plush was known for his access to the uberfamous. Nine times out of ten, he would skewer the sweetbreads of his subjects, but one time out of ten he would fawn orgasmically in the pages of *Major Player.* Entertainment industry types, preferring the risk of evisceration to oblivion, would play roulette with their careers with the prayer that they would win a Plush orgasm. Regardless of the article's content, all subjects in a game of Plushian roulette were guaranteed a huge photo spread with famed photographer Elena Molotov-Weinberg behind the lens.

The afternoon that Turnpike Bobby was found in the Pines, the airwaves were a veritable Plush-o-rama. Plush was armed with a staccato barrage of sound bites, expressing escalating skepticism about whatever alibi Bobby would eventually conjure up.

"They found two bodies charred beyond recognition, but Bobby Chin just ends up with pine needles in his briefs," Plush told the Fox News Channel, his ever-present red telephone lighting up within range of the camera. *("See how many people call* moi?*")*

"My dear Bobby-Boy has more drama queen in him than Liberace and Diana Ross combined," Plush quipped to CBS. "His stunts have gotten more audacious as his career has declined."

Plush may have been nasty, but he wasn't off base. Something wasn't right. How does one pull off a plane crash that had killed at least two people? It was one thing for Bobby to sleep suspended from bungee cords tied to a crucifix (1987), and to purchase the corpses of the house pets of world leaders for display at his Bel Air mansion (1990), but a plane crash was a big production, not just an orchestrated catharsis.

A fter dinner, I took Edie and the kids to an ice cream parlor on Ventnor Avenue. I never remembered the name of the place, only that it was next door to a slick South Jersey creature who advertised his oral-care practice using a huge glamour photo of himself (in black) with the caption:

DR. SETH MILLER
THAT'S ONE GORGEOUS ORTHODONTIST.

"That man is happy he is him," observed Ricky shrewdly.

"But he shouldn't be," Edie said. I kissed her to echo this sentiment. Edie and I were very much aligned on the subject of the local culture's penchant for undeserved self-congratulation.

In midscoop of a vanilla/Oreo cookie mix, my phone rang. Cindi. We had spoken a dozen times since Turnpike Bobby turned up earlier that day. Given her own suspicions, we didn't speculate too much on the phone about the day's events.

"He wants to meet with you," Cindi said.

"Who?"

"Bobby. He's being released from Atlantic City General Hospital, then he's going to his hotel."

"I don't get it. He survives his ordeal and he wants to meet with *me?* I didn't think he'd remember me."

"That's what his manager, Reverend Kadaborah, told me. He called me from the hotel balcony. It was really loud so I didn't hear everything very well, but I told him you'd go over."

"Did you say 'Kadaborah'?"

"Yeah. He used to be a proctologist in Pennsauken."

"And now he's Bobby's manager?"

"Uh-huh. It's complicated."

"I bet. I still don't get it."

"Please, Jonah, I'm stuck in Philly. I can't get to A.C."

"Well, I'm with my family."

"You can go to the hotel after everybody's in bed."

"Where am I going?"

There were several seconds of inappropriate silence. "The Golden Prospect."

"Why is Bobby staying *there?*"

"That's where his concert was going to be."

Click.

With big stars, there are true rumors and false rumors. As Cindi has told me during her frequent let-me-tell-you-something-about-show-business dissertations, almost all successful male stars are rumored to be gay. In fact, you're nobody in show business until you're tagged with a gay rumor, which is inevitably supported by testimony about one having a cousin who knows a hairstylist who has a lover/butt double for Colin Farrell who works in Hollywood who claims to have seen George Clooney mounting Charles Durning.

Truth is (according to Cindi), some male stars may be gay, but most are not.

Women stars are often rumored to be nymphomaniacs or dirty, as in unsanitary. Cindi insists this is true, but there's a cattiness with this one that I don't quite trust. I maintain a list of female stars that I hope will become nymphomaniacs upon meeting me, but not before.

Before going to meet Bobby, Cindi e-mailed me an article from a two-year-old story in *Major Player* magazine. A nasty piece (in the same manner that poodles are nasty), it did contain a few things that I found plausible. One was Plush's belief that Bobby was chronically enraged that he was never taken seriously as a rock star because he had been Mega Boy when he was little. This made sense. Bobby's attempt at hardass-hood by adding the prefix "Turnpike" to his name had a whiff of desperation that wasn't lost on anybody. Plush also chronicled Bobby's obsession with Bruce Springsteen, who Bobby felt was unworthy of being called "The Boss." In Bobby's mind, according to Plush, *he* was The Boss. While Bobby had an ongoing rivalry with Springsteen, no one in the solar system believed that Springsteen had a rivalry with Bobby.

The other credible Plush theory had to do with the trademark indecipherability of Bobby's lyrics. Plush believed that Bobby purposely garbled his lyrics so that they could not be ripped apart because critics had so harshly savaged his emergence in music. By singing a verse that sounded like "I put a yam in the urinal," Bobby could always claim he was a misunderstood genius who was really singing "I know I am your one and all."

As evidence of Bobby's marketing genius—something Plush didn't deny—his album sleeves never printed his lyrics. This served two purposes. One, it made people go out and buy the shrink-wrapped album hoping that the lyrics would be printed inside, which, of course they weren't. Second, it fueled endless on-air speculation about what Bobby was really saying—kind of like the charade the

Beatles were accused of pulling during the whole Paul-is-dead swindle, or what the Kingsmen did with "Louie Louie." Forty-plus years later, people are still trying to determine what the hell those guys were talking about.

No matter how one read it, being misunderstood was clearly a part of Turnpike Bobby's shtick, and while Plush was a mean bastard, he knew the celebrity pathology better than anyone working in assassination journalism.

In the Exalted Shower Stall

"The Dude hears ticking."

had first met Bobby in 1985. He came to the White House, where I was working on President Reagan's polling staff. For the photo op, the press people thought it would be neat to have other young people around the Oval Office, so I was invited to hang out and act youthful. I was twenty-two, at the top of my youthfulness game.

In the Rose Garden, Bobby sang his new single, "Let's Be Serious." His lyrics came out sounding like *"Lesbian Seagulls."* Even the President cocked his head when he heard the refrain. Afterward, Bobby and I talked for a few seconds about being from South Jersey, and he offered me a job. I didn't know what the job would have entailed, but I think he liked the idea of having a former presidential aide on his payroll. I declined, but approached his people later on when I set up my own polling firm. Bobby put me on retainer for a while. I did a few polls validating that the public thought he was "awesome."

Of all the Boardwalk hotels where Turnpike Bobby Chin could have been staying, the Golden Prospect was the one that validated my irrational sense of a divine conspiracy against me. This explained Cindi's hesitation before. My grandfather built the Golden Prospect after casino gaming was legalized. Everybody referred to it as "Mickey Price's place." Unlike the larger hotels in town, the Golden

Prospect was the last of the mob strongholds, and remained under its management until Mickey died at the millennium. Its performance arena was tiny, and I was surprised it had been chosen for Bobby's comeback concert, now aborted.

I spent my last two years of high school living with my grandparents in the hotel. This sounds glamorous, but it wasn't. Mickey abhorred displays of wealth, and his apartment was a modest two-bedroom number. He and my grandmother, Deedee, simply transferred their Eisenhower-era furniture from their house in Ventnor to the Golden Prospect. I remember Mickey proudly suggesting that some of the leftover furniture be donated to "the poor people," which prompted Deedee to suggest, "Better we should give it to some rich people, screw them a little."

Mickey, forever justifying his frugality, lectured Deedee on why we couldn't have fancy new furniture. Something about an investigation and a big deal with the Teamsters' pension. Deedee lifted up one of the worn-out sofa pillows and said, "Oh, look, Jimmy Hoffa! We were worried sick about you, Jimmy."

I didn't like being back at the Golden Prospect. It had a physiological effect on me. I'd get dizzy and depressed, as if the new life I loved with Edie and the kids wouldn't exist once I set foot inside. I studiously avoided the place so that decades of bad memories wouldn't cascade onto me.

An elderly Vietnamese man swayed on the sidewalk outside the Golden Prospect. A cheap folding table stood tenuously before him. Three shrink-wrapped mini-umbrellas rested sadly on the table next to a ripped piece of cardboard that had the words "BLOWOUT SALE!!!" handwritten in black marker. A tsunami of depression washed over me, and I wondered what had gone into this tragic piece of marketing. Was the Vietnamese man pleased with his slogan? Did he feel betrayed by America? Was he even sad at all, the way I was because I had psychically put myself in his place? It was scenes like this that reminded me to stop feeling obliged to love my job—a notion of dubious origin invented by my generation. Maybe we should just do our work, present a bill for services, and shut the hell up.

News helicopters with distended cameras circled the Golden Prospect in search of a relic of Turnpike Bobby Chin. A loose affiliation of plainclothes cops milled about the lobby unsubtly. I received more than one conspiratorial glance when a security guard inspected my driver's license and cleared me to go up to the penthouse. I resented not being more broadly recognized in a place that had once been my home. When you leave, you leave.

As I made my way through the elevator bank, a room service waiter had multiple cameras encircling his face as he answered questions about what kind of food Bobby had ordered. He would be fired soon enough—the casinos were very protective of their celebrities—but his bug eyes in the light of the cameras suggested he hadn't thought too many steps ahead. As every moment ticked by, the waiter's encounter with Bobby became more detailed, and his posture became more erect.

A teenage guest claimed before another hive of cameras to have seen Bobby in the hotel's game room. She characterized him as being "like, nice."

Hotel security people were checking the room cards of everyone who attempted to get on the elevators. A sleek, middle-aged New York woman complained bitterly about the hotel's lack of hospitality when she was forced to show her room card. She threatened that the casino's management would be "hearing from Mr. Schoen," her attorney, about demanding a refund.

On the penthouse floor, a sleek, muscular man with a few days of carefully calculated beard stubble opened the door to Bobby's suite. In his mid-thirties, he had that Hollywood douchebag patina, which balanced two contradictory messages: 1) I'm dressed casually because players like me *can*, and 2) the clothes are black and expensive, which means if you screw with me I'm the kind of guy who knows scary people. I felt a galloping desire to hurt this man badly, and it scared me.

A huge poster of Turnpike Bobby had already been mounted on the entry wall. The graphic was taken from the *Turnpike Immortal* album, and featured a gargantuan steel Bobby with millions of antlike serfs milling about his feet.

A Turnpike Bobby song, "Brigantine Sunset," warbled in the background. *"Put a petunia up his ass,"* the lyric droned. That's what it sounded like. At the time the song was popular, 1982, that's how people sang it, with sniggers. My college roommate showed me the alleged lyrics printed up in a regional rock rag. *"Put a tune on with pizzazz,"* it read. Oh.

A uniformed man from Piney Spring Water rolled out a cart of empty plastic water cooler containers. I stood back to let him pass. I shook my slick showbiz greeter's hand and said my name. He didn't say his. Ah, yes, the illusion that everyone must know who he is. The man did, however, offer an unctuous half-smile, as one does when one greets an inferior. Jonah Eastman, Cretin, backed into the suite.

When the door closed, the wall beside it vibrated, and a wall-mounted plate depicting the Atlantic City skyline fell to the floor and shattered. Señor Smarm tugged at his silky shirt and stared down at the fallen novelty plate.

"That's what they get for putting plates on walls," I said.

Smarm shrugged. Feeling badly about being the catalyst for this destruction, I picked up the three pieces of the plate and put it on a small table. Apparently this was my responsibility, because Smarm said nothing; he just kept walking deeper into the suite.

"You've got Atlantic City out here," I continued, "and they feel compelled to put a frigging plate on the wall with the skyline. Not even a painting. *A plate.* It's like putting a lawn sprinkler in your hamper. It makes about as much sense."

Smarm stopped. I wasn't anybody who could do anything for him in Hollywood, so his responses were minimalist, energy-conserving. "You want something to drink?" he asked.

Screw him.

"Water is fine," I said.

"Sparkling or flat?"

"Either. Just on a plate," I chuckled.

"Affirmative," he said, sniffing a little, a mini-laugh. Vindication. He tossed me a Piney Spring Water bottle from a refrigerator. "This is the only kind Bobby drinks."

One of the largest freshwater reserves in the country was located beneath the New Jersey Pine Barrens, a fact that never seemed to make it into the public consciousness.

"Are you ready to meet Bobby?" Smarm asked. *This must be a big moment for you,* his eyes conveyed. I choked down my pride and followed him.

Standing in white linen in the dressing area was a small, self-satisfied man of about fifty who sported a Nixonian five o'clock shadow, despite being freshly shaved. Ah, the proctologist. He wore one of those little boxy hats on his head, like the one Nehru used to wear. His matching slacks and shirt were crème-colored linen, vaguely clerical. He nodded his head in false humiliation. "I see you met my partner, Tic Turner," Kadaborah said.

"Yes, but I hadn't caught his name." Mistake. I had delivered a narcissistic wound to the smarmy Mr. Turner, who had inaccurately assessed his reknown.

"So, what do you think of the patient?" Kadaborah asked.

"Patient? I haven't seen him yet," I said.

"I like a man who treats inanimate objects with tenderness."

"I'm sorry?"

"The sofa."

"What sofa?" I asked.

"The patient. The torn sofa."

"I didn't see a torn sofa—"

"Negative," Turner interrupted. "I didn't show it to him yet."

"But you are the upholsterer?" Kadaborah pressed.

"I'm a *pollster.*" My jaw hung open, imbecilic.

"You don't repair sofas?"

"No."

"There must be some confusion then." Beads of sweat broke out beneath Kadaborah's Nehru cap. Turner started to fidget. "We had asked Cindi for an upholsterer. Bobby was distressed by the rip in the sofa and wanted it repaired immediately."

"Let me see if I follow," I said. "Bobby just survived a plane crash where two bodies have been found. He was just found alive in the Pines. The authorities are investigating, and he wants the sofa in his hotel room suite fixed?"

"That's correct."

"Okay, I get it now."

"Extraordinary people cope with stress differently," Kadaborah asserted.

"Clearly."

A shout echoed from another room: *"Kadaborah!"*

Kadaborah gazed down toward my waist. "Your watch," he began. I was wearing my running watch. "Please remove it before going in to see Bobby."

"May I ask why?"

Kadaborah and Turner exchanged impatient glances. "Bobby doesn't like watches." Kadaborah said this the way one might have addressed a dislike for cigarette smoking.

"Forgive me, but I don't understand."

Kadaborah became impatient. Apparently, one didn't ask questions. "The sound, the ticking. Bobby doesn't like it."

"This is a digital running watch. It doesn't make noise."

"Please, Mr. Eastman."

Curious now, I obliged and removed my watch, stuffing it into my pocket. I followed Kadaborah, whose hands were pressed together as if in prayer, into . . . an enormous bathroom.

My vanity is that I've seen everything, but I had never been in a meeting when the client was still in the shower having his pasty buttocks sponged off by an aide. In this case, the aide was a pixieish woman who reminded me of Tinker Bell, who did not appear to think her task was unusual. I remembered what Cindi had said about Bobby liking virgins.

With celebrities, a close examination of their person is a mandatory compulsion. Height, wrinkles, blemishes—we all need to see these things to assess how different they are, in fact, from actual people. We find it comforting when celebrities are short. It's as if we now know their secret and can blackmail them. So I studied Bobby as he stood naked as Atlas in his shower.

Bobby was taller than I had remembered, perhaps because I had been hoping the way other commoners did that he would be short. I also harbored a racial stereotype that Bobby would be short because he was half-Asian. His hair was now pageboy length, thick, flat, and black. He had one woven hair element extending halfway down his back like a tail. A small medallion was around his neck. Bobby had pale red markings on his shoulders and back, which appeared to be a cross between seaweed and veins. What kind of charismatic markings were these? Sensing I might be staring too long, I looked away.

Several more female aides, dressed in a skimpier derivative of Kadaborah's attire, emerged from the steam, climbed into the large shower, turned it off, and began to dry Bobby. I tried to avert my eyes, especially from his midsection, but caught a glimpse. I saw nothing that would have stood out in a locker room setting, which was odd because I envisioned that I had been brought in here because there was something unique to behold.

Bobby was thin, remarkably so for a man his age, but his body was largely undefined. His was a shape that was maintained either by good genes or modest appetite. This was not a form earned through exercise. I recalled Derek Plush's coining of the word "netherosexual" when describing Bobby's decidedly unmanly—but not feminine, either—features. There was no tan line around either wrist where a watch would be worn. I became self-conscious of the circular whiteness on my own arm, as if my traditional watch-wearing habit were akin to the needle marks of addiction.

"The Dude hears ticking," Bobby spoke. "Are you wearing a watch?"

"I took it off before I came in," I said.

"You still got it, though?"

"It's in my pocket."

One of Bobby's shower virgins automatically climbed out of the stall and extended her hand. I surrendered my watch as the others dried Bobby. Out of the corner of my eye, another man entered the bathroom. In his late forties or early fifties, trim as a whippet, ponytailed, and dressed in all black, the cadaverous man held a sleek video camera. He stood back and began filming. Besides me, no one appeared to find this strange.

Noticing the cameraman through the steam, Bobby bowed his head down, and he wore that geisha expression of his that begged his audience to witness his suffering and mirror back to him a cinematic recognition of his pain.

"Can you fix it by tonight?" Bobby asked, taking a sip from the water bottle the virgins handed him.

"I'm sorry, fix what?"

"The sofa," he said.

The subject matter aside, today's encounter was especially awkward, since it was clear that Bobby had no memory of ever having met me before.

"The Dude wants the couch fixed," Bobby pressed, stepping out of the shower. I determined that Bobby himself was "the Dude."

Four virgins—Bobby's fuckable Oompah-Loompahs—all in their late teens or early twenties, blew him dry with hair dryers. Bobby held his arms out by his sides like a cross between Yul Brynner in *The King and I* and a very moist Jesus Christ.

"I'm a pollster," I said defensively.

"I know, that's what the Dude wants," Bobby said.

"But I'm a *pollster,*" I repeated. "My job is to figure out what the public thinks. There must be some confusion . . . I think you need an *upholsterer.*"

"Why can't you just do it?" Bobby sneered, his upper lip twitching.

These are the kind of calls I get: A rock star in the final stages of a psychotic break demands that a once-hot Republican political operative fix his frigging sofa. Whatever the catalyst, the celebrity's ultimate request will translate as follows in Earth-logic: "I have done something awful, and I don't want to pay a price for it. Make it go away and get them all to love me again."

"I can take a poll," I said weakly. "Given your recent, uh, news, maybe I can find out how much your fans need you and pray for you."

Bobby nodded, stepping into briefs that one of the Virgins was holding beneath his crotch.

So it was that I was hired because a delusional proctologist had mistaken a pollster—a guy who determines where people stand—with an upholsterer, one who repairs where they sit.

After the conversation from Neptune crashed and burned, Kadaborah nervously explained that there must have been some confusion, and assured Bobby that the sofa would be fixed by the evening. Everyone, save the cameraman, gave me looks that were pinched with disgust. I was the poodle turd on the ballroom floor.

Cicadas

"Isn't it cool the way they just leave themselves behind?"

Back in the suite's living room, Kadaborah berated Tic Turner to have the infidel sofa removed and switched with another one elsewhere in the hotel. "Affirmative," Turner said, as if he were about to alter President Kennedy's corpse at the behest of J. Edgar Hoover. I had Turner pegged as that unique mutation of man who never outgrew his fascination with the whole Special Forces-spy-gun cult.

Bobby emerged, dressed in a straw Western cap, white pants, and a T-shirt. The ponytailed man with the video camera followed, as did an aide with a silver tray covered with water balloons. The aide wore a tentative expression, but gained confidence when Kadaborah waved him in.

"Radical!" Bobby pumped a fist, jumping up and down giddily. "You wanna wing some of these over the balcony with me?"

"Uh, I don't know, Bobby, we're really high up. The momentum of the balloon and all could—"

That's right, Jonah, try to explain balloon momentum to this psycho.

"C'mon! What's your name again?"

"Jonah."

"C'mon, Jonah, don't wuss out on me."

Bobby waved the High Priest of the Water Balloons out onto the penthouse balcony with him. Once outside, he began hurling the balloons down at the little people milling about on the Boardwalk. I looked to Kadaborah, assuming he would weigh in, but he didn't. Speechless, I went out onto the balcony, trailed by Kadaborah and the cameraman.

"Whoa, totally nailed the bitch," Bobby sniggered.

I looked over the balcony. A woman with half of her helmet hair flattened sat on the Boardwalk and stared around dazed.

"I think we should stop this," I said. "The A.C. cops get nasty about things being thrown onto the Boardwalk. Look, there's also press helicopters out there."

Kadaborah glared at me. Bobby suddenly became distracted by something on the floor of the balcony. "Radical!" he said. "A cicada! Jonah, isn't it cool the way they just leave themselves behind?"

I thought there was something poetic about Bobby's comment, so I agreed with it. The seventeen-year cycle when cicadas invaded pockets of the Eastern and Midwestern United States was upon us. They came for a few weeks, only to vanish until their fleeting and seemingly useless rebirths seventeen years hence.

"Yes, but they don't actually leave themselves behind. It's their husks. I think they're called exoskeletons."

"Whatever, but the Dude thinks it would be awesome to leave himself behind."

"Maybe, Bobby."

"The cicadas came out about the time my TV show first hit."

"What year was that?"

"1970. The Dude thought it was awesome. I came out of nowhere and turned into something else just like the cicadas. In 1987, they came out again. I was on my Immortal tour in Europe. I was huge in Europe. The cicadas always bring something awesome for the Dude, huh, Jonah?"

"It looks that way, Bobby. I remember both cycles."

"What do you mean?"

"I remember when Mega Boy first came on, and I remember when *Turnpike Immortal* crossed the ocean."

"What did you think?"

"I remember thinking that you were the first person my age to be big."

"Did you want to be big yourself?"

"We all did."

"Hey, Tic," Bobby said. "Take a picture of me and Jonah." I thought this was odd. Usually it's the sheepish commoner who requests a photo with the Gods. Turner pulled out his mobile phone while Bobby put his arm around me and snapped a photo with his phone. This amazed me. I struggled on a daily basis to figure out what buttons to push to make a call, and other people were taking pictures with their phones.

"Gimme your e-mail address," Turner asked me. "I'll send it to you."

"By e-mail?"

"Yeah."

My Big Theory on technology: the gadget should serve me, not the other way around. There is to be no learning. If it doesn't work easily, I abandon the gadget. If I'm engaging the gadget, *it* is operating *me*. I live in a world of wondrous new technologies that are useless in the true sense of that word because I cannot use them.

But soon I'd have a picture of Turnpike Bobby Chin and me. Cool.

I left the suite having no idea how I could really be of value. My summons had been an accident, and in all likelihood my visit would be forgotten as fast as one of Bobby's water balloons once it departed his fingertips.

I walked down the tastefully lonely corridor. A recessed ceiling light that hadn't been blinking before blinked now, hinting at a burnout. A man who was presumably the next visitor to Turnpike Bobby's hallucination stepped from the elevator. He was a tall, handsome man with long reddish hair that had been bleached around his forehead by the coastal sun. The man had the look of an artist, and I had the fleeting hope that he would be visiting Bobby to collaborate on some new music. My hopes were dashed when he stuck his hand out to hold the elevator doors open, pulling out a small mobile cart. An object about three feet tall sat atop the cart, covered by a rusty blanket. Whatever it was under there, it did not suggest music. I held the elevator doors open so he could slide the object out more easily. He thanked me, and pushed his cluster of weirdness down the hall to Planet Bobby.

Maggots

"Whoever tells the biggest lie wins."

Cindi appeared at our front door a few minutes after Edie and the kids headed to the beach.

"Cinderella, I tremble in your presence," I said.

"Maybe it's just gas," Cindi said, shutting the screen behind her. "So, what happened with Bobby?"

"I don't think he liked me."

"He didn't remember you from the White House?"

"I didn't bring it up. The discussion got off to a surreal start."

"How?"

"He thought I was an upholsterer. They thought that's what you said I was. There was a rip in the sofa."

"You're serious?"

"Yes, I am."

"I told them you were a pollster that could help with public opinion."

"Well, I don't know how the translation got garbled, but they were mighty disappointed when I couldn't fix the couch."

"It's incredible. This is how everything works with them. People expect this well-oiled machine in show business, but it's a miracle anything gets done. Anyhow, what did you make of the Maggots?"

"Huh?"

"That's what I call Kadaborah and Turner. When you kick over the rotting log that is Turnpike Bobby, they come running out carrying bits of his flesh."

"Tasty. What do you know about them?"

"As I mentioned, Kadaborah was a proctologist in Pennsauken for years. An entrepreneur type. Real name was something boring. Connor. Shafer. Something like that. He changed his name and started a holistic cult kind of thing, the Ong's Hat Flagellants—"

"Flatulence?" I said to annoy Cindi.

"*Flagellants*, Jonah."

An old Piney town that had its heyday more than a century ago, Ong's Hat had developed a peculiar following among the occult on the internet. It may have originated with an old Piney tale involving a young man named Jacob Ong. Ong was said to have lost his girlfriend to another man at a local dance. Upon leaving the soiree, he tossed his hat into the air. The hat got caught in a tree branch, pulling the branch down like a lever, which opened up a hole in the earth. Ong vanished forever.

In the late twentieth century, Ong's Hat had cultivated a reputation as a paranoid's paradise—secret government raids by missile-tipped black helicopters and paranormal phenomena including yawning fields with sliding boards straight to hell.

"What do these Flagellants believe in?"

"Money. Actually, they think the pathway toward redemption and purification of the soul goes through the colon."

"Who doesn't?"

"Kadaborah signs the checks, handles all of Bobby's business matters. Turner's a piece of work. He was a porn star in the eighties and some of the nineties."

"He's got that look."

"Yeah. Performed under the name Ezra Pound in *The Rodfather,*

Parts One and *Two.* Turner did *The Little Spermaid, The Slutty Professor, Apollo 13 Inches, Forrest Rump . . .*"

"Plenty of body cavities to go around with these guys, huh, Cin?"

"One can only hope. Then he was some kind of private investigator until the Bobby gig came along."

"I really liked the thing who follows Bobby around with a camera—"

"Lonesome Jake."

"It has a name?"

"Yeah, Lonesome Jake. He never talks, just records."

"Have you ever seen any of the film?"

"It's digital, Jonah, it would be a chip, not film."

"Right, a chip. Probably a, uh, Pentium microtit point five turbo-wanker gigabyte model?"

"You're stuck in nineteen seventy-five, aren't you?"

"Minus some of the hair. So, what's with your unveiling of Bobby's statue?"

"It's postponed for now. With the cops all over the place asking questions about the crash, the A.C. Chamber of Commerce wants to chill out."

"Does Bobby know this yet?"

"No, he wants to see the statue first. If he likes it, we'll try to set something else up. The sculptor was supposed to show him a mini-version last night. You were there. Did you see it?"

"No."

"The guy must have brought it after you left."

"Maybe he was the guy I saw in the elevator. He was wheeling a cart. Reddish hair?"

"Yeah, Christian."

"There was all that chaos in the lobby of the hotel, but up in Bobby's suite there was something very calm about the weirdness."

A strand of wavy black hair fell from Cindi's forehead over her eyes. She blew the strand up in a manner that made her sexy in a freestyle, Goldie Hawnish way, even though she and Goldie looked nothing alike. Cindi and I had known each other since we were kids—brother-and-sister buddies—so I felt perverted for thinking anything she did was sexy. I believe that all impulses should remain imprisoned in their appropriate compartments.

"When you've been driven through life with a police escort there are only green lights. The stopping and the waiting beneath stupid traffic ornaments is a ritual for the Unchosen."

"Well, Cin, given how we, the Unchosen, treat people like Bobby, do they even have a chance to be anything other than what they become?"

"Whoever tells the biggest lie wins."

"Until everybody loses."

"It's a business, Jonah, not a crusade. If you end up working for him, remember that, okay? Beneath it all, you're still an idealist. Don't confuse yourself with Moses. Jonah was swallowed by a big fish and got his ass spat out on the beach. Moses was the one who parted seas."

Cindi winked. My grandfather's real name was Moses.

"You know one thing I remember about you when we were young, Jonah?"

"What's that?"

"You always had a thing for office supplies."

"I still do. Turns me on. Post-its, colored plastic paper clips. I don't know what it is."

"I do. Order. You like putting things in order. And control. With office supplies you get to put everything in its place with nice little tags. You despise chaos. You get more excited by Office Depot's direct mail than the Victoria's Secret catalogue."

"Don't get me hot."

"You are mesmerized by freak shows like Turnpike Bobby because he's the world gone mad. You as a little boy fleeing the country with your criminal grandfather. Mickey telling you that the Law was wrong, not him. Chaos. Moral relativism. Today's icons become icons because they're out of control. Courtney Fucking Love, she's the currency. And you hate it because you honestly believe that goodness has its origins in order."

"What's the action item here, Cin? I'm burned out on polling."

"I'm going to be asked for a miracle, Jonah, and I may need help."

"I'm not sure I'll be able to give it to you."

Missing

"I go through life with a perpetually guilty conscience."

Knives of morning sunlight cut through the windows in our bedroom as I changed into running gear. Morning beach noises crept into my ears. I did a few stretches in front of the TV. I did them out of obligation because it was a compulsion, not because I was convinced of stretching's utility. A fluffy-haired newsman was summarizing a disappearance in Atlantic City. This is how life ends, I thought—a mannequin lowers his voice an octave to CONVEY CONCERN about something he has no feeling for. I tuned out what the anchorman was saying until he referenced the Golden Prospect.

And now the photo of the Missing One: a good-looking, Princeton-based bohemian named Christian Josi. A sculptor.

A sculptor?

I looked harder at the man's photo, which appeared to have been lifted from a website. Good Lord, he was the guy in the elevator after I left Bobby last night. His office mate, an anorexic painter who called herself Quaneefra, reported him missing. They had gone together to a Starbuck's on Nassau Street every morning for years. Christian had indicated he would see her that morning like every other. Furthermore, he had been anxiously awaiting a meeting with a potentially large commission. The prospect showed, but Christian had not.

Of course, none of this would have been of interest to anyone so soon after his disappearance had Christian not been meeting with the cynosure of the current news cycle, Turnpike Bobby Chin.

I go through life with a perpetually guilty conscience. I'd fail a polygraph and get myself convicted of the Manson murders, which occurred three thousand miles away when I was seven years old. That's how skittish I am naturally. My heart was doing a Ringo Starr in my chest cavity. If that Christian fellow got himself clipped right after I left Bobby's suite last night, well, hell . . .

I'd go for my run anyway. I'm not guilty of Jack Squat. My grandfather ordered murders and went home, watched a little *Jeopardy!*, discreetly belched, and went to bed. I didn't do anything and was having angina from just watching the news. Nah, I'm cool, I'd take my run.

Six steps onto Atlantic Frigging Avenue, Adam-12 hits the siren. Two cops get out leaving their unmarked Ford's ass half in the street. Stocky. Plain clothes. Cheapass suits and porno mustaches.

"You're Jonah Eastman," Cop #1 said. The other guy played with his shoulder holster. Yeah, Sundance, I see you've got a real live grown-up-like firearm.

"I'm Detective Rich Galen, A.C.P.D.," Cop #1 said. "Sorry to disturb your run, but can I ask you a couple of questions?"

What do I do here, say, *"Yeah, butt-lips, I mind"*? And then become a suspect in the Jimmy Hoffa disappearance? Or am I Citizen Eastman, helpful, earnest, self-incriminating?

"Sure, Detective."

"Were you at the Golden Prospect last night?"

The hotel had been wallpapered with the Law, not to mention more security cameras than casino chips. "Yes."

"Why were you there?"

"I had a client meeting."

It dawned on me when I saw the roll of fat around Cop #2's middle that my beloved exercise routine had been interrupted. What's wrong with people? You don't screw with a man's exercise. Suddenly I felt like Dom De Louise.

"Turnpike Bobby?"

"Yes. Well, he's a potential client."

"What business are you in, Mr. Eastman?" The bastard knew.

"I'm a pollster." I added, "Political work mostly."

"Why does Bobby Chin care about politics?"

"He's running for president of Murray's Delicatessen. Look, Detective, where are we going here?"

"We're investigating a possible kidnapping at the Golden Prospect."

I nodded, feeling no urge to be helpful. Mickey taught me that. These guys were here because they knew exactly who I was. Who my grandfather was. A cop could always get a little suck with the police brass in A.C. by dragging in the name Mickey Price. Around here, that name explained everything from the Kennedy assassination to the melting of the polar ice caps.

Getting nowhere, Detective Galen asked, "Do you know a Christian Josi?"

"No."

Galen took out a piece of paper with a photo on it. Josi. "Do you recognize this man?"

"He looks familiar. Is he famous?"

"Jersey famous. He's a sculptor. He was doing a statue for Bobby Chin. *Of* Bobby Chin. He was in Bobby's hotel room last night. So were you."

"I didn't see him in Bobby's suite."

"Did you see him at all?"

"I'm not sure. He looks familiar. I passed people in the casino, maybe that's where I recognize him. Why are you interested in him?"

"Because he's the one missing."

"As in presumed dead?" I became conscious of my own swallowing. *We the jury, find the defendant, Jonah Eastman, guilty of the murder of Christian Josi, John F. Kennedy, Martin Luther King Jr., Sharon Tate, and the theft of an Almond Joy bar at the Ventnor Pharmacy in 1971 . . .*

"That's what we're trying to find out. Did you notice anything strange?"

"Strange? Detective, with Bobby, that's the wrong question."

"What's the right question, Mr. Eastman?"

"The right question would be, 'Did you notice anything normal?' "

Detective Galen laughed. "Give me an example of something strange."

Help him here, Jonah, just a little. "Well, for one thing, Bobby called me in the first place to fix his sofa."

"Why?"

"Because it was ripped. And I'm a pollster."

"I don't get it."

"Exactly."

"Anything else?"

"Yeah, he's got a team of young women who get in the shower with him and scrub his balls."

"Are you shitting me?"

"Why, Detective, you don't have a staff of scrote-scrubbers?"

"Mine went on strike."

"Damned unions."

"Well, Mr. Eastman, I may be back in touch with you."

"Why?"

"Let's just say you have a pattern of being around when high drama goes down."

"Because I'm Mickey Price's grandson?"

"I don't know all the origins of the universe, but you're an interesting fellow. You worked for Mario Vanni a few years back, right before he got whacked. His consigliere vanished about that time. Then there was your work for Governor Rothman, and that little incident on your property."

"Yes, Detective, I shot a man who was coming to kill me, and I called the police right away."

"You're a good citizen, Eastman. I admire that."

"I've got a six-mile run ahead of me, Detective. You may admire me running off."

Game Boy

"This'll all blow over by tomorrow."

SCULPTOR MAY HAVE VANISHED
FROM TURNPIKE BOBBY'S SUITE

The *Atlantic City Packet* announced this little gem. The words "may have" were a virtual guarantee of nationwide pickup despite their ambiguity. Somebody at the ACPD was almost certainly winking to the *Packet,* which contained the standard cop-style allusions to "exploring all possibilities." The Maggots were sufficiently concerned that they requested my presence. It seemed, courtesy of Cindi, as if I had myself a client, but somehow I wasn't rejoicing.

Day-Glo yellow tape repeating the phrase RESTRICTED AREA— ATLANTIC CITY POLICE greeted me as the elevators opened at the penthouse level of the Golden Prospect. The tape served no practical purpose that I could tell, but conveyed hysterically that some form of police business was being taken very seriously. A grave-faced uniformed police officer, arms folded defiantly, stepped forward.

"Yeah, can I help you, pal?" he asked. His voice was all confrontation.

"I have an appointment with Bobby."

"Name?"

"Jonah Eastman."

Two plainclothes officers emerged from an unmarked doorway. The cop in uniform turned to them and sneered, "Jonah Eastman here for Bobby."

"What are you doing back here?"

"I have a meeting with Bobby."

"Are you a big Hollywood playa?" The cops all laughed. "I'm just screwing with you. I saw you on the list to be cleared through."

"So, may I go?"

The two plainclothes policemen took a few steps toward me. They were both taller than me. They looked down their noses at me as the uniformed officer receded into the elevator bank.

"Sure!" the detective said with false exuberance. "Free to go. Do as you please, Eastman. Whatever you damned well please." Both cops smirked.

I was on the receiving end of one of those cop-show ploys you see on TV. *I don't have anything on you, but I suspect your ass, so I'm gonna treat you like a convicted child molester BECAUSE I CAN.* Mickey called this phenomenon earning "psychic income," abusing people as a non-monetary job perquisite.

Inside his suite, Turnpike Bobby Chin sat on the replacement sofa in all his middle-aged glory wearing his straw Western hat and playing with an electronic Game Boy. To his left, Tic Turner, the Francis Ford Copulate of the Jersey Shore, sat flexing the sinews in his forearms. Yes, Tic, you're muscular. The Reverend Kadaborah sat in his off-white linens and fez to Bobby's right, clasping his hands together as if he were silently saying a *barucha* over lunacy. Cindi sat in uncharacteristic silence in a puffy chair that matched my own, directly across from Bobby and the Maggots.

"Bobby needs a lawyer," I began.

A huge faux pas, clearly, because Kadaborah pursed his lips. "And why do you say that, Jonah?" His hands were still clasped.

"Cops are everywhere. Even the chambermaids have Glocks. They don't believe Bobby's plane accidentally crashed. They suspect foul play with this sculptor, Christian. They don't manufacture things out of thin air. True or not, it's too good a story line not to pursue." As if on cue, a police helicopter whizzed by the window, rattling the glass.

Bobby kept working on his Game Boy. Turner shot me a hard look he plagiarized from Elmore Leonard. Kadaborah unfolded his hands, a patronizing expression flourishing on his face. "Why do you believe such things, Jonah?"

Such things. A tad British for a *tuchus* juggler from Pennsauken.

"I've been in this town my whole life, practically," I said. "I watch the news. I got a visit from a detective this morning. Those are a few reasons."

"Why would a detective visit you?"

"Because there are a million security cameras all over this hotel, not to mention police and media, and I was here last night before the sculptor came."

"A disconcerting development, unarguably, but I'm at a loss to know what this has to do with Bobby."

"Bobby," I said, "Would you please put down your Game Boy for a moment?" Faux pas #2. I was going to make it big in show business.

Cindi inhaled slowly, painfully.

"You don't have to, Bobby," Turner said. Bobby liked that, and resumed play. "Don't worry, Bobby, this'll all blow over by tomorrow," Turner assured.

This may have been the biggest lie I had ever heard in my entire life, but for some reason, it just popped out of Turner's mouth the way a gumball bounces happily from a dispenser: *Here I am, world, in all my sugary glory!*

"This most certainly *won't* blow over," I said.

"It won't. No way, guys," Cindi added. "My goddamned phone is ringing off the hook. We need to make a st—"

"Jonah, you do *not* handle Bobby as you might a regular client," Kadaborah interrupted. *Verrrrry* patronizing.

"The Dude wants to know what the hell is going on," Bobby chimed in. He snapped his fingers, and one of the Virgins dressed in gauzy white handed him a Piney Spring Water. Bobby glared at her. Recognizing her mistake, she screwed off the bottle cap and then handed it to Bobby. There was something ritualistic about it, as if a sacramental candle were being lit.

"Look, guys, I'm not a Hollywood player," I said. The Maggots nodded as if I had admitted to fornicating with a cocker spaniel. "I know I made a career mistake by telling Bobby to put down his Game Boy. But you need a lawyer, Bobby, because I sense the cops and the media want you on multiple counts of murder, and that's just the beginning. That airplane went across state lines, and some of those cutouts downstairs look Federal to me."

"And how do you have such insight for a man who is not a lawyer?" Kadaborah asked.

"Because the same crew chased my family out of the country."

Cindi let slip a nervous laugh in anticipation of the Ghosts of Eastman Past shrieking their way into the cocktail party.

"Why would they do that?" Kadaborah asked. A little concerned now.

"Because my grandfather was Mickey Price."

Dead silence. Hushed reverence. Earsplitting quiet. Think of a few more clichés to describe can-hear-a-pin-drop serenity, and you'll get the full effect. Bobby was a South Jersey Boy. Kadaborah was from here. Turner, Mr. Super Scary Spy Guy, was almost certainly a scholar of the American fringe. They all knew who Mickey was. And now, a newfound respect for the failed upholsterer—

Mafia mythology was all about what people wanted to believe. I could no more order up a murder like Belgian waffles than I could give Britney Spears talent. But the Mafia's stranglehold on the American imagination was all about what people demanded of their fantasies.

"The Dude wants it to just go away, Jonah," Bobby surrendered, putting down his Game Boy.

"Make what go away, Bobby?"

"These people who are saying all the bad things. The police."

The guy was operating on the same level as my little daughter. *All the bad things.*

"Bobby," I said softly, as if it were nappy time, "we just can't tell the New Jersey State Police, the FBI, CNN . . . to stop saying bad things."

"But we can make a statement," Cindi added.

Turner and Kadaborah were still agitated, more, I supposed, because of my coarse truthfulness than the prospect of prison. The idea of a profound consequence was beyond their ken. Or maybe there was a noncriminal explanation for all of this strangeness. I doubted it, but had been rightly accused before of seeing goblins where there were none.

Bobby, suddenly, began to engage. "Do you know a lawyer, Jonah?" he asked. His Game Boy was no longer visible, perhaps having fallen between the pillows of his newly replaced sofa.

"Yes, he's been one of the top defense lawyers in this area for fifty years."

"Do you know him through your grandfather?"

"Yes. He represented Mickey and other businessmen who were being stalked by the government. Truthfully, Bobby, we shouldn't even be having this discussion without him. Understand, this doesn't mean anybody did anything wrong," I fibbed, which was disturbingly easy, and I wondered fleetingly how many more lies would tumble out of my mouth. "It just means we need protection."

Kadaborah leaned forward. "Well, look, Jonah, I'd like to give this some thought—"

"No!" Bobby interrupted. "Who is this lawyer?"

The Maggots recoiled. I clearly had miscalculated the power relationship between these men. I had cast Bobby as the puppet, the Maggots as the puppeteers, but it was trickier than that. When Bobby had been shocked out of the Game Boy miasma that was his life, he shut the Maggots down and they cowered. It was as if his psychosis were selective, that he might actually be aware that he behaved like a Thanksgiving turkey on LSD, which would render him sane, wouldn't it?

"I think you'll like him, Bobby. He's known as the Cohn of Silence."

Bobby nodded approvingly, like a chief executive, and for the first time I respected him. "In the meantime, please, please, please stay in the hotel. No media appearances. Let Cindi talk to the press. Please."

Emergency Grown-up Outfit

"Don't be helpful."

indi and I retreated to the balcony.

"My phone messages are jammed up with media calls," Cindi said. "Christian this, plane crash that. We have to make a statement now."

"Yes. But for God's sake, keep it short. If you say too much, it can come back at us in court."

"Court?"

"This isn't PR, it's crisis management. Your instinct will be to say a lot, to be helpful. Don't be helpful, just feed the beast. The more you say, the more a prosecutor will have against Bobby. This guy has more heat up his ass than . . . I don't know, whatever has heat up its ass."

Ten minutes later, we had a statement prepared. Cindi went down to her car and changed into her Emergency Grown-up Outfit.

or years, Cindi had kept her "Emergency Grown-up Outfit" close by for just these occasions. It was a sharply cut navy-blue suit. While she changed, an intern from her office sent out a media advisory that a statement from Turnpike Bobby Chin would be forthcoming about his plane crash and the disappearance of the sculptor.

We chose the Boardwalk outside the Golden Prospect for Cindi to make her statement. We selected this venue because it was not convenient for the press. It was a bad spot for the media's light and sound people, being hard to find power sources for their equipment. It would force the press to have to hustle to studios and satellite trucks to convey their content rather than ask hard questions. It would be easy for Cindi, however, to do her spiel and tiptoe back into the hotel when she was done.

I watched the proceedings on the Golden Prospect's security camera. Cindi stepped out to the Boardwalk, where there was, despite our worst efforts, a phalanx of cameras and microphones. Cindi's face was taut with worry. Given that there was no podium around which to center the media's equipment, Cindi gave the gaggle a few moments to organize an electronic nest around her.

"Thank you for coming," she began. "I am going to give you the only authorized statement on behalf of Turnpike Bobby Chin. I know many of you would like to speak at greater length about recent events, but due to Bobby's cooperation with ongoing investigations, we are limited in what we can say."

Cindi withdrew a large index card from her breast pocket, brushing her eyes across it.

"Turnpike Bobby returned from Los Angeles on July 4 to his native Atlantic City in order to promote his forthcoming *Awesomest Hits* collection. He was scheduled to do a televised concert at the Golden Prospect on July 5. That event, of course, had to be cancelled. There are no plans to reschedule right now.

"Bobby was aboard the plane that crashed in the Pine Barrens on July 4 along with two pilots. He cannot remember much that happened immediately before or after the crash. He has referenced eating leaves and sleeping under tree branches in the Pine Barrens. He remembers the people who found him walking in the wilderness and is grateful for their help.

"After resting in his hotel suite two nights ago, Bobby was briefly visited by a sculptor named Christian Josi. Josi was working on a bronze statue of Bobby that will stand on the Boardwalk. Bobby and Christian had a pleasant discussion, and Christian left. Bobby has no knowledge of Christian's whereabouts. Bobby's thoughts and prayers are with his family.

"Bobby wants to thank his fans for their prayers. He promises to perform again for everyone as soon as he heals from this terrible ordeal."

With that, Cindi pivoted and vanished back inside the Golden Prospect. The press shouted "Cindi! Cindi! Cindi!," but she was absorbed into the bowels of the building. A wall of security men blocked the Boardwalk entrance to the casino to facilitate Cindi's escape.

Applause Machine

"We won't be able to help this client if we don't have this client."

L ate the next morning, Edie was flipping through the channels trying to find *SpongeBob* for the kids. "Jone!" she called. "You may want to see this."

"I don't get *SpongeBob*," I said from the kitchen, where I was reading an article in a gossip magazine about an up-and-coming kickboxer training for a fight in Bangkok. The owner of our beach house subscribed to these rags, and I found myself unable to resist them (and feeling as if I had squandered my Ivy League education). The most peculiar thing about the article was the photographic collage of the fighter getting his hair (including a thicket of chin foliage) bleached for the fight. Not a word was written about his athletic skills.

"It's not *SpongeBob*," Edie said. "It's your new friend. Turnpike Bobby Nutcake."

On TV, Turnpike Bobby was being mobbed on the steps of the Atlantic City Courthouse. He wore an all-black piratelike getup that must have been awfully hot in the scorching sun. Or maybe the heat was in my own lungs. Bobby was flanked by mountainous bodyguards in white linen. Very serious faces, these bodyguards. The cameras were being jostled by a throng that appeared to number in the hundreds, while Bobby climbed into his stretch Hummer.

The visuals were set to a verse from a 1980 Turnpike Bobby song, which sounded like, *"There's a ferret in my underpants."* The actual lyric was allegedly, "Took a ferry to my inner thoughts," which marginally made more sense. The only word I caught in the newsman's voiceover was "questioning." Before the vehicle's door closed, I saw Bobby touch his fingers to his cheeks as if to say, "Goodness me!" He nodded downward, conveying a facsimile of humility (his geisha face). And then he was gone.

I felt as if I had just climbed out of a freezing swimming pool stark naked in a capacity crowd at Madison Square Garden: very tiny in the wrongest of places. Just when I thought that perhaps I had gotten through to Bobby, and that beneath his mantle of madness was a core of lucidity, my illusion was smashed. My counsel had been contradicted in the most absolute way. I grabbed my mobile phone and called Cindi.

"What the hell was that on TV?"

I could hear in the background that Cindi was standing in a crowd. *The* crowd.

"Sorry about this, Jonah, but it was totally last minute."

"Well, what was it? I heard something about questioning, but nothing about a lawyer. I don't know if Bobby has even met with Mr. Cohn yet."

"Let me move somewhere quiet," Cindi said, rustling through the *lumpen*. Her voice returned, softer, conspiratorial. She sighed, "It's what we call an 'incognito.'"

I felt like I had the IQ of plankton. An incognito? "There was nothing incognito about what I just saw."

"It's part of my arrangement with Kadaborah. I alert the press that Bobby's going to be at a certain location incognito. The press shows up. Bobby is mobbed by crazed fans. Crazed fans that I hire and pay. Bobby acts surprised, but gracious."

"What's the objective here, Cin?"

"The Maggots want to keep Bobby happy."

"To what end?"

"Look, Jonah, coverage is Bobby's heroin, so they bring me in to place stories about how private he is . . . when he goes through withdrawal. If I can't get real fans, I rent the fans, and his bodyguards hold them back. The cameras pick it all up. Sometimes when I can't get any cameras to show up, I hire photographers and camera crews to crowd him. It looks like thousands of people, but it's really about fifteen. Fifty bucks a head. We ship 'em around all over. That's what you just saw."

"So, Bobby wasn't being questioned by the cops?"

"No, he just went to the courthouse and walked around while we got the crowd and the cameras in place."

"It's like *A Face in the Crowd*."

"Whose face?"

"It's a movie. Budd Schulberg wrote it in the 1950s. Andy Griffith is a TV demagogue. When his star fades, his doofus aide cranks up an applause machine. An actual machine, like a big toaster."

"That's what I am, Jonah, an applause machine."

"Cindi, this stunt puts more pressure on the police to come down on him. They can't just say, 'Turnpike Bobby roamed the halls of the Atlantic City Courthouse.' Do you know if he said anything to anybody?"

"I don't think so, but I was outside mostly."

"Did you see the Cohn of Silence?"

"No."

"Am I crazy, or didn't I recommend that he needs to be kept *out* of the news as much as we can?"

"Yes, you did, Jonah, but we won't be able to *help* this client if we don't *have* this client. You got Bobby to agree to getting a lawyer. He gave something up in the negotiation."

"How does Bobby feel about being invoiced for photographers

who aren't really taking pictures of anything and fans who've never heard his music?"

"Jonah, what about bodyguards who aren't protecting him from anything? Nobody wants to kill this guy!"

"Except me. Look, Cin, this one is pure heartache."

"I need you, Jonah."

"And I need the eighty-three grand I'm owed on this Hopkins Pond screw job. I can only consider helping out if I get money up front. My clients don't pay me once the hurricane passes."

"How much?"

"Fifty grand."

I heard a click on my phone. Another call. Another voice.

"Those beautiful children of yours," a hypnotizing rabbinical voice said. "They like ice cream, yes?"

The Cohn of Silence

"Your goal isn't to win, it's to get out alive."

The voice on the phone belonged to Stubie Cohn, who I asso-
ciated with trouble. I first met him when he paid a condolence
call to Mickey after my mother died. He reemerged a year
later when Mickey, my grandmother Deedee, and I fled the country to
duck an indictment alleging that Mickey was skimming from Nevada
casinos. Mr. Cohn was in the van when we were driven to a private
airport where a prop plane waited to ferry us to New York, and then
to our criminal diaspora.

I didn't hear a word of what Mr. Cohn had whispered to Mickey,
but it had to have been bad news. There was a look on Mickey's
face—an amalgam of concern and surprise—that suggested his cy-
clonic life was in the hands of an inaudible man who was known by
Mickey's boys as the "Cohn of Silence."

The Cohn of Silence did not have an office. He had an ice cream
truck. He didn't drive it; that task was left to his stoop-shouldered
brother Izzy. In the summertime, Izzy would hawk ice cream out of
the truck's side window, while the Cohn of Silence★ visited with

---

★The Cohn of Silence was sometimes confused with Cohen the Barbarian, the Camden Superior Court judge who was known for giving maximum sentences. The two were not related

clients inside the vehicle. Given his gangland clientele, the truck, with its steel freezers and icy walls, was soundproof. This was another of the possible explanations for his nickname. Yet another, and perhaps most apt, was that witnesses against his clients inevitably decided not to testify.

The Cohn of Silence was now in his early seventies. An immaculate little man who favored bow ties and cream-colored suits, he had a mannerism whereby he leaned in toward you and told you whatever you needed to know in the gravest of confidence. If he wanted to comment on the weather, the Cohn of Silence would meet you nose to nose, look to either side, and conspiratorially say, "Nice day."

The ice cream truck jingled onto our street, which sent Ricky and Lily into paroxysms of euphoria. Edie and I followed them onto the sidewalk. The side window slid open, and a moonfaced Izzy stepped into the light. Seconds later, the side door of the truck opened, and a bronze hand attached to a tannish cord suit sleeve emerged to wave me in.

I shrugged to Edie, who supervised as the kids' minds spun at the poster setting forth their ice cream options.

Once inside the truck, I stood before the bronze hand, which was now holding something: "Éclair?"

"Thank you, Mr. Cohn, I think I will," I said, taking the wrapped ice cream.

"You're skinny enough. Do you diet?" he asked.

"No, I run."

"From what?"

"Nothing. For exercise."

"Is somebody chasing you?"

"No."

"Nothing's chasing you, so why run?"

---

and apparently did not even acknowledge each other at the annual New Jersey Bonds for Israel charity ball.

"So I can eat ice cream."

"Good for you. I always wondered why all those people were running on the Boardwalk. 'From what?' I ask myself. I don't believe in that Chet Atkins diet everybody fusses about. How can you not eat bread? It's a whole food group down the crapper."

"That's true. Did you meet with Bobby?"

"Yes. Before we get down to business, let me thank you for this referral."

"You're welcome."

"Who ever thought when you were a little *pisher* hiding under your grandfather's sofa, you'd be sending me business?"

"Consider it a kickback for all that ice cream you fed me over the years."

"Finally, a dividend from you. I handle other musical acts, you know? Familiar with Swine Flu?

"No."

"Legionnaire's Disease?"

"That's a music group?"

"All of them are. It's called plunk rock or funky rock or something. These band kids are always wrecking hotels, chasing female guests with vibrating implements. These things become troubling for the record label, needless to say, which is where I come in."

"I'm not familiar with incidents with these groups."

"Thus my success. Now, let's talk, privileged, of course."

"Of course."

"I met Bobby and his advisors. I think they're all a few scoops short of a sundae. The Feds are looking into the plane crash, but they don't have anything yet. The A.C. cops confirmed they're looking at Bobby on the disappearance of this sculptor, but they don't have enough yet to make a move. I talked to them about this little courthouse charade. Stupid, show business *meshuggeners*. They told me you assured them I could win for Bobby. Win? I asked them to define a win. They said, 'We've got to get him back to where he was at his peak.' I said, 'Gentlemen, that's not a win, that's a hallucination.' They asked me, 'If that's not a win, what is?' I told them, 'Now, Bobby has a forty-thousand-square-foot house and he's a free man. A win is that Bobby lives in a twenty-thousand-square-foot house and remains a free man.' In these situations, the goal isn't to win, it's to get out alive. I don't think they bought it. Bobby did not do a crime, of course. But I need to start thinking of a plausible alternative scenario. I called this P.A.S. For Plausible Alternative Scenario, of course. This will be hard to find with all of these vultures and jackals watching his every move. I need to probe. Quietly. I cannot probe quietly with cameras up my client's kazoo. You follow?"

"Mostly. What are your alternative theories?"

"This is what troubles me, Jonah. Given how isolated Bobby is, it's unlikely that a great woolly mammoth climbed up the side of the Golden Prospect and pulled the sculptor over the balcony. Still, it's more likely that one of the gentry that surround Bobby did something naughty. This brings up other problems. Nobody wants to get pinched on capital murder, not even for a celebrity. Anyhow, I'm afraid it's necessary to do a little digging around."

"Enlighten me more on what's plausible."

"Do you remember that congressman, Condit? He had that affair with that nice girl from California? That case ran away with the news for a whole summer until September 11 knocked it out. Condit was a cold fish. He was guilty of *shtupping* her, but not killing her. But at the time everybody was making a whole *tsimmis* about it, there was no Plausible Alternative Scenario about what could have happened to her. Other than Condit, of course. There was no crazy ex-boyfriend, no stalker from where she worked. The only plausible suspect was that poor Condit—even though he didn't do it. If not Condit, then who? If not Bobby, then who?"

"We can investigate who else might want to hurt the sculptor, see if there's anything there."

"I agree," the Cohn of Silence said, lukewarm.

"You don't seem to be sold on that."

"Oh, but I am. What worries me is—depending on what we find, of course—is that I don't want our scenario to be one of those O.J.-Simpson-the-Colombian-drug-lords-did-it things. That's a scenario, but it's not plausible."

"All due respect, Mr. Cohn, you're jumping to conclusions before we've even investigated. Something else is bothering you."

"Perceptive. What's bothering me is show business. You see, Jonah, everybody in every walk of life is full of shit, it's just a question of how much. I'm a lawyer: I, too, am somewhat full of shit, but not completely. In show business, everybody's completely full of shit, therefore everybody's a suspect."

"We'll have to look into everybody who's close to Bobby."

"We'll have to look into the very people who are signing our checks, Jonah. If any of them presents a Plausible Alternative Scenario, my obligation as an officer of the court is to acquit Bobby, not his entourage."

"Do you think Bobby's capable of murder?"

"Jonah, did you ever see the movie *Whatever Happened to Baby Jane?*"

"Years ago. It's fuzzy."

"Bette Davis is a hag who used to be a child star named Baby Jane. After her house of horrors is discovered—dead bodies, her invalid sister all tied up—she goes running after the poor slob who discovers it. Baby Jane is screaming about her innocence and how everybody's mean to her. She screams, 'He's going to tell!' Do I think Bobby's innocent? Of course he's innocent. They're all innocent."

"Scary. I'd hate for my kids to turn out like that."

"They won't."

"How do you know?"

"Because they have parents."

"So did Bobby."

"Show business kills the parents. There are no parents in that life. Now, where do we go at your end?"

"I'd like to do some opinion research to get a handle on a strategy."

"Strategy? Do you know what Hank Aaron said about strategy? 'Just hit the ball hard, somewhere.' I thought that was marvelous: Hit the ball hard, somewhere. Do your research, but know that after we scheme, Hank Aaron's strategy is going to be our strategy, too."

"I want to reach out to some guys I've used for investigative work."

"Who does your spooking?"

"The Chief."

"I know Chief Willie. Is he taking on work outside of his casino clients?"

"He likes me. He likes me more when I have cash."

"Enlist the Chief, then. And think about this, which is the main reason I wanted to see you: Right now, Bobby's misfortune is the only game in town. Press. The authorities. Hard for us to do our spade-work in such a hot climate. I understand through the grapevine that you may be able to affect this climate."

"I have that reputation, but I'm not a magician."

"Well, *boychik,* become a magician. Get back to me with some ideas."

"I asked Cindi—"

"The PR broad?"

"Yes. I told her I couldn't do anything until I got fifty grand up front. If we keep at it, a program like this will cost a lot more."

"Understood. Your check will come from me. You are a consultant to legal counsel. That way we are privileged. *Capisce?*"

"*Capisce.*"

Shortly before bedtime, the Cohn of Silence's ice cream truck did its musical waltz onto our street. It stopped outside our house. I dashed out in my gym shorts. The truck's side door slid open, and a bronze hand extended an envelope and an éclair. The door slid closed.

I put the éclair in the freezer, and opened the envelope from Cohn Legal Services and Confections. I suddenly generated a bit more zeal for the cause of Turnpike Bobby Chin.

Derek Plush

"I want to tell Bobby's side of the story."

It was late in the day, and Edie and I took turns facing the ocean where Ricky and Lily were playing. It was my turn to face the sun, which was in the embryonic stages of its decent. My chair was a low number that only rose a few inches from the sand. On the one hand, it was more comfortable than full-sized beach chairs because it allowed me to stretch out my feet. On the other hand, sitting so low made me feel as if I had fallen on my ass, a potential metaphor for my life that I didn't appreciate.

I checked my e-mail on my laptop to see if Tic Turner had sent the photo he had taken of Bobby and me. He hadn't, and I scolded myself for my fanatical thirst.

I was wearing my radio earphones to listen to the news at the top of the hour. The newscast led with the ACPD's discovery of a security tape of Christian Josi entering the Golden Prospect through the parking garage. There was no corresponding footage of him leaving, and his car remained where he had left it.

The ACPD also made public the identity of the pilots who flew Bobby's plane, a Los Angeles–based duo, David D'Amico and Ronald Harwood. Their remains had not yet been positively identified, however.

According to the report, the Coast Guard had begun to troll the ocean and access bays around Atlantic City. Scuba divers were also searching for the sculptor's body beneath the tides. The mayor's office established a telephone hotline of volunteers to assist the ACPD in collecting clues about Josi's disappearance. To the west, I could make out State Police helicopters dotting the heavens above inland fields.

It was the cranial glow that I spotted first. Normally, bald bulletheads in the Ultraviolet Age wore hats on the beach. Not Derek Plush, whose *jihad* in life was to be noticed even if it invited melanoma. He was wearing a navy-blue sport jacket, khaki pants, and a blue Egyptian cloth shirt opened at the neck, revealing an adolescent's hairless chest. In his only compromise with his casual surroundings, Plush wore sneakers rather than his trademark brown-and-white smacked-ass Spectators that were often visible as he crossed his legs on television.

Derek Plush did not walk, he glided. He wore the perpetually self-satisfied Grimace of Olympus. This grimace seemed to say, *It's just so much pressure to be at the center of such BIG THINGS . . .*

By the time Plush arrived at my ass-in-the-sand chair, there was no awkward dance of introduction. He just stood above me awaiting a shibboleth of my awe. I removed my earphones.

"Derek Plush," I said. (I'm facile with words.)

Edie looked up momentarily to appraise the interaction, but turned back, unimpressed with Plush, to watch Ricky and Lily roll around in the shallow current. Her stock jumped a few more points in my eyes.

"Jonah Eastman," Plush said. For a nanosecond, I felt like a media insider. Then, from my lowly vantage point, I felt vulnerable, which was probably the point. So I stood, and took a few steps away from Edie.

Plush did not waste time. I sensed a disparity between Plush's words and the message of his expressions. "I'm sorry to interrupt your time with your family," he began. *I couldn't give a shit about your family.* "But I wanted to get your advice about Bobby Chin." *I want to tell you exactly what you are going to do for me because I can destroy you.*

"He's the singer, right?"

"Why, yes, that's right, Jonah." *Smartass.*

"How can I help you, Mr. Plush?"

"Derek. Jonah, I know you're working with Bobby, but I don't know exactly what you're up to."

"You make me sound sinister."

"I don't necessarily think you're sinister, Jonah. I think you're effective. I just don't know how that jibes with what I'm working on."

"And what is that?"

"A big story on Bobby. A chance for him to tell his story. I've already spoken to Bobby and that . . . Kadaborah about a huge pictorial spread in *Major Player.*"

"Wooooooo."

Plush shot me a schoolmarm look. "Kadaborah implied you're against my story."

"Against it? I didn't know anything about it. All I did was express my opinion that Bobby should lay low. I didn't know until now that you were speaking with Bobby and Kadaborah."

Why the hell was I defending myself to this guy? Because with a flick of the Send key on his laptop, he could ruin me, that's why.

"Now that you know about my story, how do you feel?"

"I'm concerned about Bobby being in the press too much."

"But why?"

"He may end up on trial for his life, Derek. It's not smart to pose for pictures in *Major Player* when you may be on the line for big crimes. We're not just pimping an album here."

"There would be more than pictures, Jonah."

"That's what worries me. The pictures are the bait. That's what draws Bobby in. Kadaborah's mission in life is to keep Bobby happy. Pictures will do that. Bobby won't read what you write, but potential jurors will. Other journalists will. People will wonder why a criminal suspect is having such a good time."

Plush frowned. He couldn't tell me I was nuts because he knew my suspicions were anchored in life experience with guys like him. "I disagree with your assessment, Jonah. I want to tell Bobby's side of the story." *I'm going to cornhole the freak because he is so OVER. There's nothing Bobby could do for me.* "How could you be opposed to that?"

"Because a photo spread in *Major Player* is very seductive. Seduction scares me."

"Does your pretty wife know that?"

I laughed. "I suspect she does. Don't get me wrong, I respond to seduction, but I worry that Bobby can be so seduced by the candy in one hand that he won't be able to see the knife in the other."

"For a political operative, you don't have much of a strategic sense, do you?"

"That's code, Derek."

"Code?"

"It's a threat. If I don't facilitate your story, you're going to train your laptop at me."

"Are you guilty of something that merits investigation, Jonah?"

"Does it matter? You can write whatever you want, and you're protected by libel law. Hell, how does anybody prove malice? Look, Derek, I'm all for building relationships with the media, but I keep feeling like the Indian shaman who hears the ground rumbling. There's a stampede over the hill that just hasn't come into view yet."

"Perhaps you're right, but keep something in mind: This stampede you feel quivering in the distant tundra was set in motion long before Turnpike Bobby wandered away from his fireball . . . so miraculously."

"You may think I know something I don't know."

"What do you know, Jonah?"

"Just what I read in the newspaper."

"Do you believe Bobby's a killer?"

"I can't imagine that."

"But you're trying to imagine it."

"That's my job."

"It's mine, too, Jonah."

The voice of my grandfather: *Things usually end up going where they're headed.*

His Flagellence

"He promised us a pictorial layout."

I went to a drugstore in Ventnor and picked up the July issue of *Major Player* to research Plush's recent targets prior to confronting the Reverend Kadaborah. I flipped through it before making the purchase. This month, the High Priest of Celebrity Evisceration had set his scalpel on a brewing dynasty. The article, featuring breathtaking photos of a sun-kissed family with the thinnest noses ever to evolve naturally, was entitled "Bottom of the Barrel." At a quick glance, I was tweaked by the words "sordid," "seamy," "reckless," and "beastio-erotic."

I turned to a regular feature comprising society photos. I was struck by the way members of the overclass were always throwing their heads back in uproarious laughter. The captions often read something like this one: "*Major Player* correspondent Derek Plush shares a laugh with Diane von Furstenburg and Brooke Astor." What's so funny? The only thing that could make me laugh this hard at a party would be a centenarian fossil like Brooke Astor falling head over heels down a marble staircase into a plate of spinach dip. *That* would be funny. Maybe it's a character void on my part, or maybe I'm jealous that I don't laugh at parties. Or maybe there's some libidinous part of me that believes I should have been invited. Why won't Diane von Furstenburg tell *me* the very funny joke?

I called the mobile phone number that Turner and Kadaborah shared and told Turner I was dropping by because I had news. I added that I was downstairs in the lobby to make it more difficult for them to rebuff my visit. I was promptly admitted past the scowling ACPD and Bobby's security people onto the penthouse elevator. A few tourists made note of my special status and, regrettably, I felt pretty cool about it. It reminded me of years ago when all of the Spandexed Americans would gawk at the White House, and I would just flip my badge and move right through the northwest gate. Twenty years ago, Jonah.

A crunchy-looking couple presumably dressed in the garb of the Ong's Hat Flagellants bowed toward Kadaborah before leaving Bobby's suite.

"Thank you for seeing us, Your Flagellence," they said in unison, and striking their own chests in a curious way. Then they left.

Turner was skulking about the dining room. Kadaborah gestured like a corrupt cardinal for me to enter the deeper chambers of his lair. Bobby was nowhere to be found.

"Thank you for seeing me," I said, bowing just a little.

"I understand there's a development," Kadaborah said.

"I got an ambush visit from Derek Plush. He said you've been co-operating on a story he's doing on Bobby."

"You seem nonplussed. I'm Bobby's business manager. Do I have to clear everything with you?" Kadaborah asked.

"If you want Bobby to survive this, it would be smart to keep those handling public opinion apprised."

"It's just a magazine article."

"Do you know Derek Plush's M.O.? He skewers."

"He promised us a pictorial layout."

"That's his snare. Look at what he did this month to the Hernsen family, the big brewers. Pretty pictures, but there's something in here about the daughter and a dachshund."

"Maybe she likes dogs."

"As *sperm donors?*"

"Oh."

"Look, Plush knows Bobby wants his picture in *Major Player*. Plush will hammer him in the text."

"Are you psychic, Jonah?"

"I grew up in a casino. I'm all about odds. Plush will kill Bobby. He sold you the story on photos by Elena Molotov-Weinberg. I know you like to keep Bobby docile, but this fix may destroy him."

"How much worse can things get? And where's the Eastman magic Cindi sold us on? Or is that an optical illusion?"

"Yes, it's an optical illusion. I'm in the reality business. What does Cindi say about working with Plush?"

"She was all right with it," Kadaborah said. "Now, what reality would you like to share with me?"

"Anything that provokes the media and the public also provokes law enforcement and a potential jury. Bobby doesn't need more enemies."

"But he does need a reason to go on living, Jonah," said Boss Flagellant.

"And that reason is media coverage?"

His Flatulence's jaw tightened. It occurred to me that there was a slim chance, very slim, that perhaps Kadaborah knew what he was doing, and I was the one who was missing something.

"Not everything is about your narrow agenda, Jonah," Kadaborah said, perhaps not wrongly.

"How could I possibly gain from giving this advice? If anything, I'm trying to do the right thing for my client."

"A good inner dialectic to engage in, don't you think?"

"Sure. Has Bobby sat down with Plush yet for his interview?"

"No."

"Good. All I ask is this: let me have a training session with Bobby. I want Mr. Cohn with me. You have to understand that anything he says in this interview is fair game in a legal inquiry."

"If you say so."

"I say so. Do we have a deal? Will you agree that Mr. Cohn and I can prep Bobby for his interview with Derek Plush?"

"Bobby doesn't *do* preparations very well, Jo—"

"Does he *do* getting raped in prison well, Reverend?"

"Fine. OK. You can prep him."

Action on Million Dollar Pier

"I had a pattern in life of getting rolled."

My routine summer morning run put me on the Boardwalk in Ventnor by seven. I could see through the little window in a newspaper vending machine that the featured visual in the *Packet* was a grainy photo of Christian Josi in the elevator bank of the Golden Prospect, the optical striptease that would hopefully lead to the money shot—Turnpike Bobby Chin doing the perp walk.

During the work week, the Boardwalk was sparse even with the exercise traffic, so I liked running here. On the weekends, it was actually safer to run along Atlantic Avenue because the chances were slimmer I would get hit by a car on the street than a bicycling yenta on the Boardwalk. My guard was always down through Ventnor because my fellow exercisers were harmless. Carbo-counting yuppies. Speed-walking grannies. Bicycling tourists marveling at the beachfront palaces bloating as they glided south toward Longport. Once I got to Atlantic City, however, my heart monitor always registered a more rapid rate despite how the thickening crowd slowed me down.

The Atlantic City Boardwalk first thing in the morning was like shining an ultraviolet blue light into the sink of a public restroom on the New Jersey Turnpike. Oddly shaped creatures squirmed about as if under a microscope like toxic protozoa. Betrayed dreams were stamped on faces, living fossils of the American spiritual underbelly. The creatures showed not the slightest intention of altering their trudge paths for me, another yuppie jogger as far as they were concerned. Especially not the two hefty rednecks leaning against a railing near Million Dollar Pier.

The blond goon, wearing a mullet and a sleeveless T-shirt stepped out directly in my running path. His darker partner reached out and yanked off my radio earphones. I tried pulling them back, but failed because the blond punched me hard in the gut, reducing me to a fetal position on the Boardwalk. The radio unit itself was still in my hand until a foot with a construction boot stomped on it hard until I released the contraption. The two men were above me now. Mullethead bent down, resting his knee on my sternum, which knocked the remaining oxygen from my lungs and onto the boards along with my reddening spit.

"Curiosity killed the bird, asshole," Mullethead said.

In my degradation, I tried to say "the cat," as in "curiosity killed the cat," but my lips died fast. At these moments, despite the emasculation, one's primary instinct is to live, not educate. Both monsters leveraged their feet beneath me, forklift style. With twin grunts, they heaved me over the side of the Boardwalk onto the beach, where I remained until a seagull landed on the railing above me and crapped a pungent purple grenade onto my scalp.

In the movies, when a guy gets beaten up, he walks around with his wounds as if they were combat medals. Occasionally he'll wince a little like Indiana Jones when the hottie he's teamed with dresses the wound. Not with Jews. We go to doctors.

I was having a hard time breathing, so I walked to the Golden Prospect and asked the concierge who had been there since Mickey's tenure to find me a lift to Atlantic City General Hospital. The hotel called ahead to make sure I was seen right away.

As I sat on the tissue paper in the doctor's office feeling like pastrami takeout, I took a moment to reflect upon my tormentors. They had been waiting for me. They knew my running route. They had delivered a message, even though I didn't know yet what it was. The bad news for me was that I had a pattern in life of getting rolled. The good news was that I had a track record of successfully figuring out who had rolled me. And getting back at them, something for which I am not the least bit apologetic.

I was thinking about Tic Turner. Porn star. Sleazoid director. Situational private investigator. Self-styled storm trooper for the gentle Reverend Kadaborah. It was a message job. *Just know, Jonah, that despite your fabled pedigree, you are touchable. Do what we tell you to do with Bobby, and it'll all be cool.*

A doctor came in and asked me what had happened because he saw no serious visible wounds. I answered the doc, adding that I didn't want to press charges. He said I probably bruised a rib or two. He prescribed a turbo dose of Tylenol and staying away from assholes. I'd try to oblige him, but this was a chronic problem for me.

Chief Willie Thundercloud

"Hard to dig when vultures circling your ass."

Everyone who practices the seat-of-the-pants art of damage control asks himself this terrible question at three o'clock in the morning: What if my client is lying to me?

I knew that Bobby & Company were withholding information, but in the entertainment business, lying was built into the dialogue, so it was hard to separate it from the everyday give-and-take.

I needed answers if I was to do my job correctly. If I wasn't going to learn about the plane crash and Christian's disappearance from Bobby and the Maggots, I'd go elsewhere for my ugly truths.

Chief Willie Thundercloud, a 1970s-era professional wrestler and authority on Native Americana, now had a unique calling. He was known as a "boomerang." His job was to make sure that money that had left casinos under suspicious circumstances (cheating) came back by any means necessary. If a casino suspected someone was scamming them but couldn't prove it, they sent Chief Willie out to "investigate." The Chief's activities, of course, were largely illegal; after all, one couldn't always find evidence of scamming. Nevertheless, casino operators felt that the message value of letting the Chief loose outweighed the risk of prosecution.

The most interesting thing about Chief Willie was that he wasn't an Indian, he just thought he was. Sometimes. He was a stocky, ruddy-complexioned half-Irish/half-Jewish Jersey boy named Marty Kramer who had done odd—very odd—jobs for my grandfather along with his ad hoc band of former wrestling colleagues, including Sheik Abu Heinous (Vinnie Santafurio) and the Viking (Stu Moskowitz).

Above Chief Willie's kitchen table, which served as the global headquarters of Peace Pipe Asset Retrieval Worldwide (motto: "We can find your ass anywhere"), was a blowup of a Gary Larson *Far Side* cartoon. It portrayed a professor outlining for a colleague on a blackboard how *four* wrongs actually *do* make a right when calculated using a particular formula.

"Chief Willie's heart grow big with return of Mongoose," Chief Willie said when I showed up at his Margate house. He was wearing his headdress. The Chief had assigned me the Indian name "Mongoose Behind the Dune" on a prior case. I pretended to cherish the gesture.

"I couldn't think of anyone else I'd rather work with. The Cohn of Silence also sends his regards."

"Ah, Cohn of Silence. A man who speaks volumes through discretion. Is he on the case?"

"Yes, I brought him in. The client is Turnpike Bobby Chin."

"Chief Willie following that affair. Stinks like buffalo shit downwind at high noon. I see Kierkegaard at work."

"Kierkegaard?"

"Kierkegaard wrote about 'leveling.' The desire by the masses to destroy the individual. Bobby is an individual. He must be cut down to keep the mob happy."

"Right, sure."

I told him everything I knew about the case, including interactions with the Maggots. "In terms of your role, Chief Willie, Mr. Cohn and I are thinking about a couple of things. For one, we're going to have to find out how innocent our client is. We'll need what Mr. Cohn calls a—"

"Plausible Alternative Scenario."

"Good. We don't know quite what to make of these characters who manage his career, Kadaborah and Turner. We'll need to learn more about them and, of course, this sculptor, Christian, who vanished."

"Chief Willie say, 'Hard to dig when vultures circling your ass.' "

"That brings us to our big challenge. The media are all over the place. In order for Mr. Cohn to have time to prepare for a potential defense for Bobby, we need to have the press looking in a few different directions. Like you said, we can't learn much when every move we make is being watched. I'm doing a few polls to get a sense of what our options might be, and will report back to you."

"Mongoose," Chief Willie said in businesslike mode. "To do what I have to do with the P.A.S., I'll need to know more about what goes on in Bobby's mind. Do you have any theories?"

"A few, but I'm going to consult with a colleague of mine who may have better insight."

"Do you have a shrink on staff?"

"No, but very close by."

"Good. I thought for a second that the Eastman wigwam grew."

"Nah, it's still only me." I shared with Chief Willie my Big Theory on employees: *One employee is two full-time jobs.* Which is why I don't have 'em. I work only with independent contractors. This way, everyone understands what the relationship is all about and there's no need for breastfeeding, which is all "management" really is. The problem with my operating philosophy, of course, is that there is no delegation. There are no buffers. There are no vacations.

"I admire your misanthropy. But I need my crew. And, Mongoose," Chief Willie patted my knee in fake patronization, "there's no 'I' in 'team.' "

"Well, there's no 'U' in 'blow me.' "

Chief Willie howled.

"While we're on the subject of my business, I need your advice on a problem I'm having that falls within your area of expertise." I told him about being stiffed for eighty-three grand by the borough of Hopkins Pond.

Chief Willie scratched his red beard and imparted his own Big Theory on business: "Chief Willie say, 'Three quarters of business talk comes down to three words: 'Me no pay.' "

Then, escorting me to my car, he shut his eyes and pinched his forehead as if making a psychic gesture. "Do you know what Napoleon said about battlefield strategy?"

"No."

"Engage the enemy and see what happens."

book two

SATURATION COVERAGE

Men are only as loyal as their options.
—BILL MAHER

All Bobby All the Time

"Nobody ever filled twenty-four hours of
cable with the words 'All's well.' "

You know the media are on to a winner when the on-air talent starts with the self-reflection. Are we covering this story too much? What does it say about us that we're covering this story so much? *Well,* the rationalization goes, *nowadays the popular culture IS news, and this is a huge pop culture story.* Navel-gazing is the passport for salaciousness. One can only serve up the nipple if one is having a PUBLIC DIALOGUE about the ROLE OF SEXUALITY in national discourse. With the exception of Animal Planet, it seemed as if every other television outlet had a hook for the Turnpike Bobby story. I caught a few of them.

The Galaxy Broadcast Channel had a camera crew outside every place Bobby was believed to have spent time during the past four decades. The owner of a Brentwood, California, stationery store where Bobby had once bought a scented candle commented about how his choice of sandalwood betrayed a gentle soul, therefore he could not have murdered Christian Josi. Murder had become a more viable cause for speculation ever since a washcloth with Christian's blood had purportedly been found in a dumpster near the Golden Prospect late last night. Despite the media's desperation to make a connection, no one could offer up a viable theory on what the disappearance of the sculptor had to do with the Pine Barrens plane crash.

GuilTV featured back-to-back former prosecutors dissecting how the ACPD had botched the investigation into the disappearance of Christian Josi. It wasn't clear what these geniuses would have done differently, nevertheless, the specter of failure was the coin of the punditry realm. Nobody ever filled twenty-four hours of cable with the words "All's well."

The Legal News & Views Channel showed defense attorneys cross-talking about how Bobby's lawyers had blown his potential defense despite the nuance that he hadn't been charged with anything yet. The call-waiting telephone features of Jewish mothers nationwide were operating in overdrive as friends and relatives were alerted about the appearances of their brilliant sons on TV.

The Apology Channel had on psychologists, grief counselors, and corporate public relations people who suggested that if Bobby "fessed up" and "said he was sorry" he could bring "closure" to all those "wounded."

QNN (Queer News Network) ran an hourlong profile of Bobby, which, in between segments of *Mega Boy* and concert footage, featured men who claimed to have slept with Bobby.

The political news channel GraftNet invited on pollster Abel Petz, who shared a helpful sound bite.: "Turnpike Bobby isn't about rock and roll, Turnpike Bobby is about a rock and a hard place."

Global World News's media critic debated the ethics of a newspaper having run a zoom-lens photo of a naked Bobby scratching his ass on the Golden Prospect balcony. The offending ass-scratching photo from the paper was displayed on the TV screen during this debate. Later in the segment, the ethics of paying interviewees was debated when it was revealed that the Queer News Network had paid the men who claimed to have had sex with Bobby. The men returned to the airwaves to defend their having been paid, and repeated the allegations.

The only bit of actual hard news was the release of a statement by the airplane charter company that flew Bobby during the day of his fateful crash that their two presumed-dead pilots, David D'Amico and Ronald Harwood, were very much alive. The Atlantic City Police Department released a statement which read, in part: "We have not yet identified the bodies discovered at the crash site, but it's obvious that they do not belong to Bobby Chin or either of the pilots whose names appeared on the flight manifest that day. We are still searching the crash area and the wreckage for potential evidence of other passengers."

Cindi e-mailed me a partial segment of an interview with Bonita Chin, Turnpike Bobby's mother, which ran on KBRO. The screen showed a blonde in her late sixties who had probably been attractive during the Buddy Holly era. I envisioned her in the late 1950s quivering on that fragile precipice that divided the cheerleader who was said to be "spunky" with the one who could degenerate into a flaxen-haired bulldog. She was standing in front of a split-level home wearing an expression that appeared to be shouting, "You're not better than me!" She spoke in the Philadelphia-South Jersey accent known as Phlersey, in which the vowels were pinched and stretched simultaneously. *Home* was pronounced *hee-UME. Moon* came out *mee-YUNE. County* was *kee-OWWN-tee.* The interviewer, the ubiquitous Al Just, queried:

KBRO: "You were an entertainer, weren't you, Mrs. Chin?"
Mrs. Chin: "I danced and I sang at Skinny D'Amato's 500 Club. I was also runner-up for Miss Atlantic County in 1958. A lot of people think the competition was rigged against me. The mob and whatnot—"
KBRO: "What caused the estrangement between you and Bobby?"
Mrs. Chin: "I was a singer myself, as I said. I was with the

Shirelles for a bit. I had a manager who said I was THIS CLOSE to becoming one of the Shirelles permanently. The thing is that Bobby was never willing to put himself out for anyone but himself. He never thought about my needs."

Her needs.

So *this* was one of the ingredients in the concoction that had souf-fléed itself into Turnpike Bobby Chin. Watching this remnant of a showgirl melt into pancake on screen made me reconsider who might have insight into Bobby's pendulum swings from infantilism to shrewdness. I'd have to accelerate my visit to Mustang Sally.

As the interview with Bobby's mother closed out, KBRO played a verse from one of Bobby's songs. Bobby voice warbled something like, *"You smell like a rare bird fungus."*

A Philadelphia tabloid ran with a photo of Bobby sitting by the Golden Prospect pool along with a caption: KILLER IN THE SUN? This, of course, was a Springsteen lyric, which must have driven Bobby to levels of madness he hadn't yet experienced.

When I put down the newspaper, there was a knock on my door. It was a courier who asked me to sign for an envelope. This had never happened while we were down the Shore. We always re-ceived our mail back home in Cowtown. The envelope was crème-colored. A law firm's name mooned me in block letters from the upper lefthand side. I had either inherited big money or was getting hosed. The arc of my life suggested the latter.

The correspondence was from the attorneys for the polling subcon-tractor I had retained to do the Hopkins Pond survey. My buddy Hank. I'd either have to pay Hank out of my own pocket, or sue the town of Hopkins Pond for the eighty-three grand they owed me. I had been hoping it wouldn't come to this, but it looked like it just had.

Neighbor Poll

"People don't process information, people process drama."

We held our first focus groups at an office building in Pleas-antville, which was just inland from Atlantic City. My hypothesis was simple: People demand drama from the news. If-it-bleeds-it-leads logic. If I could isolate what interested people and, more important, what didn't, I might be able to flesh out the Cohn of Silence's Plausible Alternative Scenario about what really happened to Christian.

This survey activity was an offshoot of a dubious science called "jury consulting," the objective of which is to identify the kind of jurors who may be friendly or hostile to your client, and the arguments that resonate and don't. What made this effort different was that Bobby was not yet a defendant. Our goal, therefore, was to influence the outcome of the process so that either he wouldn't be charged or, if he was, we would lay the groundwork for his acquittal.

The focus group that we assembled was representative of the population of a potential Atlantic City jury pool. We had eight participants, including two black men, two black women, a Hispanic man, two white women of varying ages, and a young white man.

The moderator was Eliza Baird, a seasoned psychologist I had worked with for many years who had a gift for drawing people out and obscuring the identity of our client. An attractive, businesslike woman of about fifty, most of her work was health care–oriented, Eliza having been corrupted during the 1960s into thinking she could make a positive contribution to society. As offensive as I found this attribute to be, I had persuaded Eliza from time to time to take a walk on the wild side, and probe the underbelly of the American psyche. Working with me, she had said on more than one occasion, was a spiritual extension of her board membership at a Philly-area school for juvenile delinquents.

Our first focus group was a disaster. My hypothesis was roundly trashed. This group indicated that consumers were not as interested in the sensational as I had thought: they were suffering from "salacious saturation," according to one woman.

"Could there be anything wrong with the methodology we're using?" I asked when the session was over.

"I'm not sure," Eliza said. "I was thinking that maybe one problem is that we have a group setting."

"What do you mean?"

"There's a group dynamic. In groups, people care what others think. One-on-one, there's a sense of confidentiality. We may be able to draw people out more one-on-one."

"I buy that, but something else is bothering me. Can I ask you a rude question?"

Eliza appeared suspicious.

"What kind of man do you find attractive?" I asked.

Eliza scrunched up her nose. "Where is this going, Jonah?"

"Bear with me. I'm not hitting on you. What's your husband like?"

"He's average height, like you. He's really skinny, though."

"Stereotype him."

"Stereotype? I don't like—"

"Exactly. Do it anyway."

"He's a professor at Temple. I suppose he looks like a professor."

"Have you ever fantasized about a huge, muscular construction worker?"

"Jonah! I don't see—"

"All right, I'll back off. I'm sorry. Let me tell you some of the things I think about down deep where nobody can see."

"Is this going to be gross?"

"No. Just offensive." I inhaled deeply and let go with my stream of consciousness: "If I found a sack of cash while I was out running in the woods, I'd probably keep it if nobody was looking. . . . I think Anna Nicole Smith is a loopy skank, but I'd do her. . . . When I saw those pictures of Iraqi POWs being humiliated, I really didn't give a damn. . . . I thought Kennedy was a stud and Judith Campbell was a slut even though they were doing the same damned thing. . . . I think Islamic fundamentalists hate America because they can't cut it in the modern world, not because we did anything wrong. . . . Farts are funny. . . . I've always suspected there's some trick to sex that I never caught on to, and I think about it a lot. . . . I'd rather sit home and watch a movie I've already seen ten times than travel to someplace in-teresting. . . . The United Nations is gay. . . . I think successful people are smarter and harder-working than failures. . . . The French don't like Americans, and I have no idea why I should care. . . . People who eat too much and get fat don't deserve a frigging dime from the food companies they sue. . . . I felt vindicated when I ran into a girl who ignored me twenty-five years ago and saw she now had an ass the size of the Liberty Bell. . . . Luck is everything. . . . I love my kids more than other people love theirs. . . . I thought the bursting of the Inter-net bubble was funny and liked seeing all those smug billionaire ge-niuses with their synergies and their connectivity and their e-commerce working behind the counter at Arby's. . . . There are certain people who invite me to lunch, and I don't follow through because I don't want to have lunch with them—ever. . . . Some people are just plain boring. . . . I think life's too short to do the right thing all the time. . . . I've never enjoyed a Hemingway book in my life. . . . Big companies shouldn't waste their time saying they care about people when everybody knows they don't. . . . I have a competitor, another pollster, who I hope gets caught screwing a Brownie. . . . I'd rather take a nap than go to a museum. . . . Stereotypes are true a lot of the time, or at least they give you somewhere to start. . . . Asian people drive too slow. . . . Americans who go to dangerous parts of the world and screw with savages shouldn't be surprised if they end up on the wrong end of a machete. . . . Lots of art sucks. . . . Rap music sucks, but nobody can say it because they're afraid to be called racists. . . . People who inherit money usually think they earned it. . . . Most lawyers who say they represent the little people are gangsters. . . . I cherish my free speech, but don't care if people I strongly disagree with are muzzled. . . . People want to be lied to provided it's done with finesse. . . . That's about it."

Eliza was expressionless. She studied my pupils to see if they were red or dilated. I just breathed slowly. After about thirty seconds of fearing for her life, she said softly, "I don't think I'll ever look at you the same way again."

"That's my point. I told you ugly things that I think, or have thought. I may pay a price for that in my relationship to you. The people in that focus group were just people. They have certain thoughts, but they're not going to say them out loud because there will be a price."

"Jonah, it sounds like you have a working hypothesis you're not sharing."

"I do. I don't believe these people *aren't* interested in scandal. I know there's oil down there, I just don't know how to drill to get it. If I can attach what they really feel, I can help Bobby somehow."

"The media will go with whatever's controversial and dramatic, not what's true, is that what you're saying?"

"The media won't go with controversy in a vacuum, they'll go with it because that's what the people want. Everybody blames the media. They're just retailers. People don't process information, people process drama. Nobody gives a damn about everyday life. We want to see what kind of things are happening to other people. Who's lucky in life, who's striking out, who's ahead of us, who's behind, rich people losing their fortunes, poor people winning the lottery."

"So what do you suggest?"

"I suggest one-on-one interviews, like you mentioned."

"Do you think it'll make a big difference if I ask people what they think one-on-one?" Eliza asked, backtracking.

"You're not going to ask them what they think, Eliza."

"I'm not?"

"No. You're going to ask them what their neighbor thinks."

Dismissive Apathy

*"You hear about these things that happen close
to home and you can't believe it."*

I t's not easy to turn opinion research upside-down on short notice,
but one of Eliza Baird's gifts was improvisation. The following day,
she embarked on a daylong schedule of one-on-one interviews.
These were all to be recorded for later analysis. The interviewee could
not see me, but would be told that someone might or might not be on
the other side of the one-way mirror. Each session would last about
one hour. I could handle about three of these before I would impale
myself with one of the huge magic markers that were scattered
around the table. After all of her interviews were complete, Eliza
would write up a report summarizing her findings.

Eliza's first one-on-one interview was with a Haddonfield woman
named Sarah Shackley. Sarah was a software consulting executive in her
mid-forties. Eliza began with questions about Sarah's media habits, her
news sources, magazine subscriptions, and political interests. Sarah
watched CNN Headline News every morning and listened to a local
radio talk show as she drove to work, occasionally with a colleague who
liked to listen to shock jocks and other tabloid-driven programming.

"What about this colleague? What did you say her name was?"

"Maya. I've worked with her for a long time. We carpool to the
office twice a week."

"What's Maya's particular interest?"

"Wife killers," Sarah laughed. "She watches all of those entertainment shows. I guess they're really not entertainment, but you know, those channels that talk about people like that Yates chick who drowned her kids. Or was that Susan Smith? Actually, they both drowned their kids. There was that woman right here in Jersey where the husband faked a car accident that killed her, but everybody thinks he really did it. Laci Peterson, those Mormon people."

"What do you say to Maya when she listens to these things?"

"I say, 'What's with you? Enough is enough.'"

"It's interesting that you know the names of some of these people."

"Believe me, if you spent time with Maya, you'd know 'em, too."

The second respondent was Leon Vilera of Pleasantville. A well-groomed Hispanic man in his early forties, Leon was a sales manager for one of the major casinos in Atlantic City. His job was to book and cater corporate events at his hotel. Perhaps the most remarkable thing about his interview was his reaction to the name of Turnpike Bobby Chin, which was one of a handful that Eliza threw out. Whereas I (due to my own acute biases) had anticipated overt disdain for Bobby, Leon conveyed dismissive apathy. Despite all of the news coverage of Bobby—which would have suggested a desire to gossip about him—Leon wanted to move on to other celebrities—Martha Stewart, Tom Cruise, Jennifer Lopez, George Clooney.

Yvonne Hawley, our third respondent, was a regional manager for a jewelry chain. A striking black woman of thirty-three, Yvonne took good care of herself. She had a crisp, no-nonsense demeanor about her that conveyed authority. She got her news through the

Philadelphia Inquirer, avoided television, and listened to music when she exercised, which she did four or five times a week. Yvonne's answers were short. Her smiles were economical, which was a shame because she was very pretty when she showed emotion. She reminded me of the sportscaster Pam Oliver, whose face lit up like a coastal sunrise when she smiled. The same seriousness that initially broadcast authority eventually suggested a woman afraid of someone tinkering inside her brain.

"What about celebrity news?" Eliza asked.

"I don't pay attention to it," Yvonne said.

"Do you see movies, read about musicians?"

"Not really."

"Why not?"

"I think celebrities are from outer space," Yvonne said, grinning a little.

"How so?"

"I operate in the real world, a world with deadlines and responsibilities. Celebrities . . . I just don't have patience for them and the way they live."

"Are there any celebrity stories in the news that you're aware of?"

"Didn't Jennifer Lopez get married again?"

"I'm not sure."

"See, that's what I mean," Yvonne said, more animated now. "We're supposed to care about J. Lo and there are so many more important things going on in the world, but we can't avoid her. I mean, who *cares?*"

"That's an interesting question, Yvonne. Who do you think cares?"

"I don't think anyone cares. It's like J. Lo is inflicted on us. She's dropped on me like a bomb every day."

"But you don't really follow celebrity news, you said."

"No, I don't. I don't follow it because I don't care about it."

"Yet you know Jennifer Lopez by her nickname, J. Lo."

"I can't avoid it. No one can. When I go into the supermarket to buy a Lean Cuisine, she's staring out at me from the shelves."

"You seem to have strong feelings about this."

"My sister, Lisa, and I talk about it all the time," Yvonne said, now in schoolgirl mode. "Everything with her is Puff Daddy or P. Diddy or Eminem. She's younger than I am. I don't like that music. I call it crap music. Am I allowed to say that?" Yvonne glanced around the room as if the potty-mouth cops were going to burst in and arrest her.

"You can say whatever you want."

"I don't care about who Julia Roberts is married to this week. Lisa cares. She's obsessed with it."

"Tell me more about that."

"I don't know what else to tell you. Lisa went to see the Letterman show with some friends last year. Denzel Washington and Natalie Portman were guests. So Lisa went out and rented every Denzel and Natalie Portman movie ever made. For months, all we saw was Denzel and Natalie."

"Did you watch the movies?"

"Some of them. But enough is enough. There are so many more important things to care about."

"Like what?"

"War, terrorism, crime."

"Are there particular stories you would tune into? News stories?"

"I'm not big on the terrorism stuff. After a while, I think, 'What can I do about it anyway?' But you hear about these things that happen close to home and you can't believe it—people who kill their families, hit-and-runs, missing kids, companies that go broke when the boss loots the till. It's scary."

———

Early the following week, Eliza Baird submitted her report on the sixteen respondents she had interviewed. It contained the following conclusions:

1. Respondents do not think of themselves as being interested in celebrity news or salacious human-interest stories, but awareness of subjects that respondents claim to find repugnant is, nevertheless, high. Respondents, however, overwhelmingly believe that *others* are interested in such stories.

2. Turnpike Bobby Chin is almost universally seen as a source of cultural spectacle versus substantive human interest. Furthermore, Chin does not, in any decipherable way, possess a "magnetic flaw"—a morally offensive behavior pattern that people find to be perversely endearing or charismatic (e.g., President Bill Clinton and adultery, Tony Soprano and violence).

3. Respondents have an underlying or free-floating sense of nearby danger, as if they have reserved an emotional "fund" of grief that awaits a catalyst in which to transfer these resources. Recall that prior to September 11, 2001, Americans were hysterical about a killer shark epidemic, deadly rollercoaster rides, dangerous household mold, and the fate of missing Capitol Hill intern Chandra Levy. Americans seem to demand hysteria.

And there's always the retail news media to supply the demand. "Salacious saturation," my ass.

Mustang Sally

*"Castrating smoke alarms is just ducky until a five-alarm fire
breaks out and the whole thing goes up."*

Mustang Sally had the most lucrative psychiatric practice at the
Jersey Shore. She specialized in failed entertainers, especially
performers in "tribute bands"—once they began to discover
that they really weren't Van Halen or Nirvana. She was also a director
of the Heidi Fleiss Free Enterprise Fund, whose charter was to inspire
capitalist innovation for women—retired, uh, massage therapists—
who had little chance of inventing a microchip. A handful of successful small women-owned businesses in Atlantic City had received seed
money and entrepreneurial counsel from the grants unit (the Fleiss
Board of Finance, or FleissBOF).

When I first met her in the early 1980s, Mustang Sally was a showgirl at the Golden Prospect Hotel working her way through medical
school at the University of Pennsylvania. I knew Mustang, who was a
few years older than I was, was different from the other showgirls
when I caught her reading Alice Miller's *The Drama of the Gifted
Child* on Million Dollar Pier. Sitting next to her was another chorus
girl named Mercedes or Porsche or some other wicked-cool car;
however, this hot rod was reading a pop-psych number called *Body
Language.* It was basically about how to trap men into marriage by

shaking one's ass to the left three times, or to the right four times, or whatever.

Mustang was adorable, teeny-tiny—she looked like a kid—but what made her stand out among the other showgirls was her capacity to peel back the skulls of her contemporaries and tell them exactly what was on *their* minds. My grandmother Deedee loved Mustang because neither of them could tolerate the whining of beautiful women who professed to be shocked at why they were being mistreated by men. "Because you wanna be!" Mustang would tell them, prompting a "You said it, babycakes!" from my grandmother. If Deedee was the Don of the showgirls who worked for her husband's hotel, Mustang was her consigliere.

Mustang Sally's practice was in a modestly decorated room at the Celebrity Motel in Atlantic City. The Celebrity was a two-story dive. Its logo was a giant Marilyn Monroe caricature featuring the dead star winking at passersby from atop her sunglasses while stardust fell into her cleavage. Yes, gents, the Answer is Down There. Mustang's office was sandwiched beneath the "headquarters" of Fatima the Netherworld Hell Bitch–Dominatrix and Indra the Pet Psychic, who may have been the same mental patient shuttling between the two rooms.

I knocked. No one answered the door, so I took the audacious step of opening it myself. Mustang Sally was sitting at a sleek Euro-design desk, her back to me. She was wearing earphones and a pink leather getup with matching stiletto pumps. She was looking at something online, photographs that appeared to be tapestries in various reds. A feature article on Mustang Sally's fifty-foot schooner, *Lady Sarah Tonin,* was framed on the wall beside her. I tapped Mustang Sally on the shoulder, and she jumped up, clutching her chest.

"You scared the living shitballs out of me," Mustang Sally said, removing her earphones.

"Frightening petite women makes me feel masculine."

"So, do you love me?" She hugged me.

"I'm obsessed with you in a dangerous way, Stang."

"Correct answer. You look good, gangster boy."

"Damned right I look good. You look like you just left your Brownie troop. Wanna go out for some ice cream?"

"See, this is exactly why I'm thinking of buying myself some new tits. I read about a special a plastic surgeon's got going in Margate. He's calling it Bazonga Jubilee."

"Subtle. Yet tasteful. C'mon, you don't need any work."

"Aw, you're a sweetass—"

"Are you seeing anybody?"

"I was seeing one of the fake Blowfish. From the Hootie and the Blowfish tribute crew, but it didn't work out."

"Was he a patient?"

"No, but I met him through a patient, the fake Michael Stipe from the fake R.E.M."

"I like R.E.M."

"The real or the fake?"

"The real."

"Actually, I prefer the fraud R.E.M. Their Michael Stipe doesn't look as skeletal as the real one. That whole radioactive look is NOT FOR ME."

My eyes suddenly slammed onto her computer screen. *"What the hell are you looking at?"*

"Autopsies. Slicemandicem.com."

"My God, all that red . . . it's blood!"

"It ain't Hi-C, sugah. If you don't know how they died, you don't know how they lived."

"Who's the dude on your screen?"

"Decapitation victim. Carpenter's saw. Probably a suicide." Mustang Sally winked.

"How is this related to your work?"

"It's not. I'm just fascinated by autopsies. Now, what brings you to my humble commode?"

"Can I have doctor-patient confidentiality?"

"Lay it on me, muscles."

I sat on the patient couch and told Mustang Sally everything I knew—and believed—about Turnpike Bobby. Engaged, she skipped over the news items and bore right into the interactions between Bobby and his aides.

"What do you know about entertainers, Jonesy Boy?"

"I assume they're a lot like politicians, Stang."

"With a critical difference. Solipsism."

"What the—?"

"It means the world only exists as you know it to exist. Absolute self-involvement, as if everything else but you is part of a pop-up book that exists only if you open it. Politicians have to interact with the public. There's friction. They're tested. There's a give-and-take in the marketplace. Entertainers in the league we're talking about never leave their interiors. They've got a band of sycophants around them to make sure nothing gets in that pop-up book that's not peachy-keen."

"You can figure this out by dealing with, forgive me, lounge singers and all?"

"Same principle applies, lovebug. Lounge singers have backup singers who'll tell them that the audience wasn't empty, that the real crowd was sitting just beyond the lights past where he could see. Then there's the showgirls. They've got suitors who tell them they're prettier than Julia Roberts and are destined to knock her out of the box office. These suitors are also there to nurse her showgirl ego back after the Asshole Boyfriend beats her like a piñata."

"That's pretty sick. How do you bring this back to Bobby?"

"Bobby's not just a celebrity, baby doll. He's an icon. That's bigger than a celebrity. Ten to one says he's got these handlers who run around disabling smoke detectors so Bobby can light his instruments in peace. Castrating smoke alarms is just ducky until a five-alarm fire breaks out and the whole thing goes up. What concerns me is that you haven't mentioned music. Bobby doesn't seem to love music itself. Music was a Trojan Horse to get what he really wants."

"Which is?"

"Deification."

"Christ, Stang."

"Read about Him, didja? If Bobby cared about music, Jonah, I'd say there's hope. There would be a creative outlet. But Bobby doesn't want music, he wants immortality."

"Is that why his boy, Lonesome Jake, follows him around with a camera? Is the logic that if the media won't cover Bobby, he'll cover himself?"

"The camera may be a placebo."

"That's a pill, right?"

"A *fake* pill. It's possible that Bobby has harangued his people so much about publicity that they provide him with a camera as a prop just to placate him, delay the tantrum. Constant indulgence is at the core of his *schema*. Dissonance will set him off."

"Well, that's true enough."

"Yes, the thing with small-time entertainers—my clientele—is they slam into the ground pretty fast, which is actually a good thing. It facilitates adaptive behavior. With one of these icon disasters, there is a well-financed apparatus to delay the crash. Guys like Bobby aren't allowed to hit bottom, they're only allowed to hit top—till it all goes up in smoke. When little show people crash, it's a bicycle wreck. When icons crash, it's a train wreck."

Or a plane, I thought.

"Could the perpetuation of the disaster be the goal in and of itself?"

"Maybe. Perhaps they're using this Lonesome fellow to palliate Bobby during his final days. One of the reasons why small-time entertainers crash so fast is that they are abandoned so fast. Bandmates leave, a nebbish suitor tires of a showgirl's sluttier-than-thou histrionics and marries a sane woman. Managing a megastar is big business, Jonesy Love. You have to ask yourself, who gains if Bobby lives, dies, succeeds, fails, goes to the slammer?" Mustang Sally put her stilettos up on her desk. "So, Prince Charming, how do you plan to make a morally righteous public feel good about this fruitcake?"

"Most of damage control isn't about morality, Stang. It's about attraction. Attractive people are given moral leeway—Dillinger, Gotti—"

"Clinton."

"In his own way, yeah. What worries me is that Bobby's attractiveness is buried a few hundred news cycles behind us. I can't make him attractive—ever."

"These child actors don't have good trajectories."

I thought about this. There's the porcine obscurity of the Beaver, Jerry Mathers, Leif Garrett. There are the freak show self-parodies of Liz Taylor, Danny Bonaduce, and Barry Williams. Then there's the low-rent deaths of Dana Plato, Judy Garland, that girl who played Buffy on *Family Affair* whose name I can't even remember. Occasionally, a legitimate youth talent matures into a legitimate, well-defended adult talent like Jodie Foster or Kurt Russell, but that's not the way to bet.

I handed Mustang a CD that contained Bonita Chin's interview with KBRO. She popped it into her computer. Bonita's livid face replaced Mustang's autopsy photos.

When the TV segment was over, Mustang said, "What a piece-a work she is."

"How so?"

"Classic pretty girl who got old. Probably had a million boyfriends in high school, thought her whole life was going to be an endless parade of senior proms. Got more flowers than the Botanical Gardens.

Got married on a whim thinking the flowers would keep coming in, but you know how it is, life is life."

"So?"

"So she never gets over being the prom queen, not that any of us like getting older, but this Bonita-chica just can't take it. She's *pissed*— wants it all back, wants her kid to get it back for her. That kind of thing. So what do you do, Jonah?"

"I'll keep you posted if you'll be my sounding board, Stang."

"Hell, honey, for a fee, I'll be your headboard."

The Treatment

"You seem surprised."

On the drive up to Princeton to visit with Christian's office mate, Quaneefra, I shared with Cindi the results of our opinion research.

"What's the big strategy?" she asked.

"In a personality-centered crisis, strategy takes a backseat to personality. Bobby just isn't cool."

"Jonah, are you saying that his problem isn't so much that he killed somebody as it is that he's uncool?"

"Pretty much."

"That explains a lot."

"Like what?"

Cindi blushed. I didn't understand why. "Nothing," she said.

"I don't follow, what does it explain?"

"Just . . . his lack of a fan base is all."

"Is that why you chose the Golden Prospect for his concert? Because it was Bobby's hometown, and it was a small arena you thought you could fill?"

"Look, Jonah, I already told you it was going to be a little concert. Stop with this Sherlock Holmes shit!"

"Whoa!" I said. *OverREACTION!*

When Edie got like this, I had learned that the best coping mechanism was to mentally move onto another subject. So I ruminated on my Big Theory about coolness, which was a variation on the whole Kennedy–Nixon nexus. That Kennedy successfully subverted the very foundation of democracy to steal the White House concerns very few historians. Nixon's unsuccessful efforts to undermine the Constitution during Watergate still has people spitting bile. Why? Kennedy's naughtiness had a certain boys-will-be-boys Rat Pack groove to it. Nixon, however, was seen as a chess club/marching band dorkwad. Uncool.

After marinating in my own sense of futility, I told Cindi about the little Chief Willie had learned about Christian. He was a thirty-five-year-old Princeton graduate, an art major. He had opened a successful studio, propelled largely by foundation money and batty dowagers who liked his work. He was unmarried, dated a professor of sociology off and on, worked very hard, and was a popular figure around campus.

Christian's finances were modest, but he owed money to no one. Nobody had ever sued him. While one could never tell the essence of someone's life from an initial investigation, it was safe to conclude that Christian Josi was a hard man to hate, at least for a normal person.

"So much for the he-had-it-coming-to-him strategy," Cindi said.

"My thoughts exactly."

Christian's studio was in an old wooden townhouse on Nassau Street. The front door was unlocked, so Cindi and I walked right in. The studio to the left must have been a living room prior to its conversion, judging by the fireplace in the perimeter's center. Sunlight burst through the windows, illuminating sculptures of various shapes and sizes. The floors were creaky hardwood.

The studio to the right appeared as if a Category 5 hurricane had swept through it, angrily spitting clay and paint everywhere. Sitting in the rear of that room was a spindly black woman with wild stalks of hair.

"Hello," Cindi said.

"Yes?" the woman responded, glancing up from a spinning explosion before her.

"We work with Turnpike Bobby," Cindi said. "We spoke on the phone."

"Oh, yes," she said, "I'm Quaneefra." She flipped a switch beneath her. The spinning blob slowed as she made her way toward us, hands still covered with clay. "I know you'll forgive me if I don't shake your hand."

"I'm Cindi Handler. I manage publicity for Bobby. This is Jonah Eastman, who does polling work."

"You two have your hands full, I guess," Quaneefra said.

"We do," Cindi agreed.

"I'm not sure how much I can add to what I've already told the police," Quaneefra explained, her bright eyes flickering with silver sparks.

"Did Christian tell you why he was going to meet with Bobby?" I asked.

"Yes. He was excited to show him the little replica he made of the statue that was going to be unveiled."

"To your knowledge, did he take the replica with him?"

"I helped him load it into his car."

"How big was the replica?" I asked.

"About two feet or so."

Cindi began walking around the open studio opposite Quaneefra's. "Is this Christian's place?" her voice echoed.

"Uh-huh. He's much neater than I am, as you can see."

"I saw you on the news," I said. "You said that you became concerned when Christian didn't show up at Starbucks."

"That was our ritual. He was obsessive about his routines."

"Did Christian share with you any thoughts about what he expected from Bobby?"

"He was a little nervous, hoping Bobby would like his interpretation of him. Artists have very thin skin."

"Had he talked to Bobby often about the sculpture?"

"No. They had had one meeting face-to-face. Then there were a few calls, I think. May I ask you something—Jonah, was it?"

"Yes, sure."

"Did Bobby say anything about what he thought of Christian's work?"

"No, we haven't talked about it."

Quaneefra appeared dejected. "What about his take on what might have happened to Christian?"

"Bobby hasn't said anything."

"Did he even say that the two of them met that night?"

"No, Quaneefra, I'm sorry. Bobby didn't discuss it with me." Sensing the woman's hurt, I added: "But his lawyers are telling him to keep silent."

"Do we even know that they met at all, that Christian got there?"

"Yes, I saw him myself."

"You did?"

"I was getting into the elevator when he got out."

"Seriously, you know it was Christian?"

"I saw his photo on the news later. He was pushing a cart that was covered up with a tarp or something."

"Yes, he brought a cart in his truck."

"Where is the real statue, the big one?" I asked.

"Jonah!" Cindi called from the other studio.

Quaneefra and I followed Cindi's voice through Christian's studio into a smaller room at the back of the house. This one was more cluttered. Cindi was staring up at an eight-foot bronze statue of . . . a little boy.

"There it is," Quaneefra said.

Cindi and I exchanged pregnant glances.

"Christian sculpted Bobby as a *child?*" Cindi asked.

"Yes."

"So the little replica would have been—"

"Just like this, only smaller."

I examined the sculpture more closely. There was no question, it was a young, bronzed Bobby, his head tilted to the side in that patty-cake way, the sunlight getting lost in his dimple. His bowl haircut had a three-dimensional quality, cute from one angle, pathetically outdated and uncool from another. While the statue was slick and quite accurate, there was something creepy about its ethnic uncertainty. The Asian influence of Bobby's features could be magnetic in person, but was somehow creepy when bronzed.

"You seem surprised," Quaneefra said.

"No," Cindi and I lied simultaneously, the visceral instinct of flacks.

Quaneefra's translucent eyes asked for elaboration.

"Actually, Quaneefra, I am a little surprised," I conceded. "I had it in my mind that the sculpture would be of Bobby as an adult."

"Funny you say that, so did I," Quaneefra said. "But Christian thought this treatment was the way to go."

"Do you know if someone suggested this . . . treatment?" Cindi asked.

"I'm sorry," Quaneefra said. "I don't know. I think this is something Christian came up with on his own."

"You've been so nice, Quaneefra," Cindi said. "I'm sorry if we haven't been much help. If you think of anything else, would you let us know?"

"Of course. Would you like to see some of the things I'm working on?"

For the next twenty minutes, Quaneefra eagerly showed us some of her paintings and sculptures. I nodded politely, but cursed myself for having so little appreciation of art. As much as I loved good writing, I hadn't the faintest idea what made Picasso great. I didn't know if Quaneefra was brilliant or an idiot. I knew Christian had to have some talent because his work accurately depicted people and things I knew. I knew what Bobby looked like as a boy; I knew what Martin Luther King looked like, and could say, *Yeah, that looks like them.* Quaneefra's work was all bumps and colors and flying globs. What the hell was wrong with me? Was anything wrong with me at all? Was my obliviousness to art some kind of Neanderthal gene I had inherited from Mickey? I didn't know, but had the gnawing sensation that I was doing this decent woman a terrible disservice by having no sense of what her talent offered or robbed from the world.

On the drive back to the shore, Cindi and I contemplated Christian's "treatment" of Turnpike Bobby Chin.

"That was fucked up," Cindi said.

I agreed with her completely, but wasn't sure why.

Googling Bobby

*"The coldest place on earth is the layer of ice
that surrounds the celebrity's inner circle."*

In the Golden Prospect suite, Bobby sat morosely in front of a television. Staci Chin, his sister-in-law, was being interviewed on the Starstruck News Channel. Staci was a big-haired Jersey girl in her late thirties. She was sitting in a contemporary living room of a Pennsauken apartment. Pennsauken was a New Jersey bedroom community a few minutes outside Philadelphia and Camden, about fifty minutes from Atlantic City. The Starstruck interviewer was a Carmen Electra clone whose eyes appeared to be frozen open in shock that someone as hot as she was was interviewing a world-class nobody in a South Jersey apartment.

> **Starstruck:** "When was the last time you saw your brother-in-law, Turnpike Bobby Chin?"
> **Staci (tearfully):** "It's so hard to talk about."
> **Starstruck:** "Do you miss him?"
> **Staci:** "Bobby's baby brother, Michael, and I are just so hurt. We feel so betrayed and abandoned with what happened with our dream home."
> **Starstruck:** "And what was that?"

Staci: "Bobby was just so jealous of the joy in our lives, the joy that the house brought us. When he used his connections at the bank to be sure we didn't get the loan . . . we were devastated."

Bobby clicked off the TV. He then stood up, grabbed hold of a lamp filled with shells, and hurled it out onto the balcony. Thankfully, it fell against the railing and only a few shattered shells spilled over the side. After following the trajectory of the lamp, he settled on a facial expression I can only describe as being philosophical. For about thirty seconds there was a serenity about him, a country-and-western sense of God's will at work. Bobby proceeded slowly over to where Tic Turner was sitting and leaned over his shoulder. Turner was hunched over his laptop. The Google search engine was fired up.

"Put my name in," Bobby demanded.

"Affirmative," Turner said, typing in "Turnpike Bobby Chin."

Google delivered 240,000 "hits," or references, to Turnpike Bobby.

"Yes!" Bobby pumped a fist triumphantly.

There had been no acknowledgment of my arrival.

"Type in Springsteen," I suggested.

Dagger eyes from Turner. Fear in the eyes of Turnpike Bobby Chin.

"Go ahead," Bobby said. "Type in Bruce." As if the two rockers were on a first-name basis. Buds.

Turner keyed in "Bruce Springsteen," which after an agonizing .18 second coughed up 612,000 hits.

"Motherf—," Bobby began.

"Negative. Negative. That couldn't be right," Turner jumped in, the suckass.

The silence was thick and physical in its power. Bobby appeared lost. I wanted him to. Suspense would make him more grateful for my rescue. Mega Pollster Boy was on his way.

"Tic, do you mind if I sit there?" I said. "This couldn't be right," I echoed. "I think there's a more accurate way to do this."

"Do it!" Bobby dared, the message being, *You got me into this quicksand, you get me out!*

I switched places with Turner. "Sometimes these search engines are temperamental," I said. Bobby, his eyes perched open wide nodded, as if technology was his bag.

I typed "Turnpike Bobby" into the engine. After .23 seconds, Google gave me 310,000 hits. "See, guys, we have 310,000 hits for 'Turnpike Bobby.' We had, what, 200,000 hits for 'Turnpike Bobby Chin.'

"240,000," Turner, desperate for redemption, corrected. "Affirmative."

"Right, so that's 550,000," I tallied.

Bobby began nodding like a kindergartner who promised not to get the new P.F. Flyer sneakers in the store window dirty if only his parents would buy them for him. Salvation inching closer.

"Now," I continued, typing in "Bobby Chin." This version of Bobby's name returned 305,000 hits. "How do you like that? This brings you to over 800,000 hits."

"Radical!" Bobby said. "The Dude totally dusted Bruce."

"Dethroned the Boss," Turner sucked.

"Jonah, you're really great at this Internet." Bobby clapped me on the shoulder.

"It's a gift," I said.

Turner purloined one of Bobby's sneers and shot it my way. By digging into my long-repressed political asskissing technique, I had achieved a celebrity-relations coup and faux pas at the same time. On one hand, I had Googled myself closer to Bobby, but had further provoked the wrath of his handlers. The coldest place on earth is the layer of ice that surrounds the celebrity's inner circle. And there was a multibillion-dollar industry staffed by alleged grown-ups to do this shit. Worse, it was an industry that so many actually wanted to be a part of.

I felt my lungs constrict, which I linked with the colossal dishonesty of my Google stunt. What frightened me was the ease and speed with which I performed it. Normally, whenever I pulled my tricks I had pangs of conscience. The thing with Bobby was that he brought something out in me—in everybody who came into close contact with him—that lubricated mendacity.

See You Around

"I want whatever it is that you don't give me."

E die went to the airport to pick up her cousin, Irene Grant, who stayed with us for a few weeks most summers. Irene managed an independent bookstore in Ann Arbor, Michigan. I always looked forward to her visits. Irene had a captivating, if peculiar, skill. Every time she visited us, a major celebrity died. To date, Irene had bumped off Ronald Reagan, Princess Diana, John F. Kennedy Jr., Frank Sinatra, and Bob Hope. She had also dispatched the singer Aaliyah, but this hadn't qualified as a major hit. On a recent telephone call, she betrayed that she had set her sights on the Pope for her upcoming visit. A Catholic, Irene had mixed emotions about this.

I took Ricky and Lily to the beach and watched them roll around in the surf. While Lily remained thoroughly childlike in appearance, her rounded cheeks reverberating with every step she took, Ricky had become more boy than baby. Tall, lean, and serene like Edie, he was graceful in the water. His was more than a natural athleticism; rather, it was a sense of peace with his position in space and time. I had never felt this for myself.

I adored these children madly, and it was not unusual for me to get up in the small hours of the morning to watch them sleep. The only problem with this sentimental ritual was that I didn't know what to do with myself when I felt this way. Sometimes I would walk out of the house in the dead of winter and wipe tears from my eyes alone in the woods. Once Edie asked me what I was doing outside when she felt my cold breath stalking her in bed. I said something about getting fresh air.

I had learned through excruciating life experience that men capable of such emotion are universally abhorred. Despite the claims of most modern women that they want men to be more emotional, this is just chick code that means: *I want whatever it is that you don't give me.* Edie, to her credit, appreciated my paternal affection, but too great a display of this quality would serve to remind her of my insane asylum of a childhood, which she rightly found to be one of my most acute liabilities.

As Ricky and Lily took turns throwing seashells at an out-of-commission jellyfish, a chubby-kneed little girl of about two or three ran into me and fell. She was stunned. I picked her up.

"Are you okay, little peanut?" I asked.

"I bump," she said, wiping her eyes. I put her down and brushed some of the sand from her cheeks. I looked up, and the swelling breasts of another creature entirely blocked the sun.

The woman was a blonde with a pixie cut. Her arms were muscular, but in a lean, long-sinewed way. Then there were her legs, which made me want to curl into the fetal position, suck my thumb, and sob. Not long showgirl's legs, but with a definition that suggested accomplishment on a tennis team someplace. She was wearing a red bathing suit that descended into a pair of white casual shorts. I sensed by the way she put her hand on the little girl's head that she was the responsible adult.

"Oh, thank you," my goddess, Ms. Suicide, said. "Kate runs off so fast."

She's not the mother.

"Happy to help," I said.

"You're good with children," said the sexpot, scooping up Kate in her arms.

"I have a few," I said, conveying utter domination of all the sperm in the world. I pointed to Ricky and Lily, shamefully wondering if acknowledging my children was a strategic mistake with regard to the agenda now driving my lower functions.

Then it hit me. The Ache. When confronted by feminine beauty, I felt pain. I always had, which was probably why I never did well with women in the quantitative sense. Women could detect the Ache and, in the Darwinian sense, disrespected it. *Men who ache don't propagate the species*, goes the logic.

Ms. Suicide was The Girl Everybody Wants. The problem was that The Girl Everybody Wants happens to want everybody. This was bad news for the lovesick male: if he tried to make his move, he would suffer the same fate as the proverbial Victim #1 in a horror flick—the genius who decides to investigate that scratching sound in the attic.

Ms. Suicide's eyes swept over Ricky and Lily, and she nodded. I'm not sure what I expected—some cheer, "He has sperm!"—but I was hoping for more of a reaction.

"Is Kate your daughter?" I asked, knowing the answer.

"No, I live with her family this summer."

"I thought you looked too young to have a big girl like Kate," I said, booping Kate on the nose.

"I go to Villanova," Ms. Suicide said. "I make extra money as an au pair."

Au pair. What enchanting words. Oh! Pair!

"Great school," I said. Which I would have said had she gone to Booger State. "Are you from the shore?"

"Wilmington. You?"

"I grew up in Atlantic City. I didn't go to college around here, though, but I came back most summers."

"Where did you go?" she asked.

Excellent. I had regressed to the same discussion I had with girls twenty-some-odd years ago. Progress? Only now, I had the confidence and savvy to mask the Ache.

"Dartmouth."

My inner televangelist—I called him Reverend Screed—chimed in my weakening brain. The reverend was my plagiarized version of the comedian Dana Carvey's Church Lady character. "You *admire* Turnpike Bobby Chin's sexual freedom, don't you? *DON'T YOU, CALIGULA? Need I remind you that you're a married man with children. You're twice her age. Your knees throb when you run. Beelzebub.*"

"Wow. I have a friend who goes there."

Probably some blowhard in one of those football frat houses who bench-presses four-fifty. I'm going to kill him in his sleep.

"I was going to ask you the person's name, but I graduated, like, two decades ago. (Note: I said "like.")

"Oh, Mary's still there."

Yes! *Mary.* A virgin, perhaps?

There was an excruciating silence. I was hoping she was thinking, *I'm talking to a hot older guy,* but I didn't know. I could pass for my thirties, right? I was thinking, *Run away with me.* Actually, that was a lie. I was thinking about:

- *What she would look like naked, expanses of tan lines versus winter skin;*
- *Hunting down all the horny bastards who inevitably were in love with her and eliminating them. Who were THESE MEN who got THESE WOMEN? The men fascinated me more than the goddesses they captured. There must be something wrong with me, but it's true. In the presence of THESE MEN, I felt a mixture of rage and disappointment: Him? You're with him? I'm going to kill him; and*
- *How Ricky and Lily would feel about spending weekends at the Celebrity Motel with their adulterous—and poor—father.*

"Well, I was happy to help out with my little girlfriend here—Kate," I added urgently.

"Thanks," Ms. Suicide said. "See you around."

Then the Answer to Absolutely Everything in the Whole World turned around, set little Kate on the sand, and an ass that was carved on Mount Olympus stepped onto the soft sand and out of my adult life.

Surprise Attack

"I move in stealth."

Edie and Irene had gone out for dinner. Irene left me a note that simply read, "The Pope or Turnpike Bobby Chin." This meant she had them marked for death by virtue of her visit.

I tried to go to sleep at the same time as the kids, but failed. Ms. Suicide was doing handsprings inside my cranium. Eventually Edie came home, and I saw her eyes blinking beside me. Ricky and Lily were not audibly stirring, providing an opportunity to prosecute a direct action. Irene's room was at the other end of the house on the ground floor, so we were safe there. If I rolled over toward Edie, there was a chance the bed would squeak and the kids would wake up, thereby forcing me to abort the mission. But to do nothing at all, well, where would that get us? Children, I thought: harbingers of life, terrorists of sex. Ricky and Lily were the Axis of Evil. *If I don't move now, the terrorists win.* I could not allow that. It was a time for leadership, resolve. What was Eisenhower thinking before D-Day? How could he know when the perfect time would be? He who hesitates is lost, and all that.

I breathed deeply, discretely conducting surveillance of Edie. Her eyes were still blinking, so there was life. There were no audible signs of children. A familiar breeze blew in off the Atlantic, rattling the blinds to the usual cadence, and the kids were still silent. Excellent: I had air cover. I slowly turned on my side, facing Edie. There was always that chance for the spontaneous mutual discovery that would allow matters to commence of their own accord. Alas, the target remained facing the heavens, blinking silently, unaware that my shift to the side was a warning shot.

I threw my arms around her.

"Oh, you scared me," Edie said.

"Frightened, are you? Exactly as I planned."

"What were you planning?"

"Surprise attack at nightfall. The enemy is asleep. I must move in stealth."

"Wait a minute?" Edie asked, facing me. "Who's the enemy?"

"The short people who sleep down the hall. The hour of our liberation is upon us."

A sigh from a faraway room. The Axis of Evil?

HOLD YOUR FIRE. HOLD YOUR FIRE.

Then nothing.

"You are so peculiar, Jonah."

"The Dude's in the mood."

"The *Dude?*" Edie asked, groggy.

"That would be me."

"When did this start?"

"*When you wuz out wit yo bitches, I wuz here with the little homeys . . .* Uh, actually Bobby calls himself the Dude."

"Are you serious? He calls himself 'the Dude?' "

"You got it, *dawg.*"

Edie laughed through her nose. "That's pathetic. Just like his sneer on the front page of the *Atlantic City Packet.*"

"What do you make of the sneer?"

"It's a pose," she said, not missing a beat.

"Of course it's a pose, but where did he get it?"

"It's a side effect of the ease of acquisition. God made humans for labor," Edie explained. "When your god becomes nothing but a dispenser of goodies, one resents the god."

"Interesting, but I thought women found pathetic men attractive," I said, batting my eyes.

"They don't. You, on the other hand, have some other qualities that merit attention."

"What will it get me?"

"What you came for."

Plush Surfaces

*"The paradox of damage control is that
your nemesis is usually your client."*

Hey, Chief, can I share something with you?" Chief Willie and
I met on a breezy day on the Boardwalk in Ventnor. We were
a few streets down from where Mickey and I had watched his
cabaret singer career backward over the side so many years ago.

"Lenape big on sharing."

I handed him the letter from the law firm and recounted my struggle with the council of Hopkins Pond over my invoice. Chief Willie
frowned.

"What does Mongoose say about this Hank fellow, the subcontractor?"

"A very decent man who is owed money. Just like me."

"So, do you want to pay Hank?"

"Yes."

"But you didn't get money from Hopkins Pond yet?"

"Correct."

"Mmm." Chief Willie put the legal letter in his pocket. "Who
makes the decision to pay you, Mongoose?"

"It comes down to the mayor."

"What is the mayor's name?"

"Gary Simmons."

"Mmm, white man."

"Yes, white man, Chief."

"The white man has a history of not paying fair price. Look at that whole Manhattan Island incident."

"That's true," I said. What the hell else was I going to say?

"I'll check."

I scanned the Boardwalk for Ms. Suicide. The same part of my brain was operating as it did in tenth grade when I used to station myself outside the guidance counselor's office after fifth period where a girl named Tori I liked had a geometry class across the hall. The problem was that a number of other guys—Schwartz, Squires, Janove, Di Palma, Ochsman, Auerbach, Novek, Vitelli, Reilly—had stationed themselves there, too. We all needed a lot of guidance, I guess.

Learn from that, Jonah.

If Ms. Suicide made me ache, then she made others ache, too. During the past few years, one by one, beautiful young women— girls in some cases—were kidnapped from American streets, but returned to life only on our television screens. Laci Peterson. Chandra Levy. Dru Sjodin. Little Carly Brucia and Elizabeth Smart. They were all killed, save Elizabeth Smart, who turned up with that hairy monster couple somewhere out west. We ached for them in different ways. Elizabeth Smart and Carly Brucia were our daughters. Laci was our pregnant wife, the mother of the child or grandchild we always wanted, but would never have. Dru—enrapturing like April— was hope and lust entwined in an unforgivably sad tale. Dru was the spring-summer love we never had, but believed we deserved— eliminated by life's snipers. Regardless of who we were, we had a stake in our lost girls.

Then it hit me. The way "it" hits Wile E. Coyote—a scheme to nail the Road Runner. It's genius, one of those ideas that are good for the few at the expense of the many. It's so wrong, just like what I feel for the au pair. I can't do *her,* but I can do *this.*

"Mongoose, you look far away," Chief Willie said.

I told him where I had been.

M y e-mail pinged. Cindi. There was an invoice attached with all kinds of line items. It was from a company called DEVIUS, or Delaware Valley Interactive Uplink Systems. Never heard of them. My eyes glazed over at this crap, so I e-mailed Cindi back: "?????"

My phone rang. Cindi.

"What was that invoice you sent?" I asked.

"It was an invoice I wasn't supposed to see. It was attached to an e-mail I got from DEVIUS about a video news release we'd been planning for the Bobby statue unveiling. I asked a summer intern there to send me what they had in their files so I could rejigger the script given all that's going on. One of the things I got was this invoice, which is for a Web site they're doing for Bobby."

"So?"

"So, did you see the bottom line on it?"

"I didn't scroll down that far. I hate attachments."

"Well, it's for $724,620. Almost three-quarters of a mil for a Web site."

"Must be a bitchin' Web site."

"You're the one with an innate sense of grift. It may be worth having one of your henchmen look into it."

I sighed.

"What's with you?" Cindi asked.

"I've always wanted a henchman."

Derek Plush was beamed into the *Hello USA* morning program from his private home studio into the network's faux kitchen set in New York City. The host, the pandering Ken Dahl, was questioning Plush about Turnpike Bobby Chin's family. I loved the way Ken Dahl punctuated his question with a sip from his coffee mug, as if to underscore that he was having breakfast only with us.

"Well, Ken," Plush began, "Bonita Chin, Bobby's mother, is a notorious résumé fabricator. One of her favorite stories is that she was one of the Shirelles. The Shirelles, of course, were a wonderful African-American quartet from North Jersey. What they'd want with a white girl like Bonita who had a voice like a lawn mower running over a squirrel, I couldn't tell you."

"Wasn't there something about Bonita Chin getting a record contract?" Ken asked.

"No fewer than a half-dozen sources, Ken, confirmed for me that Bonita Chin had been pressuring Bobby since he was a boy to get her a record contract. She had apparently tried when she was younger, but nobody wanted her. A few people vaguely remember her, but say that at one point in the late 1950s, she stopped showing up for performances, gave up, I suppose. Eventually, Bobby got fed up with her, and stopped seeing his parents."

"Derek, what about Bobby's brother, Michael, who's in the restaurant business?"

"That's putting it rather generously, Ken. Michael Chin is a seven-time-failed restaurateur. The tabloid version of Bobby's estrangement with his brother is that Bobby bought a dream house from under Michael and his wife, Staci. The real estate records in Camden County paint a different picture. Transaction records show that the couple put a $2.6 million bid on a ten-thousand-square-foot house on the posh east side section of Cherry Hill. When it came time to submit a financial statement, the Chins referred the mortgage company to

Bobby Chin's management office. The fact is, Ken, that Michael and Staci Chin didn't have two pennies to rub together. They thought they were owed that mansion because they were in the blood-orbit of Turnpike Bobby. Bobby declined to buy the house for them, thus the estrangement."

Okay, process this, Jonah. What does this guerrilla theater tell you? Plush, I knew, wanted an interview with Bobby. He was sufficiently concerned about getting that interview that he had rattled my cage when he believed I might be an obstacle. While Plush was prone to hyperbole, he was not a Jayson Blair–style wholesale fabricator. If Bobby's family were as desperate a lot of losers as Plush said they were, they'd sue if Plush weren't accurate, and my money said his report was probably spot-on. Following the logic, would Plush, knowing how badly he wanted the Bobby story, attack Bobby's family in this manner if he thought it would spike his big interview? Probably not, therefore, it was safe to assume Bobby would be all right with seeing his family trashed.

The question was, had Plush once and for all nailed down his *Major Player* interview with Bobby? Who knew with this guy?

The paradox of damage control is that your nemesis is usually your client.

Losing Kaylee

"Not again."

Her name was Kaylee, and she didn't come home. Actually, one couldn't definitively say *home* because no one was sure yet where Kaylee was from. There was only one thing known for certain: a pudgy home economics junior high school teacher from Hammonton saw Kaylee pushed into a black sport utility vehicle by a vulpine man with tattoos.

"He just . . . took her by the neck, and he said, 'C'mere, c'mere,' and shoved her into his truck and drove away," according to Evelyn Wallace who was in the drugstore parking lot when it happened in Atlantic City. Her jowls were shaking, her hand was pawing at her ear. "He wasn't that big. He was wiry like a starving wolf. And he had tattoos all over his arms, from top to bottom. Oh, that beautiful girl."

By the time the evening news came on, the police had a sketch, and it was awful. The man had shoulder-length dark greasy hair. He wore a bushy mustache. He had long sideburns and about a week's beard stubble. His cheeks were hollow. The term used was *hatchet-faced*. His pocket T-shirt was dark. You see guys like this at rest stops in rural areas, and you stay away from them, because what they lack in size they make up for in menace. There's that wild-eyed, tightly wound mien that challenges you to challenge him. He *wants* you to

try to kill him, he's that important, his grievances that profound. If
you have rudimentary survival instincts, you won't make eye contact.
For Christ's sake, don't look at him.

By nightfall, someone who knew Kaylee e-mailed a photo of her
to KBRO. The black-and-white photo, which was to become iconic,
displayed a hauntingly exquisite woman of about twenty. She wore
her hair very short, pixielike. Kaylee had a broad, toothy smile that appeared to react to something humorous she had just seen or had been
told. It was a spontaneous, active expression, as opposed to the forced
smile of a Sears photo. Her light features suggested Scandinavian origins, or a direct delivery from Mother Earth herself to Iowa. Someplace where tall corn grew.

Then there was the intangible. There are different brands of
beauty. There's femme fatale beauty that inspires lust, fear, and resentment, depending upon one's sex. Kaylee's was a different allure. She
didn't provoke, she haunted. Men would agonize into old age how
they might have played things differently with Kaylee. *If I hadn't been
so shy, then maybe . . . If I hadn't been such a tool, then maybe . . . If I had
only been a jock . . .*

Even women who might be jealous of the gift she had been given
would find Kaylee hard to hate. In fact, they would feel ashamed of
their hostility because Kaylee was so *nice.* A young woman would go
to confession and ask forgiveness for resenting Kaylee's soul. The resentment wouldn't dissipate, but the feeler would know it was wrong.
No such doubt was felt with conventional resentment.

Can one calibrate another's soul from a photo? Of course. In a
photo, we take all of the divine attributes a person can possibly have
and assign them to a face that warrants all of these good things. As
with art, the derivation of a soul from a media image is fair game.

In the proverbial "hastily called news conference," Atlantic City
police chief Sean Desmond, flanked by grim-faced uniformed men,

assured the public he would direct "a Herculean effort to do every-thing in my power to ensure Kaylee's safe return."

KBRO's Al Just ended his broadcast by saying, "Kaylee's vanishing, as if in a film by Philadelphia's own M. Night Shyamalan, leaves us a united community asking 'Why?' and shuddering, 'Not again. Not again.' "

Digital, Not Film

"How exactly are you about peace?"

The Maggots had been denying to the Cohn of Silence and me
that an interview with Derek Plush had been confirmed. We
both felt they were lying, but the relationship was sufficiently
precarious that neither Mr. Cohn nor I saw much benefit in accusing
them directly of being liars. With someone like Bobby, job security
was tied directly to a combination of proximity and having fulfilled
Bobby's latest outrageous request. By that logic, the power belonged
to the Maggots. As a gesture of compromise, however, Kadaborah set
aside a time for us to media train Bobby to handle the proverbial Bar-
bara Walters–style interview. We took this opportunity because it was
one step up from pissing directly into the wind.

In his hotel suite, Bobby was visibly distracted. My gangland clair-
voyance told me that Kadaborah had primed Bobby to have a bad atti-
tude about our session. It was Bobby and the Maggots versus the Cohn
of Silence, Cindi, and me. Even though we were trying to save him, we
were The Enemy because we were making him unhappy.

The Cohn of Silence began, "Now, Bobby, I cannot stress enough
that it would be my strong preference that you not speak with the
press during this police inquiry. I also understand that you must do
business and intend to sit down with Derek Plush. If you do this, it is

essential that you not answer any questions at all relating to the unfortunate disappearance of Christian Josi or the plane crash. Do you understand that?"

"The Dude understands."

"Who's the Dude?" Mr. Cohn asked, looking around.

"Bobby's the Dude," I said.

"Oh," Mr. Cohn said. "So, Bobby, if you are asked about the case—no matter how many times—you must answer, 'I am unable to discuss anything involving a potential legal case.' OK?"

"OK."

Lonesome Jake emerged from an unknown room, whipped out his digital camera, knelt before Bobby as if he were about to administer a hummer, and began to record.

"Excuse me," the Cohn of Silence said. "I don't want this to be filmed."

"It's not film, man, it's digital," Lonesome Jake said.

"Does it memorialize Bobby in any way?" Mr. Cohn asked impatiently.

"Memorialize?"

"Does it record him?"

"Oh, yeah."

"Please, no recording of any kind."

"This is bullshit," Bobby said.

The Maggots tried to calm him down by giving him assurances that the session would not last long. Lonesome Jake backed off with a quiet, pale rage that I registered.

"Bobby, I'm going to play the role of Derek Plush," I began softly.

"Role, like rehearsing for a movie?"

"Exactly. I'm playing Derek Plush and you are going to rehearse the interview you're going to do with him."

"The Dude's going to be in a movie, you know?"

"You are?" I said this employing the kind of voice that one might use with a three-year-old who is happy to announce that he's three years old. *You ARE? What a big boy.*

"I'm starring in a movie that Reverend Kadaborah is putting together. It'll do like two hundred million the first weekend."

"That'll be great," I said. "Now, here goes. I'm Derek Plush, remember?"

"Yeah."

"Bobby, tell me about the movie you're working on." I'd start easy.

"It's about a hero in a village who's been gone since World War II in Vietnam. Everybody thinks he's been dead that whole time, but when these ninja polluters start wrecking the village, the Dude comes back."

"You said World War II in Vietnam. Which war did the hero fight in?"

"Vietnam. In World War II."

Cindi was expressionless. The Cohn of Silence nodded, as if Bobby's sense of history pleased him. Cohn's eyes spoke: *Better he fuck up history than his legal defense. Let it go, Jonah.*

"We haven't heard any music from you in almost twenty years. Don't you write anymore?"

"Artists don't write, we *originate.*" Bobby pronounced the word with excessive clarity, pleased with his vocabulary.

"Okay. What's the difference?"

"Writing anyone can do. Originating is rare, it's a gift. I don't need to put things on pieces of paper to originate. I originate all the time. I'm originating now."

"What are you originating?" *Other than a steaming mound of goat shit.*

"Wait and see. Just wait and see." Bobby spread his hands out mystically.

"But the public hasn't seen anything, that's the big complaint, Bobby. Nobody has seen creative product for twenty years."

Bobby rocked in his seat. The Maggots shot me nuclear-tipped missiles. Cindi pressed her fingers against her temples. The Cohn of Silence was still.

"That's not what I'm about!" Bobby shouted.

"You're a musician, Bobby."

"I'm not about some *product,* like you call it—"

"Then how else will the public connect with you? They knew you first as Mega Boy and then as a very gifted artist."

My "gifted artist" gluteus smooch brought Bobby back to his seat.

"It's about peace, you know. I'm about peace."

"How exactly are you about peace?"

"There's just so much war in the world, anyone who can bring peace and joy should bring it."

"I understand, but tell me how you bring joy and peace."

"Just my presence shines light. There's just so much light to shine, so much to give."

"What do you give, Bobby?"

"Just so much, so much." Bobby's voice dissipated like steam, and he placed the back of his wrist against his forehead. I thought of Bette Davis. I forgot, Bobby was going to be in a movie.

"Are there any issues you feel strongly about?" I asked.

"Like what?"

"I don't know . . . like fighting cystic fibrosis, or supporting euthanasia."

"Look, I can't help *everybody.*"

"I don't follow."

"I care about youth and all, but it's not like I can save every kid in a whole other country."

"That seems fair." *Oy.*

I wanted to come back to his flagging career before sucker-punching him with something that would drag him into dangerous legal territory. My ultimate goal would be for the Maggots to see the danger Bobby was in and allow the Cohn of Silence to call off the interview with Plush. Any way I examined a potential *Major Player* story, I saw disaster.

"Do you have plans for new music?" I asked.

"The Dude doesn't plan. The Dude originates. Planning is for tightasses in cubicles. The Dude doesn't live in a cubicle. There are stars and planets. The Dude makes up the universe."

"I don't quite follow. You are part of the universe, that's what you're trying to say?"

"No, no, man. The universe is made from parts of the Dude—"

"Can we just stop here for a moment?" I said. "Bobby, are you sure you want to say the universe is made up of you? That may come off as a bit egotistical, don't you think?"

Bobby threw an ashtray. It shattered one layer of glass on the sliding door behind him. We all jumped in our seats. Only the Cohn of Silence didn't jump.

"This is over, Jonah," Kadaborah said. "Enough."

"I'm pitching wiffle balls here, guys," I said. "If Bobby can't deal with these, Plush will kill him. Kill him."

"I have the whole wardrobe picked out!" Bobby shouted, standing.

"Wardrobe for what?" I asked.

"The pictorial," Bobby said. "Elena Molotov-Weinberg is shooting the pictorial."

"Jesus Christ," I said.

"Do not take that Dude's name in your veins," Bobby slurred. I contemplated for a moment whether he was drugged.

"Excuse me?"

Tic Turner put his arm around Bobby. Kadaborah reiterated that the training was over, adding, "Bobby meant that one doesn't take the Lord's name in vain."

Oh.

Feeling as if life on one of Jupiter's moons would make more sense than this dialogue, I decided to continue with my line of questioning: "Bobby, do you know a man named Christian Josi?"

"I know who he is," he answered.

"What was the nature of your relationship with him?"

"He did a statue of me. Total piece-a-shit—"

"Bobby!" the Cohn of Silence interjected. "You cannot address Mr. Josi in any way."

I continued. "Did you see the statue?"

The Maggots, following Bobby's reengagement, backed off.

"I saw some little thing," Bobby said with a sneer.

"Bobby!" Cohn interjected. "You must go back to what we talked about. You must say, 'I cannot discuss anything that may involve a potential legal case.' If you can't remember that, just blame me. Say, 'My lawyer won't let me talk about that.'"

"The Dude gets it! I get it already!"

"What happened to your plane, Bobby?" I asked.

"A missile from the government."

Cindi slapped her forehead. Turner withdrew into his vast repository of facial expressions from his porn days and faked an orgasm. Or something.

"Why would the government shoot a missile at your plane, Bobby?"

"Because of peace. I'm all about peace, and the government knows that."

I was at a total loss. I envisioned a huge banner hanging out of Bobby's suite with one word: Tragedy. The best legal and public relations talent money could buy was at Bobby's immediate disposal, and there wasn't a damned thing we could do other than pray that Derek Plush had an aneurysm. I had no qualms about manipulating a reporter, but preferred to stop short of killing one. The idea of diverting Plush occurred to me, but it was of no use. He'd come back to

Bobby, or *Major Player* would assign somebody else. Bobby was too good a story. Everybody in the room knew it. Especially Bobby.

When Bobby retired to his bedroom with two of the Virgins, there was a brief, but calm, argument between the Cohn of Silence and the Maggots. The essence of the argument was that the likely outcome of an interview with Derek Plush was an eventual conviction in court. The best thing that could emerge from an interview would be a foundation for an insanity plea for Bobby.

"But Bobby hasn't been indicted," Kadaborah said, doing one of his prayer things with his hands.

"A technicality," Cohn said. "An indictment is certain. Bobby's conduct since Mr. Josi's disappearance makes him an even more attractive target. It's worth it to them to indict him at this stage even if they lose in court. There's nothing more I can say."

Holy Trinity of Icons

"The reverend believes in rich congregants."

The TV screen framed silvery helicopters circling a South Jersey field, their noses tipping down like seagulls. The photo of Kaylee appeared in the lower left half of the screen. The black-and-white photo when juxtaposed with the full-color frame of the search created a stark contrast between majestic life and banal, final death.

The helicopters were replaced onscreen by a collage of young women and girls who had gone missing in recent years. The cavalcade of names was rehashed. Laci, Dru. KBRO's Al Just clarified something that hadn't been clear before. The only reason why the press knew the woman as "Kaylee" was because the one witness to her disappearance, Evelyn Wallace, claimed to have heard someone in the convenience store where they were shopping refer to her by that name. Whoever had sent the digital photo out confirmed her name. An anonymous caller had, according to a source at the ACPD, indicated that Kaylee's last name might be Hopewell.

As the news of Kaylee's kidnapping metastasized nationwide, an avalanche of sightings had commenced. Kaylee was seen leaving a building with the name Trump on it, which wasn't helpful because this described half of the buildings on the East Coast. Kaylee was also walking the cliffs of Big Sur in California. "A friend of a friend," according to the state troopers' patrol, had just phoned in claiming to have been with Kaylee at a bar on South Street in Philly the other night. The ACPD was so inundated with information that they requested the help of other police and fire departments in the region because numerous tips had suggested Kaylee worked for a babysitting service affiliated with the casinos.

The State Police had descended upon anyone driving a black SUV. Many of these searches were covered by local news teams in the hope that a body would roll out from under a seat. Vehicles of this description were being inspected as they came and left Atlantic City in particular. Police dogs were shipped from densely populated North Jersey to sniff out the trucks being pulled over. The place looked like Baghdad.

A tip from campers led to the search of the field where the helicopters were hovering. According to the witnesses, a black SUV had mysteriously been seen pulling out of a nearby clearing the night before. So far the search had yielded nothing.

The crisis enveloped the national news like a weather system. A holy trinity of icons made their way into every story, print or broadcast. The Kaylee Trinity was comprised of the black-and-white photo, an eerie rendering of a generic black SUV, and the sketch of the terrible tattooed man. This trinity had precedent: the O.J. Simpson homicides had hijacked the news more than a decade earlier with the "bloody glove," the "White Bronco," and the dueling photos of gorgeous Nicole Simpson provoking sex with her eyes while Ron Goldman burst with vitality so palpable that his tie-dyed headband seemed required to restrain him. Three strong knocks overwhelmed the current broadcast. I opened the door, and Chief Willie stood there wearing a mosaic headband, a matching Philadelphia Eagles jersey and shorts, and moccasins. "How!" he said.

"Zy gezunt."

"How do mongrels like Kadaborah and Turner find each other?' " he asked.

"Mongoose say, 'They sniff privates til they find friend.' "

"You are wise, Mongoose."

"What do you know, Chief?"

"Thaddeus Nicholas Turner. That's Tic. Born February 11, 1965, in San Bernardino—"

"Excite me. No collateral, Chief," I said.

"I apologize. College degree from San Diego State in film. Adult film star in about sixty films. *The Porn Identity, Lawrence of a Labia, Whore of the Rings, The Slutty Professor, Home Abone, Tush Hour*—"

"Keep going."

"Stage names—heh—include Tic the Wick, Ezra Pound, TNT (his initials), Paul Satingrod—"

"Paul Satingrod?"

"*Pul*sating rod. Get it now?"

"Yes, nice."

"Oscar Mayer—"

"Okay, I get the picture."

"Turner made good money as swordsman. He refers to his as 'Excalibur' from his performance in *Guinirear*. Set up private investigations firm in 1990, Turner's Privates, still chartered. Hollywood clientele. Divorce work. Transportation."

"Transportation?"

"Yes, sir. Mongoose, Turner is a pilot. He can fly jets."

"I'll be damned." I went into a brief trance wondering how Turner's aviation experience might translate into the airborne antics of July 4. After all, the ostensible pilots on the manifest that day had turned up alive.

"What about Kadaborah?"

"He's been with Bobby for about three years. Real name is Ernest

Miller. Proctologist for twenty-five years around South Jersey. Some entrepreneurial stuff with holistic colonics he did went bad in the late nineties. He was censured by whatever New Jersey board they've got for sphincter samurais. Kadaborah, as he calls himself, founded the Ong's Hat Flagellants, a religious sect for holistic mumbo-jumbo. They get tax breaks and all. He conducts seminars out in a big lodge in Ong's Hat. You know the place, Mongoose?"

"Pine Barrens. Middle of nowhere."

"There aren't many members in the formal sense, but my guys did some sniffing around out there. Heh. All we could find was that the characters who show up for his seminars tend to come in Range Rovers and Jaguars."

"The reverend believes in rich congregants. Do we know what they do inside this lodge?"

"No. We can try to find out, though, slap a beacon on Bobby's motorcade, see when they're on the move."

"Put it on our to-do list. I'd like to know what Bobby does in there, if he goes. I may want to join you."

"Chief Willie not sure. Chief Willie say, 'Pollster not prepared for colonic ambush in Jersey woods.'"

"Let's just think about it." I handed Chief Willie the Web site invoice from DEVIUS that Cindi had sent me. "Also, see if we can find out anything about these guys."

Chief Willie glanced at the invoice. "For this kind of wampum, Chief Willie want Web site that can give America back to Indians."

"That's what I was thinking. Sorta."

Chief Willie left. So Tic Turner was a pilot. I called an old associate of Mickey's who was the manager of the Golden Prospect. The casino owned an airplane.

Untouchable

"Why do you sneer?"

I stopped by the Golden Prospect to give Bobby and the Maggots a sense of where things stood with regard to public attitudes toward Bobby's saga. I could have done this a week ago, but I had no intention of telling them anything of value, so I wanted to wait for an opportunity to visit that would serve my interests.

"Bobby's meeting with a few dancers," Turner said in a way that implied I was missing the bigger picture.

The Virgins were nowhere to be seen, so I lasciviously suspected Bobby was busy at his avocation. The bigger picture painted itself when Bobby emerged from his bedroom with two "dancers" I had never seen before. They were all laughing, jiggling, glugging Piney Spring Water, making no attempt to conceal what they had been doing. There wasn't the slightest trace of shame, although I sensed forced joy on Bobby's part, as if he were saying, *"C'n you believe this?"* I locked my eyes blatantly on their legs—long and athletic, aerobic legs—and felt my own cardiovascular system bump into another gear.

Reverend Screed incanted in my head: *This is not what you want, Jonah.* Momentarily, I felt morally superior at my collusion with Reverend Screed for my clean lifestyle. I had not succumbed to temptation.

I bore in again on The Legs. Something about the tone of the women's quadriceps, the way the muscles were defined as they sloped into the knee, overpowered Reverend Screed's voice. *This is exactly what you want.* Pig. The only thing that stands in the way of you and The Legs are basic impediments, logistics. *You are shy with women,* Reverend Screed reminded me. *The idea of a ménage is beyond your operational ken. Tell me, Jonah, what would you do first, huh? Then there's the consequences issue. You can lie to the masses from a distance, but you're honest on an intimate basis.*

I imagined my life without impediments. Turnpike Jonah.

The thing is, that's not what I would do even without the impediments. Multiple chicks? No, that's not me. Chalk one up for Reverend Screed. One at a time? That, I could get into. Reverend Screed on the ropes. Turnpike Jonah kinda diggin' da life wit' Bobby . . .

The Legs exited the suite. Bobby, freshly showered, asked what was up. I identified a couple of brown-nosing points from the focus groups and relayed them.

"Despite all this bad news, Bobby, people don't dislike you," I said truthfully. At first Bobby looked wounded. Then he looked angry.

"That's the best you've got?" Turner asked, accurately reading Bobby's disappointment.

"What I meant was, uh, people don't think you did anything wrong." This was a lie. It just fell out of my mouth. I had seen Bobby's face, had felt the room chill off, so I lied to climb back into the happy womb. "I think we have to work with that to beat this bullshit investigation." I pumped my arm at the word "beat." Rah-rah, Jonah. These were not the behaviors of a maverick pollster. Whatever the opposite of a maverick was, that's what I had become in the last thirty seconds. I tried to think of what the opposite was, and kept coming up with rodents—weasel, mouse, gerbil. At this moment I was no mongoose.

"What are you doing now?" Bobby asked.

"My kids have a little play at camp. I'm going there."

"Radical! I want to see it," Bobby said, apparently seriously.

"You want to see my kids' play?"

"Yeah."

"It's fine with me, but we can't do the whole security thing. It would have to be low-key."

"That's cool," Bobby said.

Turner pushed back. "Negative," he said. He didn't want Bobby with me. He was probably afraid I'd screw things up by reverting to telling the truth. Or, even worse, perhaps I'd lie better than the Maggots did. Turner raised security concerns, and something about a call with a record label, which I knew was horseshit. Finally, Bobby glared. It was the cold glare of lost icon affection, lost revenue. The message: No more Hollywood for you douchebags. Turner, envisioning a return to a skanky Econo-Lodge in Van Nuys, backed down.

Let me state, lest there be no ambiguity, that TURNPIKE BOBBY CHIN WAS IN THE PASSENGER SEAT OF MY CAR. We had smuggled him out in a laundry bin, a technique Turner had down pat.

Bobby rested his head against the window. He wore a faraway expression tempered by a mild sneer. I imagined him picturing himself appearing on a movie screen being REVEALED TO THE AUDIENCE accompanied by a COOL SONG. The audience, in Bobby's mind, would think "ooooh" as George Thorogood's "Who Do You Love" pounded the theater. How many times had Bobby played this one out in his mind? He had been revising his screen entrance ever since he saw Scorcese pioneer the technique in *Mean Streets,* when Robert De Niro's Johnny Boy entered the bar to 'Jumpin' Jack

Flash." All that hair-trigger sexual kinetics, not knowing when the wild man would blow.

Midway to Margate, Bobby belted out a slurred line from one of his songs that was big when I was in college: *"Don't break wind on the patio."*

"I remember that song. They used to blast it from my dorm all night," I said. "What's the lyric again?"

Bobby said it slower: "Oh, take the wheel again, Daddy-O."

This was cool. Asking Turnpike Bobby Chin about one of his trail-mix lyrics. BECAUSE HE WAS IN THE PASSENGER SEAT OF MY CAR.

"Right, *Daddy-O*. Loved that song." It only took me twenty-three years to realize it wasn't about methane.

Bobby's medallion had slipped out of his shirt.

"Is that a saint?" I asked.

"Yeah. St. Jude. The patron saint of lost causes," Bobby laughed.

"Bobby, can I ask you something?"

"Lay it on the Dude."

"Why do you sneer?"

"I don't sneer."

"Yeah, you do. You do this." I showed him.

"That's just my face."

"I looked at pictures of you when you were young. You didn't used to sneer. Same face. Same guy."

"No, I'm not the same guy. I never got to be a real kid. Maybe that changed my face somehow when I wasn't looking."

"I know what you mean. I didn't get to be a real kid either."

"How come?"

"My parents died when I was little. I was raised by my grand-parents—"

"Mickey Price. Musta been cool."

"Why?"

"The big gangster, man. You're, like, untouchable."

"We were chased out of the country. That's pretty touchable."

Bobby shook his head in dismissal, as if to say, "Nobody suffers the way I suffer."

I decided to abandon my pursuit of Bobby's sneer, but not my line of inquiry altogether.

"You got what everybody wants, though, Bobby. We're not supposed to admit it, but a lot of people want fame. You got it, but it makes you miserable. It changes your face."

"That's because they always try to take it from you."

And there it was. The tragedy of fame was not what it brought, but the terror of its loss. It was socially appropriate to blame misery on the deprivation of a childhood, but it was harder to blame it on the theft of fame, which should have been a guarantee due to one's intrinsic uniqueness, I suppose.

Right then, I nailed my Big Theory on the American Dream: For our grandparents, it was about prosperity. For my generation, it was about notoriety. We tethered ourselves to the altar of the insatiable Lilith, the Press that was labeled free, but was the ultimate enslaver.

Tick-Tock

"He will make peace."

Camp Absecon's mascot was the stallion, and in a mutation of gender concepts and equestrianism everywhere, the camp's girls were known as the "Lady Stallions." Lily, being a tenacious horsewoman, could not abide this name and, according to her counselor, devoted much of the day to arguing about the impossibility of the mascot—a beautiful bucking white horse with Betty Boop eyelashes.

Bobby had dressed down—khaki shorts, loafers, T-shirt, baseball cap, and oversized sunglasses. His long hair had been tucked up under his hat, which revealed his neck. I caught a glimpse of veiny marks on his neck, the ones I had seen on his torso in the shower that time. What the hell was that? I had never read about Bobby having a skin disease; he had never done one of those you-name-it-and-I've-got-it confessionals that Cher did whenever she fell off the cultural grid.

Edie and I drove separately, and stood on opposite sides of the gathering. Parents milled about with cameras, counselors lined up campers, and frenzied food service workers set up tables of punch. Everyone at Camp Absecon was focused on something other than Turnpike Bobby Chin. He was essentially unrecognizable without his entourage, which had perhaps become the defining feature of his identity. I worried for a moment that he might flip out—the kind of concern one has when breaking the news to a child that there will be no ice cream after a poorly eaten dinner—but Bobby seemed docile. That's a good boy.

The play itself was an abbreviated version of Peter Pan. Lily was the Indian, Princess Tigerlilly, who was to be rescued by Peter, who was played by a child I didn't know. My Tigerlilly was tied (with strips of paper) to a totem pole presumably made by the other Lady Stallions. Ricky wore the paper head of the crocodile, followed by an unfortunate child who carried a cardboard paper tail. The croc didn't speak; however, Ricky repeated "*tick-tock*" as he approached Captain Hook. The Captain, a popular counselor in a silly nautical getup, met his fate as the ticking croc approached. Princess Tigerlilly broke free from her paper constraints. Before my dangerous son the crocodile reached his prey, Peter and a fuzzy team of Lost Boys jumped on Cool Counselor/Captain Hook. The paper crocodile split in two and joined the flesh pile to the delight of everyone. Everyone, that is, except for Turnpike Bobby Chin, who was weeping quietly beside me.

As the audience clapped at the resolution, I put my arm around Bobby. "What's wrong?" I asked.

"Promise me. Just promise me," he said through his tears. His breathing was heavy.

"Promise you what, Bobby?" The other parents were gravitating toward the stage with their cameras, which left me alone to deal with Bobby, thank God.

"Don't make them be onstage."

"Who, my kids?"

"Don't force them."

"I didn't force them. It's just a little play."

"I know, but what if they can't get off? See, they're all up there still." There was something childlike and helpless about his cadence, as if he were saying, "There are monsters under my bed."

"They're having fun, Bobby," I said.

Bobby wiped his eyes. His breathing slowed. "Just be careful is all."

On the way back in the car, Bobby sat between the kids in the backseat. There had been nothing in his behavior to date that could have prepared me for how good he was with them. Postcatharsis, he was focused, wise, and articulate. It reminded me of when Deedee had Alzheimer's: for weeks, she would talk nonsense, or say nothing. Then, for a brief moment, she'd be sharp as a switchblade, offering commentary on current events.

I dropped the kids off at home. Edie and Irene had gotten back first, and helped them out of the backseat. Ricky and Lily both spontaneously hugged Bobby. When he hugged them back, his face fleetingly contained surprise that switched to joy. If I could use one expression to describe Bobby's demeanor at that moment, I would say he was starstruck. Edie and Irene shook hands with Bobby and, thankfully, Edie was able to restrain whatever disapproval she felt for him.

I drove him back to his hotel feeling a sense of spiritual achievement. What was that saying from the Bible I had learned in Hebrew school? *Ya'ase shalom.* He will make peace, "He" being God. I had choreographed a small redemption here at the Jersey Shore.

I rehashed the kids' play, trying to pinpoint the catalyst for Bobby's reaction. I never saw him as a man capable of sentimental emotion, unless, of course, it was about him. Was it the children singing or laughing? I shuddered, thinking of Ricky's little face—*tick-tock, tick-tock.* It did not occur to me until I crossed Jackson Avenue into Atlantic City that I had seated my children beside a man who could be a murderer.

A Quiet Man Speaks

"Can't talk no more."

After I dropped Bobby back at the Golden Prospect using Turner's laundry bin ruse, I tried to shut the door to the suite behind me, but felt resistance. The door opened wider from the inside. It was Lonesome Jake, who deftly slipped out into the hallway.

"Mr. Eastman, can I talk to you?"

"Sure."

"You mind if we go down the hall?"

"No."

Lonesome Jake walked with me toward the elevators. He nervously brushed his mouth, as if clearing crumbs.

"Are you okay, Jake?" I studied his eyes. The lines fanning out from them reflected a topography of suffering, not unlike what you see on maps of Mars when scientists try to show there had once been life there. His narrow features conjured up life in a mobile home out on the plains. I recognized that despite my travels across the country, my inexperience with the actual lives of America's homegrown aliens was limited. I was feeling uncharacteristically liberal, a man with heightened sensitivity to the plight of those who were nothing like me. Pleased with my sense of diversity, I cocked my head, Clin-tonesque, to hear his answer.

"You won't tell nobody?"

"No. No," I assured.

"You're lookin' into what's goin' on with Bobby." Lonesome Jake said this without inflection. I listened for a beat. Hearing nothing else, I saw no downside to answering, "Yes."

"Somethin' you may wanna look at."

"Okay."

"You won't tell?"

"No."

"Bobby owns a music library. Lotsa music from old times up til now. He gets royalties. Lots. There's old movies in there, too, where that street corner music was sung. Somebody's tryin' to take control over it. Look at that."

"Who's trying to control it?"

"It's all I know. What I said. Can't talk no more."

Lonesome Jake wiped his face again with his fingers, pivoted, and walked briskly down the hollow hall, his feet against the carpet echoing as the elevator door opened.

I called the Cohn of Silence.

The ice cream truck pulled up to our beach house, and the side door slid open.

"I had a peculiar encounter with Lonesome Jake."

"You talk to cartoon characters often?" said the Cohn of Silence, sitting on his vinyl seat.

"No. He's the guy with the camera who follows Bobby around on a leash."

"I didn't know he spoke or had a name."

"He told me that Bobby owns a music and film library and that somebody's trying to take control over it. The implication, given how nervous he was, was that there may be some tie to the thing with Christian. Maybe it's our Plausible Alternative Scenario."

"Or it may be a nobody from noplace looking to be a somebody."

"Whatever. I thought I'd pass it along."

"I know some of Bobby's business lawyers. I'll make inquiries."

"I will, too. I'm also writing up some talking points to keep Bobby on message if and when he does this damned interview with Plush. Where do you want them delivered?"

"Drop it off at Bobby's hotel. Mark it privileged and confidential attorney–client correspondence."

"I will."

"Keep your eyes open, Jonah."

My eyes were very much open and fixed toward my TV. There was a commercial for a sexual dysfunction pill. I've been accused of being overly analytical about basic pop culture communications, but I asked myself in a slow, opaque way, *Just where are all of these old people humping?* Was it possible that the old people had just surrendered, and it was actually the young guys popping Viagra, Levitra, and Cialis, kind of like adding a racing stripe—not necessary, but slick? I had a tough time picturing the Cohn of Silence chasing an arthritic Mrs. Cohn of Silence around the house shaking a vial of Levitra.

When my mental engine began whirring too fast on an unconstructive analysis, I flipped the channel to a regional cable station. The reporter, Freddy Zane, walked like a runway model up to the porch steps where a worried-looking middle-aged man stood. Zane, who resembled a 1980s-era porn star, contorted his face into a mask of sympathy behind his neatly groomed mustache. He wanted the worried man to be assured that he was sharing his feelings with a friend, a comrade-in-arms, who wanted to defuse some of his worry over the fate of the missing girl.

The camera panned a modest two-story house where Kaylee Hopewell was raised.

"Kaylee and her friends practically grew up on these steps," the worried man, Stan Hopewell, told Freddy Zane. Hopewell was a slim man with thick blond hair turning gray. "Since my daughter disappeared, I can't even come out of the house this way. I can't look at these steps."

Hopewell pulled a handkerchief from his pocket and dabbed at his eyes beneath his wire-rimmed glasses. The camera panned back, and Stan Hopewell walked Freddy Zane around his house, his voiceover intoning that Kaylee had last been home to see her father just two weeks ago. Zane watched as Stan Hopewell tied a yellow ribbon around a pillar on a white wooden beam on the front porch.

The television cut to the ubiquitous Kaylee witness, Evelyn Wallace, who was tying her own yellow ribbon to the door of the Atlantic City store where Kaylee vanished.

"The yellow ribbon," Zane returned, speaking to the audience, "a symbol of hope for return, a prayer for an answer for those who love and miss Kaylee Hopewell. This is Freddy Zane in Riverside."

Doo-Wop

"We don't need flashbulbs and badges."

I parked in the underground lot at the Golden Prospect, and dropped off my proposed talking points in an envelope for the Cohn of Silence at the business office. When I returned to my car, two huge figures resembling totem poles emerged from either side of a concrete pillar. They were both Indians. Long black hair, turquoise, and everything. A burgundy Cadillac STS came careening around the corner. Indian #1, tall and slim, slid into the back seat and said, "Join me." Idiotically, I looked at husky Indian #2 for guidance. He put his arm around me and said, "Join him." I don't know why, but I didn't even think about running. Maybe it was because I liked Indians so much. I got in.

"Where are we going?" I asked.

"See Doo-Wop," Geronimo, on my left, said.

"We're going to a concert?"

The two Indians beside me laughed, as did the little Irishman driving up front.

"Nah, you never hearda Doo-Wop?" Sitting Bull, on my right, asked.

"I know the music."

"Now you know the guy."

"There's a guy called Doo-Wop?"

"There's a guy called Doo-Wop," Sitting Bull grunted.

We drove through the forgotten towns of the South Jersey pinelands. I attempted to inquire about my fate several times. The response was always the same: "Talk to Doo-Wop." I was concerned, but for some reason, I wasn't terrified. A sane person would have been terrified. I must not have been a sane person. There was a breed of strength to these men, but also an intangible warmth. With killers, they are just ice. Behind a killer's eyes there is not rage, there is nothing. When I met the eyes of Sitting Bull and Geronimo, there were faint nods back.

"I know some Indians," I said, in an effort to convey my multicultural qualifications. "Maybe you know them. Are you guys Lenape?"

Sitting Bull and Geronimo looked at each other.

"Who do you know?" Sitting Bull asked.

"Freebird," I said. I was serious. Mickey had done business with Indians.

"Heard of him," Geronimo said. "How you know Lenape?"

"I've known Lenape Indians all my life. My wife is one-quarter Lenape."

"No shit. What's her name?"

"Her maiden name was Edie Morris. Her Lenape middle name is Seven Angels."

"Morris," Sitting Bull said. "Lawyer in Cowtown?"

"Yes, that's right. Edie's father."

Both Indians nodded.

This was good. We were playing the age-old game of Indian geography. It was like this with Jews and Indians. Everybody was one step away from knowing somebody else, and even if you really didn't know who the other people knew, you felt like you had skinned a deer together. *Oh, sure, the Silvermans of Skokie. He's the orthodontist, right? Nice people. Right, the Running Deers of the North Platte River. How are Broken Feather and Rhoda? Whenever I need a bison in the Badlands, I know just where to go.* No, these guys weren't going to hurt me, we were *mischpocheh!*

Or maybe not. If they weren't going to hurt me, then what were we going to do? Had they just wanted to talk, we could have talked in the parking garage. Now here we were passing through collateral towns headed west. Lots of places around here to bury a body.

Keep them talking, see what you can learn.

"Should I know who Doo-Wop is?"

"Lots know Doo-Wop," said Geronimo.

"But I feel kind of stupid, like I should know him, too."

"You'll meet."

"I'll actually meet Doo-Wop?"

"Uh-huh."

"Where are we meeting him?"

"House."

"Why couldn't you just call me and ask me to meet him there? I would have come. It would have been rude not to."

"Must be sure."

I had held back my hole card long enough. Here we go: "My grandfather did a lot of business with Indians."

"What kind?" Sitting Bull asked.

"Gambling."

The Indians exchanged glances. The little Irishman in the front checked the rearview mirror. Reaction. "Oh, sure," I continued. "My grandfather and his partners did business for years with the Indians. Here in Jersey. Out west, even."

"Your grandfather," Geronimo said. "That's how you know Freebird?"

"Yes."

After a silence that lasted a millennium, we came to the Walt Whitman Bridge. A billboard advertisement for a law firm displayed two puffy-haired men in early middle age grinning smugly at the toll booth. The sign read:

DEMARCO & KLINE
WE'RE HUGE.

Sitting Bull frowned at the billboard, inhaled deeply, and sprung the question: "What's your grandfather's name?"

"Mickey Price."

The Caddy accelerated across the bridge and sped west on the Schuykill Expressway toward the great breast of Philadelphia's Main Line.

The house was immense, but old, not like the tract mansions that were being put up everywhere. All stone. I think we were in Wynnewood, where the Annenbergs had a place. Not the ideal ambience for a hit. Geronimo, Sitting Bull, and Paddy O'Brien led me up a narrow flagstone staircase toward the pool house, leaving me alone with the Ache. Who are these people that live in these homes? What was I doing wrong? Imagine driving home from work every day and being SERVED SERVED SERVED. Reverend Screed reminded me that this was not an attractive part of my personality, that I was supposed to scoff at such excess. *Good God, what kind of philistine needs all this?* But the Ache is the Ache, and all that I feared momentarily took a backseat to all the stuff that I wanted.

I felt warmth and motion of another presence. Standing by the pool in a terrycloth bathrobe, scooping debris from the water with a pole-extension net, was a compact man who looked vaguely familiar.

He was in his fifties, with horn-rimmed glasses and thinning salt-and-pepper hair. I could see from the opening in his robe that he was wearing tennis shorts, which made sense because there was a tennis court just beyond a set of hedges. While in the car with the Indians, I had been envisioning an encounter with Jabba the Hutt or *Pulp Fiction*'s Marcellus Wallace, or a *Star Trek* mutant with a pulsating brain, but the man before me was anything but frightening. He reminded me of the college professor everyone befriended, with the exception, of course, of the two amazons in bikinis and stiletto heels reclining out of earshot on the other side of the pool.

"I've got frogs," the man finally said. He did not look up. "You spend all this money for such a nice pool and then you get frogs. It's not even Passover. Heh. Nothing you can do about it other than to scoop them out. It's a compulsion with me," he said, scooping out a dead frog from near the drain. "Poor thing," Doo-Wop said, flinging the dead frog past the amazons-with-stilettos into the hedges.

"I understand that," I said. "Don't the Annenbergs live around here?"

"Used to."

"Close by?"

The man pointed at his own house. "Real close by. I met you at your Bar Mitzvah reception." The man finally looked up at me. His eyes were focused and warm like herbal tea. This was good. In the killing end of the trade, they had eyes that were focused and cold like hail. Mickey's partner Blue Cocco had hailstone eyes.

"My Bar Mitzvah?"

"No, Frankie Valli's. Of course, yours. You had the ceremony overseas when your grandfather-rest-in-peace had his trouble, but the reception was in A.C. when you got back. Terrible what the government put your grandfather through, just for selling saltwater taffy."

"Are you the Doo-Wop I'm supposed to talk to?"

"Doo-Wop's my Hebrew name. Heh."

"I'm sorry, but I don't remember a Doo-Wop."

"Do you remember a Norm Ornstein?"

"Orn—yes, I do. My grandfather used to talk about a Norm Ornstein. In the music business."

"That's me. I'm Ornstein."

Doo-Wop waved me into the pool house, which was furnished like Versailles. He gravitated toward a panorama of black-and-white pictures, and pointed toward a pompadoured trio. "Recognize them?" he asked.

"They look familiar."

Doo-Wop flashed disappointment. "Dion and the Belmonts. This picture over here is Dion DiMucci with me."

"Oh, sure. Would you look at that?"

"I am looking at it. See all these people? They were my life. Check out these guys." Doo-Wop pointed to a black group wearing tuxedos.

"Familiar, too, but—"

"Lee Andrews and the Hearts. Over here we have Jerry Gamble and Jean Huff. The Philly Sound. Brilliant producers. I was very proud of them. Here I've got the Dovelles—"

"The Bristol Stomp."

"Good! There's hope for you yet. This guy over here is Jerry Butler. Here I have the Intruders. Harold Melvin and the Blue Notes, of course. Drifters. O'Jays. Spinners. Tokens. Brenda and the Tabulations. I dated a Tabulation."

Doo-Wop was wistful, vulnerable even. He loved these people, and I barely knew who they were. I felt like a criminal on trial.

"This is Jerry Blavat and me," he continued.

"The Geater with the Heater."

"Yes, good."

"I know Jerry."

"Mazel tov."

"Hey, wait a minute," I said. "It just hit me. Norm Ornstein.

Aren't you the one who came up with that big new recording technique back in the sixties?"

"The Floor of Noise. That was me," Ornstein said proudly. "I handled Mickey's interests in the tunes trade. We also had some motels in Wildwood. Mick felt it was important to diversify away from saltwater taffy. Great man, Mick. Gave me my start when I was heading in the wrong direction when I was a kid."

"What direction was that?"

"Politics. Dirty business."

"I know. May I jump ahead, Mr. Ornstein?"

"Doo-Wop."

"What did you want to discuss with me, Doo-Wop?"

"I understand you've been asking questions about ownership of a music catalogue."

Nowhere to hide. "That's true. Are you concerned about that?"

"Yes and no."

"I gather you want me to stop poking around in Turnpike Bobby's properties. I guess I hit too close to home, which is why I'm here."

"You're exactly wrong. I don't have anything to do with Turnpike Bobby. Who can listen to that shit? Do you know what he's saying? I don't. 'Orthodontists suck on pickles?' What could such a verse mean?"

"I don't think that's the lyric. 'Orthodontists suck on pickles.'"

"Yeah, then what is it?"

"I think it's, 'Oh, Donna's love can be fickle.'"

"If that's the verse, why not just sing it like a normal human being? Anyhow, I like to know what something means. Different music means different things. Doo-wop meant that life makes pretty promises, then breaks them. Sweet melodies, then heartache out on South Street. Rock was about rebellion. I respect that, but couldn't get into it. The rockers were hard to get under your thumb. Who needed it?"

"What about rap? That's the big thing now."

"I need you to tell me that rap is the big thing now? Is this what you're telling me? Listen, my Ivy League friend, rappers aren't rebelling against anything. Rappers are the ultimate conformists. They want what the Man has always wanted—cash, flash, and gash. They call it bling. There's never been anything more corporate than rap. It's just the publicity of rebellion. I admit it's a good sales hook. At least with doo-wop, we had the integrity to say that all we wanted was what the Man had."

I found this genuinely interesting, but not as interesting as returning home alive.

"But why am I here?"

"This Bobby nonsense. It stinks. He's got an Elvis thing, a Belushi thing, a Judy Garland thing going. He's going to *plotz* soon, am I right? I've seen a million hotshot so-called musicians collapse," Doo-Wop said.

"Here's the thing," he continued. "When Bobby goes down, regardless of how it happens, there's gonna be all kinds of pain-in-the-ass flashbulbs and badges scratching around. I don't need that. Our guys—old guys in your grandpop's field—are still getting royalties from the doo-wop scene from the fifties and sixties. I keep that all going. I tell you that candidly because you're family. We don't need flashbulbs and badges. The more dirt you turn over about Bobby's catalogue, the more shit I'm going to have to answer when things go boom with Bobby."

"So, you're saying there's no connection between your boys and Bobby?"

"Jonah, you know Bobby's crew. Can you do business with those schmucks?"

"It's hard, Doo-Wop."

"It's impossible. Whatever it is you're looking for, it doesn't come back to us, capisce?"

"I appreciate knowing this. Why do you think someone wants me to believe his doo-wop library is ripe for acquisition?"

"I'll give you a guess. Maybe it's because this little birdie who whispered in your ear knows who does own doo-wop catalogues and old film titles, and wanted you to go poking around because it might lead to health problems for you."

"The guy who made the suggestion is probably being used. He's a naïve type, low on the totem pole."

"How long's he been with Bobby?"

I hesitated. I had never told Doo-Wop that my source was with Bobby. This Ornstein was just like Mickey, knew everything. "A long time, I think."

"If he's been with Bobby a long time, he's in show business. If he's in show business, he's not naïve. Got it?"

"Got it. Any theories about what he might have on Bobby?"

"Yeah, Jonah, I have a theory. Guys like me. Like your grandfather. We're business people. That's all. These Bobby people you're running with. *Not* business people. See, guys like me are just looking for a buck. That's all. Whoever gave you the music catalogue tip probably believes all that Mario Puzo-prick-your-finger-swear-to-a-burning-saint bullshit, which is why they set you up. We're out for a buck, not for blood. This Bobby crowd, they're looking for self-actualization, a drug, something. Very dangerous people. At least with us, you can do business. You can't do business with people trying to set up shop across the street from God. If your grandfather were here, he'd tell you what I'm telling you. Stay away from these fruitcakes."

Don't Be a Schmuck

*"The reason why you had a gun was because one day
people would come to kill you."*

I like revolvers. I've fired semiautomatics before, but they've got too many moving parts and requirements—cock this, chamber that. Loading the bullets into the magazine of a semi scrapes up my fingers, too. I'm a real badass.

Mickey had a revolver, a thirty-eight special. Actually, he had more than one. There was one beside his bed and another in the glove compartment of his car. The revolvers were always loaded (Mickey: "If they're not loaded, what's the goddamned point?"), and when I was a kid, they didn't have any of the safety features you see on guns nowadays. Mickey made no secret that he had guns, his "safety feature" being the declarative statement: "This gun is loaded, and if you screw with it you'll kill yourself, which means you're a schmuck, so don't touch it."

For the most part, I listened. A few times, however, when Mickey and Deedee went on trips, I went into the woods near Pomona and shot up a tree. When I got back home, I'd replace the bullets, which Mickey kept in his tiny shoes on a high shelf.

I never asked Mickey why he had guns because I always knew. Some people learn that the world is a dangerous place in an incremental, lockstep way. Not me. The reason why you had a gun was because one day people would come to kill you. My parents died young, so cause-of-death ruminations were academic to me. Someday they would come, so don't be a schmuck.

I owned a three-fifty-seven magnum, which also held thirty-eight rounds. Mine had a four-inch barrel. The good thing about a four-inch barrel was that it helped with accuracy. The bad thing was that it was a big mother to carry. I drove back to Cowtown to retrieve it because with my recent beating and kidnapping, it had become evident that I had gotten myself involved with another unconventional polling assignment. I put the gun in the shoulder holster, strapped the apparatus over my undershirt, and threw an oversized safari-style shirt over it so it wouldn't be as obvious in the middle of summer. I put the little bedside strongbox in the trunk of the Caddy, and drove back in great discomfort to the Shore, asking whether I unconsciously sought trouble or trouble premeditatedly sought me.

In the middle of the night, I felt our bed rumble a little. My heart raced momentarily until I recognized the critter that had sabotaged Edie's and my slumber. It was Lily, who had developed the habit of coming into our bedroom in the middle of the night because she had been having nightmares. Her particular phobia these days was big-headed team mascots. She had seen a mascot on television with an oversized baseball head, and had hidden under the sofa. As Edie and I spoke to her, she specifically recalled seeing the Baltimore Orioles' mongo-headed bird.

Regrettably, this fear may have been genetic, because I had my own issues with large-headed things. There was a midget who worked on Steel Pier when I was little. He operated a concession. He said hello to me when I was with my parents, and I was frozen in terror for the remainder of the evening. I distinctly recall my mother characterizing my reaction to the gigantic-headed little man as a "prejudice" on my part, which caused me to panic that I might be destined to join the Ku Klux Klan, a group I had just learned about with terrified fascination in a TV documentary. Anybody who could burn a great big cross like that or organize hooded people in perfect marching lines and circles had to know what they were doing.

I returned Lily back to her room. I didn't want her anywhere around my gun. I fell back into pained semi-sleep, and had a series of Tony Soprano–style nightmares that night and well into the morning. It was as if my inner nightmare director had retained a videographer from MTV, because a bunch of my current obsessions were hastily attached in quick cuts, non sequiturs. There was Ricky and Lily in the ocean; little Kate running into me; me nibbling at Ms. Suicide's tummy as the family in her care sat watching *The Little Mermaid*; and me at forty-five thousand feet in a Gulfstream V lying to Bobby while chowing down Vienna Fingers cookies. And there were always attendants around. Sometimes we're in a huge mansion. It's my mansion, only I'm pretty sure it's really Doo-Wop's.

There was another aspect of the dream that was odd, and that was the voiceover. That's right, my dream had a voiceover. The voice belonged to a kindly man named Tom Carvel, who had owned a regional chain of ice cream parlors that bore his surname. The ice cream, custard, and cakes the outlets sold were really good. The thing that was disturbing, however, was Carvel's voice. In a display of the kind of vanity that only company owners and faded actresses can possess, Carvel voiced his own TV ads. The camera would pan over his products while he would opine about their greatness (*"Look at the happy smile on CookiePuss, isn't it marvelous?"*). His was a scratchy voice that made me want to clear my throat and hock a lung biscuit into the nearest sink. And here this nice fellow was haunting my sleep, having morphed into ghoulishness.

To make my mind more like a Salvador Dalí painting, I went downstairs and paged through one of Edie's women's magazines and came upon a letter to a health editor that began: "Dear Editor, I was born with a genital defect that is extremely obvious. I have three nostrils." I read it over five times to see if I had it right. Yup.

Nothing was adding up.

book three

GRAVITY OUTLAW

"New Jersey villages where even Sunday is only a restless lull between the crash of trains."
—F. SCOTT FITZGERALD, from his notes

Kurt Rossiter

"Bobby sees, Bobby does. Jonah sees, Jonah wants."

I waited on a bench outside Mustang Sally's office for her to complete her session with a patient. Today's *Atlantic City Packet* featured a front-page story above the fold about the effect the kidnapping of Kaylee Hopewell was having on the casinos. I read the first few paragraphs.

CASINOS SUSPEND CHILD CARE SERVICE
by Charlotte Baldwin
Staff Writer

Atlantic City—In response to safety concerns following the kidnapping of Kaylee Hopewell, the major Atlantic City casinos have suspended their babysitting services.

"The hotels are full, but guests are canceling reservations for babysitters in droves," said Nina Zucker, spokeswoman for the Boardwalk Monte Carlo Hotel and Casino. "People don't want to delegate responsibility to anyone else in the wake of the Kaylee kidnapping."

Lorraine Marsh, who is on vacation with her family from Chicago, said, "We just feel better having our kids with us. I know the hotels only hire responsible people to babysit, but until this Kaylee situation is resolved, I just don't feel right about leaving the kids."

The Atlantic City Business Council has publicly criticized the slow pace of the Atlantic City Police Department's investigation. "It's amazing to me that they don't know anything at all about what happened to that girl," said Eva Schwartz, the Business Council's executive director. "If they don't make progress soon, this may impact summer business in a big way."

According to a casino executive who asked not to be quoted by name, "The unspoken problem here is liability. While we vet our babysitters carefully, the bottom line is we don't want to get sued."

"What's your hourly rate, Stang?" I asked.

"For therapy?"

"Of course."

"Three large."

"Three *thousand?*"

"No, three hundred."

"*Large* means *thousand.*"

"No kidding?"

"I heard it enough from my grandfather."

"I'll be damned. You have a patient for me?"

I pulled out my wallet and dropped three hundred dollars on her table. Twenty-dollar bills from the automatic teller.

"Take it back, I'm making enough from you on our other work."

"I insist."

"Fine. Lay it on me, gorgeous." She let the cash sit on the table, blowing in the automatic breeze from the air conditioner.

"I think it's this Bobby project. This is so embarrassing."

"It ain't more embarrassing than looking at autopsy photos during one's free time."

"Stang, there's something wrong with me. I think I have a real live mental illness."

"Symptoms, please?"

"I was walking down the beach the week before last. A little girl ran into me. I helped her up, and all of a sudden, this gorgeous au pair—"

"Here we go."

"What do you mean, 'Here we go?' "

"You said it all with those three words. *Gorgeous au pair.* The perfect stranger. Men your age are a mess. You are who and what you are. You're as big as you're gonna be. Go on, doll."

"I started talking to this gorgeous college girl like I'm in college myself, and I'm insanely jealous of every guy she's ever talked to. I'm angry. I'm having these dreams. Then there's Bobby. It's so easy to lie to him. On the one hand, the guy makes me sick. I actually had a dream that I kicked him senseless. I know he's a tragedy. On the other hand, I'm fantasizing about servants, airplanes. I want dancers in my hotel suite—girls—I want to be oblivious. Then there are moments like this, now, when I'm thinking, 'Am I nuts?' Yeah, I'm really going to end up with this college girl and she's really going to want *me*. It's this virus, this *longing*. Stang, where the hell does this come from? Am I going to lose everything? Sometimes I think I'm going to fall on the floor and start crying."

"When did we first meet, Jonah?"

"Late seventies, probably."

"That sounds about right. As long as I've known you, you've had dramas going on in your life and in your head. You were living with your grandparents in the casino. Your parents were gone by then. These theatrical productions and conflicts are the rule with you. You're not big on intermissions."

"What are you telling me?"

"Babies shove everything they find in their mouths. They understand the world orally. Bats are blind but have good hearing. They understand the world through their ears. Dogs smell their way through life. You, Jonah, can only engage a subject if it triggers agony. It's not a sense *per se,* it's an operating system like a computer. Let's start with that. Quick question: Did you have an imaginary friend when you were little?"

"No, not that I can remember." I laughed involuntarily.

"What's funny?"

"I had an imaginary nemesis when I got older."

"A nemesis?"

"Yes."

"When you got older?"

"Yes. Kurt Rossiter. His name was Kurt Rossiter. I dreamed him up in high school."

"*High* school?"

"Yeah. He was this sandy-haired guy, total hedonist stud from the Main Line. Square jaw. Ryan O'Neal in *Love Story.* Jude Law in *Mr. Ripley.* Drove an old Jag. E type. Long front. Jack Kennedy in the modern age."

"Long front? OK. Interesting."

"Whenever things wouldn't go right with a girl, or I was worried about competition getting into a good college, I'd blame it on Kurt Rossiter. My grandmother asked me why I didn't invite a girl I liked to the junior prom. I told her Kurt Rossiter got to her first."

"Did your grandmother know you made him up?"

"No."

"What was it that you admired about Kurt Rossiter the most?"

"He had no conscience. He could fake it when it served him, but Kurt didn't hesitate, he just moved."

"When was Kurt at the top of his game?"

"College."

"When did he die?"

"I didn't think about him as much after college. Maybe a little. Then he just died off."

"Guess what, sugar cube?"

"What?"

"He's back. Kurt Rossiter is back in a more gonzo form—Bobby Chin. Look, babe, if you were a normal patient, I'd be asking you a lot of questions, questions that would take months if not years to sort out. But you're not a normal patient, you're in my life. What I'm saying is, I know you, so I'll give you the *USA Today* version: You're at a fucked-up age. You're not young and you're not old. You're who you're gonna be, but you've still got options. A successful man is basically an adolescent with geometrically expanded options. It's the options thing that's riding up your kazoo like a thong made in China. Now, when did your mother die?"

"When I was ten."

"No, what time of year?"

"July."

"Where we are right now, right?"

"Hmm."

"These milestones reach out for you. You're looking around at you and what other people have and you're asking yourself, 'Could I have that?' Maybe yes, maybe no. There's no reason why you couldn't have an under-the-Boardwalk quickie with an au pair other than the price you'd pay. Unfortunately, our generation defines a good marriage as getting all of one's fantasies met, which is a big part of the problem. So, what to do? You may never be Bono, but it's possible to embark on some campaign to get rich, to have servants and planes, but would it work? On one hand, you can't be faulted for dreaming. Christ, love, you're alive. Dreaming is what living people do. On the other hand, are these obsessions worth the risk of whatever you'd have to do to get them? For every pantload CEO staring out at you from the cover of *Fortune* magazine, there are thousands of ninnies who crashed and burned. Still, it wouldn't be wrong of you to conclude you have the freedom to try. Now, these objects you think about—do you want them or do you just think you want them?"

"I don't know, planes, gorgeous dancing girls—"

"I remember a Jonah who hated to fly."

"I'm scared to death of it."

"Then what, dear Lord, are you going to do with a plane?"

"Point made."

"And the dancers. How would you feel if they, uh, went dancing with other men?"

"It would kill me. I'm very conventional. What does this have to do with Kurt Rossiter?"

"Kurt Rossiter is everything you wanted, but couldn't have. He's the guy who plays with fire and never gets burned. See, Kurt Rossiter moved like a panther to get what he wants, but Bobby's like a hyena whose brain has been rotted by syphilis. You created Kurt—your very own Mega Boy—so you sculpted him smooth, like you'd want to be. Kurt has Jonah's id, but also his sophistication—Kurt can channel his impulses. Bobby's all spontaneous id with no control. Bobby Chin is Kurt Rossiter raw. This makes you very anxious. Bobby sees, Bobby does. Jonah sees, Jonah *wants*. Jonah doesn't *do*. That makes you civilized, that balance between passion and restraint. That's one measure of a man—what he doesn't do that he *could* do. You've got that sexual capital now that you didn't have when I first met you, and, naturally, you want to spend it, but you're terrified of losing control, being your grandfather, losing your family, being a disgrace."

"Mickey had a lot of self-control."

"Not in how he made his living. I don't know the facts, doll, but I imagine if somebody got in his way—"

"I know. I know what happened when somebody got in his way. Another thing about Bobby: he's obsessed with what everybody thinks."

"He's obsessed with being the center of attention, like a child, but he doesn't care how it's done. He has no awareness of consequences, whereas consequences—the eventuality of shame—are all you think about."

"Do you know what I was thinking about last night? I'm about the age President Kennedy was when he was elected."

"See, the fact that you know that says it all. Now, even though you're getting older, you're not so old that other opportunities are out of the question. In fact, your options have expanded exponentially. Other careers, strange playmates. You know what I'm saying. You're coming to grips with the basic fact that life is what it is. You're also thinking about risk. Then along comes Bobby with his planes, suites, dancing girls. You are *in* that life, but not *of* that life. Making sense?"

"Oh, yeah, this is good. I was wondering if I was getting self-destructive like Bobby—"

"N-n-n-n-no. Let me stop you right there, Hoss, with this self-destructive bullshit. That's a cliché."

"What is?"

"That celebrities are self-destructive. Self-destruction is an outcome, it's not a cause. In fact, it's almost impossible to be self-destructive with intent. It gets back to our discussion about options. People who have a lot of options, well, take a lot of them. That's what killed young Kennedy. Thinking he could fly, nobody saying, 'No, hot pants, you don't know how to do this!' That's what killed Belushi. He wanted more drugs and there was always somebody on hand to throw some more his way. Elvis, too. Self-destructive? Oh, come on. Self-indulgent? You betcha. Human beings want more."

"Are you telling me I'm going to weigh four hundred pounds and keel over eating a Whopper on the can?"

"No, you won't. See, Jonesy, you sit up at night and make yourself sick worrying. The Worry Paradox—it's bad and it's good. It's bad because you suffer. It's good because it shows an anchor in reality—

that you're aware that outrageous behavior can go too far. The Bob-bys, the Belushis, the Elvises—they don't worry, they just *do*. Every-body around them worries, which is the problem."

"Stang?"

"Yes, sweetheart?"

"Did you know I killed a guy?"

Mustang frowned, and twisted one of her bracelets. "I heard there was an intruder in Cowtown, right?"

"He came to our house to kill me. He worked for a lobbyist who wanted something covered up that I was on to. Edie came out of nowhere and brought him down with a shotgun. Once he was down, I ended it, point-blank. Two shots from my three-fifty-seven. One in the throat. The other one took off the top of his head." I pointed to my throat and the top of my head in the event Mustang Sally needed to know where one's throat and top of the head were.

"You defended your family, Jonah."

"Yes, I did, and the police agreed."

"Do you regret that?"

"I regret that I don't regret it."

"I don't follow, doll."

"Edie shot the guy—a big Piney albino—before he could shoot me. He had a gun out. He probably would have died from her shot-gun blast if I had let it go, but I didn't want there to be any chance of him coming back. You don't want the pricks coming back. I wanted him to know who was finishing him off. I shot him in the throat first because I knew he would survive it for a moment—recognize, process what had happened, comprehend his fate. Then I shot him in the head, and it was over. I defended myself . . . but I played God there for a minute. And, no, I don't feel any remorse. Do you follow now?"

"Are you wondering what you're capable of?"

"Hell, yes. How easy would it be to do it again? How else might I decide to play God, take what I want to take?"

"Which brings us back to Bobby."

"I don't know what he did or didn't do, Stang, but here I am, as a man who exercised his free will, now working on a case where—"

"The same thing may have happened."

"Right. See a pattern here?"

"Jonah, doll, there's a difference between wanting to kill a man who posed a mortal threat to you and your family, and wasting a guy who ticked you off in some impulsive way."

"I don't know what Bobby did or didn't do."

"Fine, but there is no reason to believe that a sculptor posed a mortal threat to—"

"Maybe he did. I don't know. What I do know is that I don't feel badly about what I did to that albino in the woods. I'm nervous that I may not know where the brakes are. There's a slippery slope."

"You have a conscience, Jonah. Your conscience is the brake. This torture is evidence of that. Now let's talk about lying to Bobby. Why do you think you do it?"

"I'm not sure it's actual lying. Maybe it's some form of asskissing."

"No, darlin', it's lying. Why do you do it?"

"Maybe to keep his business. Maybe because I don't want to be tossed out of his orbit. Maybe I like breathing that rarified air and don't want to lose that oxygen. Another slippery slope to climb—or descend—to get what I want. It's not rational."

"Maybe lying to Bobby is a perfectly rational way to interact with him. You've seen how he responds to the truth. He goes apeshit. So, let's conclude that one of the reasons for your lying is strategic."

"Let's."

"If it's strategic, why not just lie to him until the end of the project?"

"Because I really want to help this guy."

"*Aha!* I thought so."

"You thought what?"

"Well, my little gangster boy, you are an idealist. That's why you'll never be Kurt Rossiter or Bobby Chin. You want to save Bobby. Bobby is sick of making his nonsensical music. You're sick of making your nonsensical mischief and calling it 'opinion research.' To save a burned-out man your age—an icon, no less—is to save yourself. It's to stay young forever and live those fantasies forever. It's to not have choices, only a limitless buffet of options. With choices, something is forfeit. With a buffet, you can have everything. This anxiety is the cruel clock ticking. Your anxiety is your wisdom talking, a recognition of the *price* for grabbing, grabbing, grabbing."

"I just hate seeing him destroy himself."

"Yes, Mr. Sentimental, it's sad. But there's something even sadder: time. Now, don't be too hard on yourself, we all try to hustle the clock. Look, love, over on that table. It's a whole titty catalogue. I feel like I'm looking at colleges again. I know what I'm doing."

"Then why are you doing it, Stang?"

"Because, doll, who's it gonna hurt? Nobody! Nobody gets hurt when I call up Dial-a-Boob. What's the risk? None. These things that our not-guilty rock star friend Bobby does—risky, risky, risky."

"Shouldn't I feel worse about the lying?"

"You already feel like hell about the lying, don't kid yourself. What, are you looking for a pain certificate? I'll whip one up on my new computer graphics program. It'll say, 'Heartache Certificate is hereby awarded to Jonah Price (as in the criminal) Eastman. Who suffers.' We'll do a little award ceremony outside Lucy the Elephant. We'll throw brown plastic trash bags out the window in her ass and have them land on you to symbolize your suffering, how's that?"

"Is there something I can do?"

"You can do what is doable. Listen, you're a passionate man, you're *alive*. You can't change what you dream about, but you can focus your passions. On your family. On your work. On your health. On things you can actually do. That may not help you much, but trust me, love-bug, it's good advice."

"You're a work of art."

"Soon to be a thirty-four D masterpiece. Look at these mommas right here." Mustang pulled two translucent spheres from a drawer. "These are what D cups look like." She held them up to her chest. "Saline. Too big?"

"Yes, way too big."

"Bless your heart. I'll throttle back to Cs, then. I'll let you grab 'em as soon as they're in. You can bring Edie, that way there'll be no subterfuge, just a red-blooded American clinical experiment with two saline independent variables."

"Thanks, Stang, this helped. Really."

I meant it, too.

Nevertheless, insight does not equal cure, and I was not cured. I had been weaned by a murderer and had, in fact, once killed yet another bad man in addition to the albino intruder. I hadn't brought this killing up with Mustang Sally. One can only relate so much in a single session.

A Courteous Exchange

"I have a hundred and eighty-six hits on Google, you know?"

Despite my latent fantasies about being a tough guy, if ever there was evidence I was deluded, it was presented to me shortly after I turned onto Wissahickon Avenue in Ventnor during my morning run.

The early stages of my run from Margate had been going great. No knee pain. Heart-thumping songs pounding out of my earphones—"White Rabbit," "Long Cool Woman," "Magic Bus." The Dude was invincible. A skywriting airplane was painting the heavens: B-O-R-G—. Oh, Borgata, the new casino. What a job, skywriting, I thought, paying too much attention to outer space.

About ten steps before I reached the ramp up to the Boardwalk, I felt an astonishing blow between my shoulder blades. To the extent that my brain was functioning, I envisioned that a prehistoric bird had dive-bombed into me. My earphones were stripped away, the doors of a van opened up, and I was dragged inside hyperventilating.

As I lay against the scratchy carpeting, I reflected not on the blessing of my survival, but on what a fraud I was. A real tough guy would not have decided to carry a firearm to protect his life only to abandon the weapon when it became inconvenient to carry, such as during a six-mile run. But no, my assailants wouldn't assail me while I was running because that would be rude.

I took my idiocy a bit further. Would a genuine hard case be running with music blasting in his ears, rendering one of his key survival senses useless? I think not. Yours truly liked the *idea* of being a Navy SEAL on the run from armed guerillas, but I had no capacity to execute this fantasy because I was a complete tool.

I opened my eyes when the van rounded a turn. A jolly-looking goon with a gap in his teeth and neutral eyes sat on a seat above me.

"What hit me?" I asked.

"It was a beanbag gun. Are you all right?"

"Compared to what?"

"It's just supposed to knock the wind out of you."

"It succeeded."

"Well, you look fine."

"Thank you. I don't believe it. I'm being kidnapped again. Twice in one frigging week."

"You're kidding," a new voice in the front of the van said. The driving cabin was obscured with tinted windows, so I couldn't quite make out the features of the men there.

"Who are you guys with, Doo-Wop?"

"Nah," the voice said, while Mr. Jolly nodded.

"The Flagellants?"

"No, sir."

"P.L.O.? Al Qaeda?" It was worth a try.

"No."

"Dammit."

"Sorry, Mr. Eastman."

"Where are we going?"

"Just gonna chill out a little while," Mr. Jolly said. "You'll be fine."

"Do you guys want money?"

"No, thank you."

"You sure are polite for kidnappers."

"You're very kind to say that."

"Are you sure you want *me?* I may not be the right guy."

"Oh, yes, we want you."

"I have a hundred and eighty-six hits on Google, you know?"

"No kidding," the voice from the front said. "That's terrific."

I sat up from the floor. Nobody objected. "May I sit in one of the seats?"

"Absolutely."

Mr. Jolly helped me up. The slim, polite man in the passenger seat of the van slid the tinted window back and moved beside Mr. Jolly to face me. The mountain who was driving didn't appear to have any interest in the goings-on in back. I noticed that the slim Mr. Polite had a laptop on his knees.

"Let me set a few ground rules," Mr. Polite said. "Our little adventure doesn't need to be difficult. We're going to ride around for a while. Nothing is going to happen to you. Nothing is going to happen unless you try to escape before we're through. I wouldn't want my associate here to put a tap in your ass."

Mr. Jolly opened his sports jacket, providing optical evidence that he was armed.

"I think you mean that you don't want to put a *cap* in my ass," I clarified. "A *cap.*"

"I always get that wrong," Mr. Polite said.

"Would you gentlemen bear with me for a moment?" I asked.

"Of course."

"Of all of the people who have kidnapped me this week, you're my favorites, and I mean that."

"We appreciate the feedback."

"But if there's something you're looking for—money,

information—I could get home to my family faster if you'd just make the request now."

Mr. Jolly and Mr. Polite exchanged glances.

Mr. Polite typed my name into Google. "Wow, there are a lot of hits for you. It says here you worked in the White House."

"When I was much younger."

"What did you do there?"

"Polling."

"Did you like it?"

Let me take a moment to rehash: I had been shot in the back and knocked off my feet while on my morning run by the type of device bounty hunters used. I was dragged into a van, which sped away. My kidnappers didn't want money. They were making cocktail chitchat with me. There was something harmless about them. Jesus, I had been snatched by the Huxtables.

There were a few possibilities: 1) I had gone insane; 2) they were stalling until we arrived at the place of my murder; 3) there was something going on that my pea brain couldn't comprehend. I decided to buy time, get my kidnappers to like me.

"I liked politics enough to make a career out of it."

"That's good. It's important to love what you do. Let me see what else they say about you. Hmm," Mr. Polite said. "You were reprimanded by the Polling Board. What was that about?"

"I used an unconventional polling technique."

"What was the technique?"

"There was an election in the South. The Deep South. I had my interviewers sidle up to the voters and ask them questions about a racist candidate. My interviewers didn't disclose that they were interviewers. They pretended to be just normal people standing in line at the supermarket. My guys pretended to like the racist candidate, and it turned out that a majority of the voters in that state liked the racist, too. I released the poll, and people in the state went nuts that they looked like racists."

"Who was your client?" Mr. Jolly asked.

"I can't tell you. But if you were going to torture me, I'd tell you now if you'd promise not to torture me later."

"Why would we torture you?" Mr. Polite asked.

"Okay, that's a relief. Let's just say my client wanted it to be known that the racist candidate had more support than people thought he did. Anyhow, a group of pollsters got together and said my methods were flawed."

"If the people were racists, then they were racists," Mr. Polite said.

"That's what I said! I just found a sly way to tap into that."

"Let's see what else Google says about you. There's something under famous New Jerseyans."

I had a feeling I knew where this was going.

Mr. Jolly asked, "Why would you be listed under famous people?"

"Maybe Google just returned an answer because I was mentioned next to somebody who is famous. That happens sometimes."

Then Mr. Polite said it: "You're under a section on Mickey Price."

"The mobster?" Mr. Jolly said. The husky driver turned his head when he heard the name.

Mr. Polite read aloud the section on Mickey:

Mickey Price. Atlantic City mobster. Born in Romania in early 1900s to Jewish parents, perhaps as Moses Prinzcowicz. Died in 1999. Pioneer in bootlegging and gambling. Using loopholes in Prohibition law that allowed the stockpiling of alcohol for medicinal purposes, Price operated numerous bootlegging stills throughout the Pine Barrens under the auspices of South Jersey Medical Elixirs. When molasses was discovered in a 1928 police raid, he claimed it was used for the manufacture of saltwater taffy. Price's ostensible job was as the proprietor of the Taste of the Shore saltwater taffy shop.

Authorities estimated that Price's mob was responsible for roughly half of the bootleg alcohol sold in the United States. Dozens of murders were attributed to Price's gang, but never confirmed. His lifelong partners were Arturo "Blue" Cocco, the underboss of the Philadelphia "family" of La Cosa Nostra headed for many years by Angelo Bruno, and Irving "Irv the Curve" Aronson, a former aide to the notorious Dutch Schultz of Newark. Price was widely believed to have engineered the murder of Schultz in conjunction with Abner "Longy" Zwillman of Newark.

Price was believed to be a major investor in Havana casinos along with his partners Meyer Lansky, Harry "Nig Rosen" Stromberg, and Charles "Lucky" Luciano. He was questioned in the gangland-style executions of John "Legs Diamond" Nolan, Benjamin "Bugsy" Siegel, Albert Anastasia, Willie Moretti, and Angelo Bruno, and in the disappearance of Teamster's boss Jimmy Hoffa, with whom he had close ties.

The diminutive mobster fled the country in 1975 to dodge an indictment for skimming and settled for several years in France. Some organized crime experts believe that Price engineered the legalization of casino gambling in Atlantic City through political graft. Shortly after the construction-accident death of the main witness against him in the skimming case, Price returned to the United State in 1978 with his wife, Dorothy (Deedee) and grandson, Jonah Price Eastman, the political consultant, whom Price raised after the death of his only child, Ann Price Eastman, of cancer, the boy's mother. Eastman's father died under mysterious circumstances shortly before his wife.

Price operated the Golden Prospect Hotel and Casino from its inception until his death, despite his official title of "Bell Captain." The fate of Price's empire and his fortune has been rife with speculation, some believing both evaporated after his death, others arguing that it fell into the hands of a younger and better-educated generation of criminals—perhaps even Price's grandson, Eastman. Shortly after Price's death (of natural causes), Philadelphia mob boss Mario Vanni was gunned down in a hail of bullets,

and his top henchman, who is believed to have attempted to extort East-man, has never been found, and is presumed murdered.

Mr. Polite flexed his jaw muscles. Mr. Jolly looked at Mr. Polite's jaw for divine guidance. I asked myself, What would Mickey do here? The amateur's instinct would be to talk mob talk, tough. Scare the bastards. The move here was to go in the opposite direction. Screw with these guys. Get them wondering. Talk nice. But I wouldn't talk first. I'd let them talk first, get control of things. Confidence.

Mr. Polite closed his laptop. I met his eyes calmly. My face was expressionless, and my eyes registered nothing. Not cocky, not scared. There was silence for what seemed like an hour. During that time, I contemplated what Google had vomited out about me. While I had heard cutesey speculation that I had "succeeded' Mickey—mobophiles love the idea of an invisible new generation of Ivy League-educated gangsters—I had never seen it memorialized so blatantly. Who wrote this crap? Didn't they know that the Jewish racketeers yearned for respectability, that they would give their lives for their offspring's legitimacy? The answer didn't matter; the sexiest narrative did. It was all virtually unstoppable. Someday my children would read this, or something like it, and I'd have to explain to them that their father was not a criminal. But would they believe me, and should they believe me?

The tinted glass behind the driving cabin revealed enough of the landscape that I knew we were moving, but I had no idea in what direction. The driver occasionally turned his head, I assumed, to hear what we were talking about.

Mr. Polite chuckled nervously. "Your grandfather, huh?"

"I'm sorry?" I asked, feigning confusion.

"Price."

"Oh. Yes."

"They leave out things sometimes," Mr. Jolly, the less bright of the two, said under his breath. This acknowledgment of poor planning earned dagger eyes from Mr. Polite.

"What did they leave out?" I asked.

"Nothing," Mr. Polite said. "He was talking about something else."

"I'm beginning to get concerned, gentlemen. My family is going to worry about me. I'm starting to worry about me."

"We told you not to worry," Mr. Polite said, a little testy, but I sensed that the testiness was not directed at me. I just happened to be sitting there when the man realized he had been taken. Whoever had put them up to this had left out the detail of their target's pedigree.

"You seem like decent men, not kidnappers, not murderers."

"How would you know about us?" Mr. Jolly said, trying to recoup from his earlier faux pas.

"I don't know anything about you," I said. "I don't, and I don't need to. I know what it's like, that's all."

"You know what what's like?" Mr. Polite asked. I saw the driver's profile. He was listening.

"My grandfather had a proverb he used to tell me all the time. 'Entrances are wide, exits are narrow.'"

"So what?" Mr. Jolly asked. "What's that supposed to mean?"

Mr. Polite's jaw was tight.

"I only know what it meant to me," I said. "It meant that we're all human. We're all capable of getting ourselves into things we can't get out of. Me. You. Mickey knew I was proud, cocky even. He worried that I wouldn't be able to know when to fold up, you know, even when I could."

There was more silence. I began to detect a familiar landscape.

Eventually, Mr. Polite said, "Now, Mr. Eastman, we are going to pull up to a familiar location. You are to sit up, open the rear door of the van—without turning around—and get out. Once you are out,

please don't turn around to look at the van or we'll have to put a—
what was it? Oh, yes, a cap in your ass."

Without any explanation, and just in time for Irene's lunch of
lentils, cucumber salad, and cheese with freshly baked sourdough
bread, I was dropped off at the end of my street.

"Have a pleasant day," I heard a voice say.

The Cohn of Silence
Is Not Impressed

"If Bobby gets in trouble, that may be good for somebody."

The Cohn of Silence was waiting for me like waxen fruit in a booth at Murray's Delicatessen in Margate. After serious deliberation, I decided against bringing up my encounter with Doo-Wop, not to mention my other kidnapping. My fear was that Mr. Cohn would think I had been investigating clumsily in pursuit of Lonesome Jake's music library theory, which would have infuriated him. Doo-Wop and Mr. Cohn almost certainly knew each other, and the last thing I needed was any perception that I was a loose cannon slamming into big shots while I was supposed to be discreet. There would be a time and a place to discuss Doo-Wop, not to mention my latest kidnapping.

Mr. Cohn was dressed in a cream-colored suit and cherry red bow tie, appearing lickable. I met him halfway in couture with khakis and a navy sports jacket. No tie.

"You look sharp, *boychik*," Cohn said.

"I'm going for the Knesset look. They never wear ties."

"You're Israeli all of a sudden?"

"I'm feeling a little *sabra* today, frankly."

"Good. They know how to survive. It's a good skill. Your grandfather had it. He had a little Ben-Gurion in him."

Cohn reflected, then added: "Why do you think Mickey survived so long? Irv the Curve, too. Both made it into their nineties." Irv the Curve had been Aaron to Mickey's Moses.

"You want a history lesson? They survived because they could keep secrets. Not only did they make money, they knew where it came from and where it went. If you get rid of the guys who know everything, especially in *that* life, you've got a problem."

"Who knows Bobby's secrets, Mr. Cohn?"

"Everybody!" the Cohn of Silence laughed. "You can read 'em in the *Enquirer.*"

"But given the stuff this guy pulls, who knows enough to hurt him?"

"Those . . . what do you call them? Maggots."

"They've just been on the scene for a few years."

"That leaves us with his family."

"Maybe. I came across an invoice to Bobby for a Web site. It's for almost three quarters of a million dollars."

"I don't know much about internets."

"I did a Web site for my firm a few years ago. I paid about four grand."

"Someone's raping our client."

"Right."

"What is the significance to us?"

"It's so outrageous, Mr. Cohn, it suggests Bobby has no connection to the reality of his business affairs."

"This is to be assumed in show business. I just heard on the news that some brain-dead prizefighter who earned upwards of a half-billion—that's billion with a *b*—in his career, is broke. If you're on to something here, don't muddy up your hunch."

"If somebody's making this kind of money off Bobby, there's incentive to keep gouging him. If Bobby gets in trouble, that may be good for somebody."

"Or bad for somebody."

"That's true, but it gives us somewhere else to look."

The Cohn of Silence picked up a pickle and studied it respectfully as if it were the Oracle at Delphi. "I'm convinced our client is oblivious to his finances, not to mention everything else that occurs on our fair galaxy. I believe we need to keep digging, but my socks haven't been blown to Newark by this invoice discovery. It could cut too many ways. If someone benefits from Bobby's largesse, wouldn't it stand to reason that they'd want him healthy and free?"

"It would."

"So the questions become, if someone wants him in trouble, who gains by it? Or, if someone's gouging him, is this systematic, and does it help us with our Plausible Alternative Scenario?"

"I don't know, and I don't know anything more about the music library angle yet."

"Fine. If someone is just gouging him, well, I'm sorry to say that's unfortunate, but it's not our commission to resolve."

"It just doesn't add up."

"Okay, Hercule Poirot, get out a calculator and make it add up. In the meantime, how's our Plausible Alternative Scenario?"

"The cops haven't taken Bobby in, correct?"

"Correct."

"Then we're doing all right."

"No, we're just buying time. You've moved us from the fifty-yard line to the forty. We're still a ways off."

Losing Control

"Trouble begets trouble."

The idea behind being a handler was that you learned about breaking news *before* you turned on the TV. That's because in concept you were the one breaking the news. With Turnpike Bobby, I could bring peace to the Middle East before I could control my own client.

As I was flipping through the channels, Fox's G'ina Mardell nailed an exclusive interview with Derek Plush. I knew the news had to be pretty big because Plush was on the Fox set as opposed to being hooked in remotely from his personal Bat-studio. I felt a surge of heat shoot up my spine because the Bobby news beat had been cold for a couple of weeks.

"Now, moving on from the bizarre and uncertain fate of Kaylee Hopewell, we have a Fox exclusive with Derek Plush of *Major Player* magazine, who had his own exclusive interview with the ever-outrageous Turnpike Bobby Chin. Derek, welcome."

"Hello, Gina. You know, I've spent thirty-five years on the celebrity scandal beat, and I've never faced a subject who has so many unfolding layers of fascination. Jackie Onassis, of course, was interesting because of what she didn't reveal. Turnpike Bobby, on the other hand, is fascinating for what he does."

"You're doing a big feature on Bobby for September's issue of *Ma-*

jor Player. That's some timing given his being a 'person of interest' in the disappearance of sculptor Christian Josi."

"It really is, Gina. One of Bobby's most amazing revelations related to my questions about the disappearance of Christian Josi is this one: I asked Bobby about the public perception that he is, for lack of a better term, 'losing it'—that he has outrageously bad judgment. Even if he is innocent of any crime, he made some comments that will be hard to explain away."

"Can you give me an example?"

"Well, in response to my question about 'losing it,' Bobby said, and I quote, 'Losing control is an artistic act. It is an expression of character, of who you are.'"

"That might be interpreted a number of different ways."

"No question, but it may be hard to explain in court."

"I suppose Bobby's lawyers will just claim he was misquoted."

"That'll be hard, Gina. The interview was tape-recorded."

Within fifteen minutes of Plush's interview on Fox, the Atlantic City Police swarmed into the Golden Prospect Hotel to question Bobby about his "losing control" remark. The police had alerted the media, and marched into the hotel wearing their best we're-not-screwing-around faces. The Cohn of Silence was there, and had instructed Bobby to say nothing. Cohn characterized the "losing control" remark as relating to creative expression, nothing more, nothing less. The ACPD, predictably, scoffed.

"If you don't have a warrant for my client's arrest, we have nothing to discuss," the Cohn of Silence said.

The police promptly left. The purpose of their visit had not been an authentic interrogation, but theater. After Plush's report, they had to save face over their lack of progress by visibly pursuing justice given the provocative nature of Bobby's remark. The district attorney, an abrasive young local named Linda Renetti, announced her intention to seize Plush's audiotape of Bobby's interview. This, too, would fail in court—the Constitution gives near-absolute protection to journalists—but the on-camera tantrum made for good optics.

T he Cohn of Silence discussed this with me following his firefight at the Golden Prospect. My cell phone rang within seconds of the interview's conclusion, the seasoned voice on the other end saying, "Care for an ice cream sandwich?"

Very calmly, the Cohn of Silence spoke twenty minutes later inside his ice cream truck: "You saw that our client Retardo Montalban granted an audiotaped interview with Mr. Plush, I take it?"

"Yes. You're remarkably calm, Mr. Cohn. I'm impressed. I'm having trouble breathing myself."

"You're still young. When I was your age, I was still under the impression that I controlled the solar system, too. You learn."

"Bobby clearly had his interview with Mr. Plush."

"I suspect, Jonah, he had the interview even before our hopeless training session."

"Why do you think that?"

"I put a few things together. One day I couldn't reach Bobby and Kadaborah for a while. It was that day they were doing all that skywriting for the Borgata."

"Son of a bitch. That was the day I was kidnapped."

"Kidnapped?"

"The day they were skywriting for the Borgata, I was taken in a van and driven around for no reason. I've got to tell you, the kidnappers were pretty courteous. Anyhow, after a few hours, they dropped me off back home. They must have wanted both of us out of commission for that interview."

"Do we look like guys who want to spend our lives farting in elevators?" the Cohn of Silence asked the heavens.

"Sometimes I think Bobby wants to go to jail."

"No. He likes to exercise the symbols of his status. *'See what I can get away with?'* His life experience, of course, has rewarded this."

"What's our action item?"

"I'm going to have a little discussion with our cuckoo-bird friends of the life's-too-short variety. I'm going to recommend that I remain in a transitional role behind the scenes, dealing with the courts and supervising our investigation to the end. What Bobby needs now is an attorney of the rock-and-roll species, someone young who wants to be on TV independent of the legal craftsmanship. I felt that since you were the original point of contact, I would tell you about my decision."

"I respect the decision, and your willingness to handle this discreetly. My own tenure is winding down, too, I'm afraid. You can only be ignored, not to mention kidnapped, so many times."

"How are you coping with your kidnapping trauma?"

"I'm going to stew on this, deal with it in my own way, Mr. Cohn."

"Just like your grandfather. Mickey never threatened when he got adverse news. He just said, 'I'm sorry to hear that.' He went through a cycle of thought that was always a thing of beauty. He would feel aggrieved first. Then he would become enraged. Then he would cogitate. And just when you thought he had laid the matter to rest, something would happen. The cliché about Mickey was that he was not vindictive. Not true. He was vindictive, just very patient. All I ask is that nothing derail our efforts to date."

"I'll cogitate on that. What do you think will happen when Bobby's case gets to trial?"

"It'll never go to trial."

"No? You think you'll cut a deal?"

"Oh, no, no deals. Not on murder. Jonah, forgive me for sounding overly biblical, but trouble begets trouble. All we can do is delay the inevitable. That's what the neighbor said about Atticus Finch in *To Kill a Mockingbird*. That poor black man will be convicted, but Finch will keep the jury out longer than any other lawyer could, the neighbor said. I can't tell you what the inevitable is for Bobby, but will suggest two things. I cannot foresee Bobby in prison, and I suspect that Bobby—he's prescient in his own way—knows this. Second, these chronic deferrals of the inevitable suggest to me that his enablers are covering some dark secret."

"Such as Bobby's guilt?"

"Maybe. Maybe not. It's collateral to what we're discussing. All I'm saying is that as the jig is up, the desperate will run for cover. I assume that our little investigation is proceeding?"

"Yes, but I haven't found that dark secret yet."

"Fine. I'm inclined to have you keep digging. For humanitarian reasons."

"I don't follow."

"Bobby cannot go to jail, Jonah. The more you dig, the more earth will shake loose, and the more you shake loose, the quicker the inevitable will come to its natural conclusion."

"I always thought Turnpike Bobby would end up like Howard Hughes. Old and crazy."

"Hughes was crazy, but clever. I did some work for him out in Vegas. Bobby is crazy and impulsive. Not optimal survival skills. Anyway, I'm sorry if I'm playing sage too much, but it's not genius on my part. It's life experience. And another thing. I know a bit more about this entertainment library issue. It's true, Bobby owns a library. Hundreds of doo-wop songs going back to the fifties, his own music, plus some of those, uh, bikini movies. It would be worth tens of millions if it were on the market, which it isn't."

"Who wants it?"

"I don't know that anybody wants it, but it doesn't really matter. You can't just take it, or do a hostile takeover. It's private."

"Kadaborah and Turner seem to have so much control over Bobby's affairs. Maybe it's them."

"You're missing my point. Bobby is the legal owner of that library."

"Maybe somebody can pirate it. You see what's going on on the Internet."

"If someone's willing to break the law, then maybe they can make mischief, but I'm just not seeing the Plausible Alternative Scenario in this."

"I seem to be failing you."

"I'm frustrated."

"Lonesome Jake gave us a bum steer. He was just trying to help, poor guy. He's a simple man."

The Cohn of Silence shut his eyes, as if he were a *Bewitched* character trying to conjure up a hurricane. "I've been in and out of the entertainment racket for almost fifty years. I've never met a simple man in that world yet."

The Cohn of Silence looked tired. Perhaps it was the way the streetlight knifed through the truck's windshield. I had seen how my grandfather and his partners aged, how they grew tired. When they were tired, they got defensive—and wrong. I had been traumatized the first time I detected cracks in these men whom I had seen as monuments, carved from granite. Perhaps the message I was getting was that I needed to do my own investigating without consulting the Cohn of Silence at every turn. I was growing up, still, even in my forties.

"Maybe you're right, Mr. Cohn."

Standstill

"A community waits another endless summer day for word from a friend."

One vehicle for a new wave of unwanted publicity was an overweight fortyish woman who claimed to be president of the Turnpike Bobby Chin Fan Club. She was contemplating filing a lawsuit because she wanted a guarantee that she would get a seat if and when Bobby scheduled his concert at the Golden Prospect. She was afraid that the small size of the performance venue would cause tickets to be allotted only to "insiders," whatever that meant.

The other source of Bobby news was, of course, Derek Plush. The central question being debated was what Bobby meant by his comments about losing control being a form of artistic expression. "Bobby is shrewd," Plush mentioned archly. Was this a confession, the pundits asked? Was it admissible in court, the on-air attorneys squabbled? The answer didn't matter. The debate was sucking up valuable airtime, plus making it harder for Chief Willie and his merry band to dig around.

These were the news items that greeted me on the TV as I entered Ozzie's Restaurant in Longport.

"Chief Willie frustrated," the big man said, sitting at the counter in a turquoise T-shirt and khaki shorts. He brushed aside the latest edition of *Philly!* magazine enumerating the region's "Top 100 Sluttiest Middle-aged Hostesses."

"What's happening?"

"I know now what I knew last time we met. Christian is clean, the Maggots are dirty, but not radioactive. It must be some kind of government conspiracy," he said dismissively.

"Have you ever *met* someone from the government?" I inquired.

"Chief Willie say, 'Touché.'"

"This guy, Bobby, is amazing. He's our client and our nemesis at the same time. Plush says Bobby is shrewd. Where does he get that crap? Why does the press need to make their targets cagey when they're not?"

"Chief Willie say, 'Always make bear bigger when you tell hunting story.' Chief note words of Rudyard Kipling: 'Power without responsibility—the prerogative of the harlot through the ages.'"

Hearing this, I found it hard not to contemplate my whereabouts in the cosmos: Sitting at a Jersey Shore greasy spoon with a retired half-Irish/half-Jewish professional wrestler who occasionally believed he was an Indian chief—and who could quote with precision philosophers and Boardwalk hustlers. No wonder I had been having nightmares.

"Hey, Chief, what do you make of the lawsuit by this woman to get tickets to Bobby's concert if he reschedules?"

"Don't know."

"I don't get why they would schedule a concert in a puny auditorium like the Golden Prospect. I can't get a straight answer out of Cindi, either. She flips out whenever I bring it up."

Chief Willie rubbed his temples. "Did you ever think about asking one of your grandfather's old friends who are still at the casino for the inside dope?"

"Yes, but I decided to use my guy there for a bigger favor."

"Well, then, I got a degenerate gambler who works in the Events office. He's due for a whoopin'."

"Are you serious?"

"Let's go."

Why are we waiting in the garage?" I asked Chief Willie. We were standing in the parking garage of the Golden Prospect Hotel.

"Randall gets off about now. He'll be headed for his car, the Saab over there. Do you know Randall Podge?"

"Never heard of him. Why don't we just meet him in the hotel?"

"You'll see." Chief Willie grinned like a kid who had just rung somebody's doorbell and bolted.

A few minutes later, a squat-looking man of about thirty-five waddled out of the elevator. He had nervous little squirrel eyes, which appeared humorously at odds with his garish brown pompadour. He looked like an obese fox that had wound up on the wrong end of one of Aesop's fables.

I turned my head to either side when I discovered that Chief Willie was gone. He was slippery for a big guy. I stood next to Podge's red Saab convertible having no idea what to do with myself.

As Podge drew closer to me, he eyed me suspiciously. Without warning, a terrible GRRAAAAAGH! shattered the *clop-clop* of footsteps against pavement as Chief Willie jumped from atop a repressed little sport utility vehicle that was sandwiched between two sports cars, one of them being Podge's Saab.

Podge screamed and covered his ears as Chief Willie tackled him.

"I didn't do nothing," Podge screamed. Clearly, a man who was accustomed to being accused of things.

Chief Willie picked Podge up by his collar and threw him against the Saab.

"You'll dent my car!" the fastidious Podge shrieked.

"Mr. Genovese," Chief Willie said to me. *Mr. Genovese?* "This is Randy Podge, the man you asked about, sir."

My jaw hung slack for a second, as no one had ever addressed me as "Mr. Genovese" for any reason before in my life. So I nodded like a Mr. Genovese might. Slowly, like I had all the time in the world in between garrote strangulations.

"How are things going in Events, Randy?" Chief Willie asked.

"Fine, look—"

The Chief slapped poor Randall Podge on his pompadour. Podge looked as if he might cry.

"Randy, I don't want to spend any more time here than I have to, so I'm going to ask you this once: Why did Turnpike Bobby Chin's people book the Golden Prospect for his comeback concert?"

"I don't know."

With one liquid move, Chief Willie kicked out one of the Saab's taillights.

"No, c'mon, man!" Podge yelped. "All I know is that Cindi wanted the Prospect. I thought it was a strange venue, but a booking's a booking."

"What else happened with the booking?" the Chief asked.

"I don't know, not much until it was cancelled. After the crash."

"What do you mean, not much?" I asked.

"Not much means not much," Podge said impatiently.

Chief Willie pulled a stiletto out of his pocket, and flicked the menacing blade into its ready position. He held it against the driver's-side door.

"Don't! C'mon, man!" Podge begged as the Chief prepared to vandalize the Saab. "All I know is that the theater was only a quarter booked a week before the event. Cindi freaked out. She said Bobby would go apeshit when he heard about an empty room."

My heart fell.

"Let me get this straight," Chief Willie said. "The event was only a quarter booked?"

"Yeah, man, yeah."

"Let's go, Mr. Genovese." Chief Willie waved me on.

We abandoned poor Randall Podge in a tragic, expanding puddle around his loafers. My head was throbbing. I ruminated on three words: *an empty room.*

"You probably thought that was a little harsh," the Chief said. "What you gotta understand is that guys like Podge are always guilty of something, so you got to just play it, you know, see what they put out. Now, follow me."

I followed the Chief to another level of the garage. He came to a pickup truck and said, "Keep an eye out, wudja?" He crouched down and fiddled with something beneath the truck, then got up and wiped his hands.

"In case you don't know," he said, "the Cohn of Silence doesn't trust this Lonesome Jake fellow. I just beaconed his truck. I hit the Maggots' vehicles a few days ago. This way we'll know where they go."

In addition to Bobby's kamikaze cannonball back into the news, the coverage of the Kaylee Hopewell affair had taken a turn. After a few weeks of All Kaylee All the Time, the authorities began to voice frustration over their lack of progress. Of particular concern was their inability to identify who Kaylee Hopewell actually was. According to an ACPD spokesperson, a few Kaylee Hopewells were tentatively identified in the United States, but they were total misses. There were no suspicious ex-boyfriends categorically denying foul play. No evidence at all that the missing woman was actually named Kaylee Hopewell. Chief Desmond of the ACPD stated at a news conference that his case wasn't growing cold, it was growing "hinky."

Oh, no, you don't Chief, I thought. *Never screw with the narrative loco-motive. The consumer public wants to love the victim and hate the villain, and here you go trying to recast the players . . .*

Desmond's "hinky" remark was instantly interpreted as a squandered attempt to spin the failure of his detectives to make progress. One national cable TV show promptly convened a panel of political spin doctors who roundly lambasted the ACPD's botching of the Kaylee matter's public relations.

"In these situations, the most important thing is to show sensitivity to the community," said Brooke Weber of Perception Management, Inc. "The police chief blew it big-time."

Observed Todd Hersh of Hersh Communications, "The police chief should apologize to the community, to the casinos, and to the guests of Atlantic City."

It was hard for me not to laugh. Nowadays, whenever a terrible event occurred, the media covered it not as a terrible event but as a public relations fiasco. There were no acts of God, only powerful bastards who botched things. There was no stronger impulse in the contemporary human being than the impulse to blame. This epidemic of covering not just the event, but how the handlers were mishandling the event had bred what was perhaps the most malignant side effect of saturation coverage: it was wiser for anyone in a position of authority to do nothing at all than do the right thing. Action begat risk, risk begat failure, failure begat scrutiny, and scrutiny begat your ass being fired. It was far more prudent to play possum, dead on the side of the road, and allow one's institution to be ravaged—all the while retaining the eunuchs of the PR industry to preach the rhetoric of apology—than it was to seek an ugly truth in a rough situation. Nobody ever got fired for showing sensitivity, but nobody ever cracked a case for it, either.

The great irony was that if one examines snafus closely, those who apologize are seldom forgiven, while those who lie and spin their asses off usually survive. We were living in the age of the tactical apology versus the Judeo-Christian one. Basketball player Kobe Bryant issued the gold standard of tactical apologies to the woman who had accused him of rape IN EXCHANGE FOR her refusal to testify against him, not to mention countless millions of dollars.

In the Judeo-Christian apology, there is suffering and damnation, and who the hell wants that?

The countdown began in my own mental clock to Chief Desmond's tactical apology. Watch your poor white ass, Chief.

The furor within a furor inspired protests on the steps of ACPD headquarters. A placard held by omnipresent kidnap-witness-turned-crusader Evelyn Wallace read, "WHERE'S KAYLEE?" Another asked, "IS KAYLEE HINKY?" Yet another ridiculed Chief Desmond as "CHIEF HINKY."

The protests were widely covered, and the media's appetite for Kaylee was nonetheless swelling. WHOA-TV in Philly led into commercials with person-on-the-street interviews with pretty much anybody who was seen walking with a young woman or girl. Not wanting to be seen as being unprotective, there was a natural inclination for those being interviewed to underscore that [protective parent/manly boyfriend] were walking with [hot chick/young girl] OUT OF CONCERN, as opposed to, well, just happening to be walking down the street with them.

On another TV channel, the reporter, Freddy Zane's, brow was furrowed in empathy as he spoke to a raven-haired college student named Eden. They were both seated on a swing set in a neighborhood park near where Eden was in college. Eden's chin quivered as she described on camera her last encounter with her "best friend since kindergarten," Kaylee Hopewell.

"We used to talk all night long about how we would be best friends forever," Eden said. "We promised we'd always live next door to each other, no matter how old we got."

"Tell me about the last time you saw Kaylee," Zane asked, playing the attractive-but-distant-older-guy-who-lived-down-the-street.

"She came home, like, two weeks ago. She was all excited about her senior year in college. Kaylee was thinking about studying overseas, like, in France before hitting the real world." Eden laughed through the phrase *real world*. "It just doesn't make sense," she summarized. "It just doesn't make sense at all."

The camera then captured Eden tying a yellow ribbon around the rusting pole that connected the earth to the horizontal pipe from which the chained seats swung.

"And so," Freddy Zane said to the camera as Eden tied her ribbon in background soft focus, "a community waits another endless summer day for word from a friend, a friend named Kaylee Hopewell. This is Freddy Zane reporting from Fairview."

Out of My Mind

"If they see him with the emotions, who knows what they'll do to him?"

A sensation overwhelmed me, a feeling that time was melting. I had not solved the disappearance of Christian Josi; I had not brewed a Plausible Alternative Scenario for his vanishing; and I had not rescued my unrescuable client. Hemingway had said that one should never confuse motion with action. I had been generating a lot of motion, but little action. A sickening conviction that this case had become a metaphor for my career was taking root. *Tick-tock.*

I had a long talk with my mother, which was odd because she had been gone for more than three decades. It was vivid, however, despite its having occurred when I fell asleep sitting up while Edie and Irene watched a foreign movie featuring overly sensitive people overly examining their lives.

I never used to fall asleep sitting up. That was something the elderly and senators did. I never used to understand how, in fact, it was possible for someone to fall asleep sitting up because sleep was an unconscious activity, and didn't sitting up require voluntary choices? I thought about my procession through my forties as if it were a war that barred any turning back. As my eyes fell catatonic, my mother drew me in to her side of whatever plane divided the lost from the living.

"I'm relieved you're a sole proprietor," my mother began. She held a cigarette. Marlboro.

"Why, Mom?"

"I always worried about you in environments with other people," she said, blowing out a cloud of bluish smoke. "You were never a joiner. I remember how verbal you were when you were young, even before your other little friends, who were no dummies. Your teachers—the ones who spent time with you one on one—raved about you. Even your grandfather's friends—you know how tough they were—called you 'Senator.' When you were two years old—two!—you told Mickey and Deedee they should ask not what their country could do for them, but what they could do for their country.

"This didn't come through in the classroom for some reason," my mother concluded, emitting another blue puff of smoke, this one cloudier than the last one. "You weren't exceptional when you were in a structured environment. I watched you in class once through those skinny windows they had at the school. Remember those? I was doing a PTA thing, I think. First grade. You looked lost or angry, I didn't know which. I was thinking, What's with him? Why don't they get him?

"Anyway, what do you make of this Kaylee situation?" Her streaked blonde hair was pulled back from her face, displaying a regally high forehead. Her eyes were as blue as a lake in the north, and bright.

"It's sad," I said. "I can't take my eyes off that picture they keep showing of her."

"She's stunning, isn't she?"

"You bet."

"She's really not your type, though. I never knew you to carry a torch for blondes, but I don't take that personally," she assured me. "You've always liked the ones like Edie."

(This, of course, was an impossible observation. Outside of elementary school play dates, my mother had never seen me interact with women because she died before that aspect of my life had budded. Despite her ghostly unreality, I still cared what she thought.)

"What exactly is Edie's type . . . as you see it from where you are?"

"Physically, a thoroughbred. Tall, legs as long and lean as Chile against the Atlantic. You're not breast-obsessed. Character-wise, they are intelligent, but quiet. Strong. They are stable and like to nest, but they're soft on praise. Edie keeps your world together.

"Your grandfather and I always thought you were God. Mickey—Dad would never let you know that. He thought all my encouragement of you was making you soft. I'd say, 'Dad, we don't want Jonah in your business. How tough does he need to be?' He would just wave his hand down at the ground the way he did. Do you remember that?"

"I remember the way he swatted his hand down, yeah."

"Say 'yes.' "

"Yes."

"You were such a magnificent child. People would stop us on the Boardwalk and say, 'That boy should be in the movies.' So handsome! Does Edie think you're handsome?"

"I don't know. We said stuff to each other when we first met, but you know how it is. We've got kids, I have work. It's not like you sit around all day at this point in your life and compliment each other."

"She's wonderful with those children. Ricky has her temperament. And that Lily—with that *bondit* mouth and red hair—we know who she is, don't we?"

"She's Deedee to the core."

"It's terrifying. I watched her as that princess in her Peter Pan play. She doesn't have to say a word to fire up that whole stage. Do you have any idea what it's like that those children will not know me?"

I felt my throat close up and ache—that precrying sensation. I heard Mickey in the background saying, "Don't start with the sensitive mishegoss!" "He's allowed to be sad, Daddy," my mother shot back. "It's tough out there." Mickey parried: "If they see him with the emotions, who knows what they'll do to him?"

"I think about it every day, Mom."

"Do you tell the kids about me?"

"I try, but I'm afraid."

"Why, what do you think I'm going to do to them?"

"You? Nothing."

"Oh, come on."

I thought about it. Her face had grown thinner during the course of our talk, the way it did about a year and a half into her sickness. During the disease's early stages, she felt terrible from the treatment, but became heavier, puffier. Her Germanic appearance softened into jolliness, a description I never would have applied to her. Then she became thin and angular, and I no longer believed she was my mother, but a wraith who had entered through the basement of one of Mickey's Boardwalk rat holes, and taken over our family.

"I don't know, Mom, sometimes I'm afraid you won't praise them. Other times I'm afraid that you will praise them too much, make them think that the world is an extended womb only to have it torn apart while they nap. That's what happened to me. I was safe. You weren't just my mother, you were a genie, Santa Claus. Then you were gone. Then I go out there and nobody saw me the way you did, and it was cold."

My mother sighed. "I see," she said. "Do you think I did it to you on purpose, like a trick?"

"I used to because that's the way it felt. I went from sultry April to cold February. For the last thirty years, I'm asking myself, 'Where the hell is April?' And then I answer my own question, 'Oh, yeah, April died.'"

"Is that why you're so preoccupied with this lost girl, Kaylee? I saw some report on TV out of Franklin with an expert on abductions. Do you think you'll save her or she'll be found, and you'll make it April again?"

"Jonah," a voice from outside the cottony plane said. "Jonah!" it repeated. I opened my eyes. Edie and Irene were grinning tenderly at me. "You were snoring."

When I opened my eyes, I found the Saul Bellow novel *Herzog* opened to the first page. I had had the book for years, but had never progressed beyond the opening sentence: "If I am out of my mind, it's all right with me, thought Moses Herzog."

Get going, Jonah.

Aerodynamics

"If you jump out in front of propellers or engines, you're shredded wheat."

Sidney Blintzes got his nickname because he loved my grand-mother's blintzes. He had been the general manager of the Golden Prospect since Mickey opened it up in 1978. The new owner, Angela Vanni, had kept Sidney Blintzes on after her father, Mario, reputed boss of the Philadelphia-South Jersey La Cosa Nostra, won an operator's license with my assistance a few years ago, but that's another story.

The Golden Prospect owned two aircraft, a Challenger jet and a helicopter for short, high-roller runs. Accordingly, the company employed pilots. I wanted to have a word with a pilot Sidney trusted, one who wouldn't go blabbing about my inquiry. "I gotcher guy," Sidney Blintzes told me. "Keep your boxers on, boobie, he'll call you." Given their travel schedules, it took longer than I had hoped to set up a meeting, but finally, an amiable man who flew the Challenger named Bucky Calhoun agreed to meet with me for lunch at Murray's in Margate.

"I met your grandfather, but never flew him," the sandy-haired Calhoun said. I put him in his late forties. "We didn't have the Challenger then. Some guy, Mickey. He always remembered a person's name. That's the thing I remember. Not like these corporate people running things. Sidney, of course, is a good man. Old-school. Despite what they say about these old-timers, in a way they had more soul than these business types."

"Mickey used to say that gambling will be respectable when they run the Italian and Jewish boys out of the business."

Calhoun laughed. "Everything that used to be a crime is now a conglomerate."

We both ordered club sandwiches and I told Calhoun about my involvement with Turnpike Bobby. "How does one person survive a plane crash like that, but two others don't?"

"He doesn't."

"But how do you account for airport records showing that Bobby was on that plane when it left Los Angeles? The police have already put Bobby in L.A. that morning. The police here found two bodies, presumably the pilots."

"The pilots flying the jet would be registered."

"But the pilots who were on the manifest turned up alive and kicking in L.A. Is it possible to play switcheroo with pilots?"

"Things have gotten more strict since 9/11, but it's possible. You know how things are: if a security guy has known a person for a long time, they may not read his credentials so close. That kind of thing."

"Okay, let's assume that you get a pilot on the plane. Is it possible to stop somewhere in between L.A. and Jersey and put more people on and take some off?"

"Very hard. Like I said, the rules since 9/11 are brutal. This is just the kind of thing they're looking for."

"So, where that leaves us is that whoever got on the plane in L.A. either died in the crash or survived somehow."

"Mr. Eastman, did you ever think about skydiving?"

"No, I hadn't. You can't jump out of a jet, can you?"

"Sure. Military does it all the time. It can be tricky, though."

"Don't jets go too fast or too high?"

"Not necessarily. Most jumps are out of prop planes. You jump out the back end of the plane, the propellers are in front of you. If you jump out in front of propellers or engines, you're shredded wheat. That's why military jets have those big openings in back of the plane. When you jump out the back, that plane is two city blocks away the minute you wave sayonara."

"What about jumping from a corporate jet?"

"Possible, but stupid."

"Why?"

"You enter the plane usually from a door on the front left of the plane. That means if you jump out, there's a chance you can get clipped by the wing or sucked in by the engine. It depends on the door configuration, how high you're flying, how fast you're going, how experienced you are."

"What could cause a plane like Bobby's to go down?"

"That was a G-Five. Their safety records are spectacular. I don't think one's ever been lost. When I heard that news, I didn't buy it. I'd say pilot error is the first place I'd look."

"If not pilot error, then what?"

"Sabotage."

"What about a flaw? Give me percentages."

"Design flaw. One percent. I'd bet on sabotage of some kind given what a looney-ass this guy is. Who knows who they attract in Hollyweird?"

"So you'd include monkey business by Bobby himself in your sabotage theory, Bucky?"

"Monkey business is your specialty, Mr. Eastman. Would you?"

"I'm leaning that way."

"You don't think it was some play for publicity, do you?"

"Yeah, I do. I just don't know to what end, or how you pull it off."

"My Lord."

"All right, so on one hand you're telling me that there's no way Bobby could have survived that crash on impact. Again, percentages."

"No way, not that crash. Zero percent."

"But it's very unlikely that he could have gotten off the plane somewhere in a civilized fashion."

"Extremely unlikely. Five percent. Too much recordkeeping. Weakest link with private planes is point of entry. It's possible that they gave bogus names or something in L.A. That's my bet. With a high-end piece of equipment like the G-Five, it's pretty safe to assume that regulars—celebrities especially—come and go with their own crews all the time. There's a lot of kissyface with stars and whatnot, so they may not be too tough on 'em there. But Bobby probably *did* get on in L.A. if the records say so. We just don't know where he got off."

"What about jumping out of the plane?"

"It could be done. Maybe thirty percent—"

"Really?"

"Sure."

"Well, let's play our odds."

"I'd have to look at how the G-Five is configured. Where the wreck was found, that kind of thing."

"I'd be grateful. And you'll get more than a club sandwich out of it."

Apple Sauce

"I'm a lot hotter than you are, no doubt, but there's something about you."

I received another crème-colored letter about my lack of payment to Hank, the subcontractor on the Hopkins Pond medical waste/child-impaling poll project. Chief Willie hadn't gotten back to me, either. I hadn't wanted to pressure him because it was a personal matter, and he had been doing so much Bobby work for me that I didn't want to distract him.

I hated doing it, but I called the Chief on his mobile phone.

"How!" he answered.

"Chief, it's, uh . . . Mongoose. Forgot my name for a moment."

"Greetings, warrior."

"Look, I hate to bother you about this because you're so busy, but do you remember that letter I gave you on that personal matter?"

"Chief Willie remember. No buffalo droppings in big cheese's wigwam," he said. Translation: He couldn't find any vulnerability on the Hopkins Pond mayor, Gary Simmons. "Very clean."

"Damn."

"That could be good," the Chief chuckled. "Invite him to dinner. Be conciliatory. Tell him you'd like to work something out."

I was disappointed. "Work something out? I want to get paid."

"I'll talk with Sheik Abu Heinous and the Viking. We have an idea. First, smoke peace pipe with white man. Trust me."

"Okay, I'll call him. Hey, do you know anything about what goes on in a computer when you e-mail a photo?"

"No. But I work with a hacker."

"Dorkus?" I asked.

"You know Dorkus?"

"We go way back. Anything new to report on Turnpike Wackadoo?"

"A little. I think you'll like this. Remember that Web site invoice for seven hundred large?"

"Yeah?"

"Lissen-a this—"

Chief Willie told me what they got and how they got it . . .

I n a Society Hill, Philadelphia bar, a young graphic designer who worked for DEVIUS, the Web site firm, sat at a raised table with a few friends. The kid was known as Apple Sauce because of his knack for spilling food on his clothes.

A Gina Gershon lookalike named Martina Collins sat with an equally smoldering friend at an adjacent table. Martina made fleeting eye contact with Apple Sauce and delivered a branded coy smile, the one that said, *"I'm a lot hotter than you are, no doubt, but there's something about you, Apple Sauce . . ."*

Apple Sauce caught the vibe, and gave his friends a look seeking confirmation. Was SHE looking at ME? To be sure, he took a sip from his beer, and looked through the glass to see if Martina was glancing his way. She was.

"You work at DEVIUS," she said to Apple Sauce. "I had a meeting there once. You were walking around doing something or other. Some celebrity thing."

Apple Sauce's friends' jaws hung slack. SHE is talking to HIM?

"Yeah, I work there. Yeah," Apple Sauce said, in desperate pursuit of a casual gesture.

"So, when you're not hanging out with Springsteen, you hang out here," she said.

He didn't deny the Springsteen allegation. Good work, Martina, always work the guy by making him feel *above* his station.

"I come here sometimes," Apple Sauce said. Dead meat.

Martina and her friend abandoned their table, and migrated to the domain of the mighty Apple Sauce. Apple Sauce da playa. Apple Sauce the hero of his friends. Apple Sauce buying rounds for his posse and da ladies. Apple Sauce drinking. And talking about the people he knows, the work he does. About Turnpike Bobby Chin, and who authorizes payment for Bobby. That would be Tic Turner. Apple Sauce, you magnificent bastard. Apple Sauce, you tool.

Martina, one of Atlantic City's most lethal shills, drops a dime to her contractor, Chief Willie Thundercloud.

"Funny how a kid in a bar can't wait to tell you about the celebrities he does work for," Martina said.

Chief Willie said to me, "If Turner can order up what Bobby wants and approve payment, who knows what else he can do?"

Total Whore

"You cannot educate a person beyond his life experience."

Bobby had a wall of televisions installed in his Golden Prospect hotel suite. All twelve of them were on. Bobby sat on his newly upholstered couch gazing ahead at no screen in particular. I told Lonesome Jake out on the balcony that I wasn't able to find anything nefarious with the music library, but would keep my ear to the ground. He nodded in mild dejection, but his eyes conveyed a deeper hurt.

"I'll keep digging," I assured him. He gave me a look like a poet whose submission had just been rejected for the millionth time. I patted him on the shoulder—Jonah, fellow celebrity dung-hauler, Comforter of the Downtrodden.

There was grainy footage on GuilTV. Bobby wasn't paying attention to it. I stupidly grabbed a remote, aimed it at the screen, and pushed the volume up. All twelve of the TVs got louder. I pushed the volume down, and all twelve of the TVs got softer. I manually pushed the volume up on GuilTV in order to hear the report. Bobby was unfazed.

The mother lode had just dropped. Footage had been released from a disgruntled employee at the company that handled security for the shopping center where Kaylee had been abducted. It was short, but chilling.

The footage opened with a grainy shot of the side of a nondescript brick wall with a door. The door opened suddenly, and a varmint-featured man shoved a pretty blonde woman into a black SUV. The quality of the footage was bad, but it was enough to place several South Jersey police departments in the crosshairs of an apoplectic news media.

Why had it taken so long before the police contacted the security firm?
Why didn't the security firm hand over the tape sooner?
When did the police find out a tape of the kidnapping existed?
Who knew what when?
Why couldn't the police find Kaylee's friends and family?
How many other women were at risk while the cops dawdled?

Inflaming the situation was the discovery by a Harrisburg, Pennsylvania, TV station of a local bartender who recognized the kidnapper from the news as Wayne Hatfield. Hatfield, said the bartender, used to drop in a few times a week. He was from coal country. A mean drunk, said the bartender. The news catalyst—the videotape and the fleshed-out portrait of Kaylee's kidnapper—set the satellites and cables of America ablaze.

"She looks like a whore," Bobby barked when the black-and-white photo of Kaylee flashed before us.

"Who, Kaylee?"

"Whatever the hell her name is, I don't know. All I see is that bitch."

"She sure is pretty," I said.

"Total whore. Look at her."

Kaylee's image began to fire up on the insect-eyed screens. Bobby stood. One by one, he angrily shut the TVs off.

Bobby's eyes narrowed when he looked at me. My first inclination was to look away because I was uncomfortable. I tried to read him, wondering if he was on drugs. It wasn't drugs. The sonofabitch was jealous. Of *Kaylee*. All of a sudden, she was everywhere and he was nowhere. This made her the whore.

Bobby blinked back to the present once the TVs were off. Businesslike, he said, "Listen to this song I just wrote, would you? It's called 'Gravity Outlaw.'" He had a printout of lyrics, which I followed.

"Sure, I'd love to." My shock at the whore comment gave way to building excitement. I had visions of myself telling friends that I was "there" when Turnpike Bobby Chin test-drove his latest hit.

Bobby tuned his guitar competently, reminding me for the first time in our relationship of the discreet talent that anchored his success.

> *I can't fly forever*
> *When terra firma says no*
> *Can feel the Jersey Devil*
> *Pulling me below—*
> *Flameout!*

Bobby's voice was scratchy, but it worked. The lyrics were audible and simple, but that was okay. He was going somewhere.

> *I'm a gravity outlaw*
> *Dancin' naked on a polar cap*
> *Nature's an afterthought*
> *Can't drain the Dude's sap—*
> *Flameout!*

There was a ferocity in Bobby's voice when he belted out the one-word chorus, "Flameout!" I could envision an audience of thousands pumping a fist to it in RFK stadium in Philly, as if "Flameout" were a battle cry, something ennobling. Then again, Bobby's music always had the skeleton of regular-guy defiance even though this was a man whose tragedy was rooted in outrageous privilege.

> *Slaughter of trivialities*
> *Flap, rudder, aileron*
> *Comin' for me anyway*
> *Where am I gonna run?—*
> *Flameout!*

Bobby set his guitar down and awaited my reaction. My intrinsic disapproval of him had primed me to criticize his work, but the truth is always more cunning than an agenda-driven dismissal will permit. The fact is, prior to his crash into my life, I always thought he was a good entertainer. His beats could make a senior citizen tap his feet, and his lyrics, however interpretive, were a cocktail of oscillating grandiosity and emptiness.

"Geez, Bobby, I really like it. It seems like . . ."

"Like what?"

"It seems like you're not sure."

"About what?"

"About whether or not you're gravity's outlaw. In one verse, you're worried. In another, you're a badass."

Bobby sprung up to his feet. "You just don't get it!"

"I like it, Bobby, I really do!" I assured him defensively.

Bobby stomped his foot. "You're jealous is all."

"I like it, Bobby. I'm just trying to figure out if you're gravity's outlaw or a flameout. I was really struck by the acoustic sound. Did you ever think about going that route, playing in a smaller arena?"

Huge mistake.

"You don't know shit about music, Jonah."

"You got me there," I conceded, and made a mental note of my

Big Theory on advice: You cannot educate a person beyond his life experience. Sometimes you just have to end futile conversations. It was vanity for me, the great persuader, to believe I could offer insight to Bobby, whose life was a monument to not learning. *Smaller* arenas? He had failed to fill a small arena, as I now knew. How many brain cells had I lost? Despite the laws of nature, this guy wanted BIGGER arenas, flameout or no flameout.

"It's a scary thing to see genius in motion this close up," I said. A shameless wet kiss, but, as I was learning, there was no such thing as shame in celebrity relations.

Bobby sang another line, which I couldn't find on the printout. *"Bon Jovi ate my nephew . . ."*

"What was that lyric?" I asked, incredulous.

"Put on those jaded new shoes," Bobby said. "Just a line I'm fiddling with."

"Oh. Hey, can you do me a favor?" I asked.

Bobby nodded, a little surprised, and took a swig of Piney water, as if it were a nerve-strengthening tonic: "Sure."

"Would you mind asking Tic if he'd e-mail that picture he took of us to me?"

"He never did? That was weeks ago."

"No. I have a lot of people who really want to see it."

"Dammit! *Tic!*"

Tic Turner Online

*"I had timed my ass-kissing jubilee to land
right before I made my request."*

While I was in Bobby's suite, sitting at Chief Willie's kitchen
table in Margate were the great non-Indian himself and a
kid we called Dorkus. I never knew Dorkus's real name,
but had been calling him Dorkus since he was a teenager. He didn't
seem to mind it.

Dorkus was about twenty. A student at Swarthmore, he was a
computer hacker. Tall, thin, pale as a ghost and pumpkin-headed,
Dorkus could commit unspeakable acts with a laptop. Over the years,
I had enlisted him in various capers, including the creation of a
huge—and utterly bogus—online grass-roots campaign for the Mafia
boss, Vanni, who wanted a casino license. I had also personally witnessed Dorkus transpose the photographic head of a girl who had declined his junior prom offer onto the nude body of an adult film
actress in flagrante delicto; edit the article content of mainstream
newspapers on their Web sites; and eavesdrop on the debating points
of rival political candidates.

Today, the task was a little different. The laptop Dorkus had before
him was mine. Assuming that Bobby would throw a fit when he
heard that Turner had never sent me the photo of the two of us—the

photo he wanted taken—I figured he'd demand that it be sent immediately. I had timed my asskissing jubilee to land right before I made
my request. The Maggots, who insisted that one of them always be
near Bobby when a third party was around, would almost certainly be
on hand.

Turner expressed confusion when Bobby confronted him. "I
thought I sent that a month ago," he lied.

"Maybe you did, but I never got it," I said, sad, *wike a wittle boy.* "I
was really excited about it."

Turner opened up his laptop, hooked his phone to a port, and began pointing and clicking. Concurrently, five miles south, Dorkus's
fingers worked my keyboard like a tarantula in heat.

"I can't believe you can send a photo from a phone through a
computer and then through a phone line again," I said to Turner.
"Tic, do you have a lot of tech training?"

"Not really," Turner said.

"Do you have to have a special kind of computer?"

"Just the right software."

"Can you take a picture of somebody, say Bobby, and then put it
on the Internet?"

Bobby came alive at the other end of the room. He walked over.
"Sure," Turner said. "There are all kinds of webcams where you can
watch what people do in their house. Some celebrities put footage of
their appearances in streaming video on their own Web sites."

The combination of Bobby detecting an unexplored opportunity
to expose himself in a new manner and Turner's chance to redeem
himself by demonstrating his worth via his computer wizardry kept us
online for about forty of the dullest moments of my life. After twenty
of those minutes, back in Margate, Dorkus ejected a CD-ROM from
my laptop and handed it to Chief Willie with a nasal hiccup of a geek
laugh. Dorkus left with a semester's tuition in an envelope.

Professional Shot

"This photo was sent in anonymously."

I awoke to a frigging front-page photo in the frigging *Atlantic City Packet* of Bobby sound asleep in his underwear on his frigging Golden Prospect sofa, similar to the one I was destined to re-frigging-upholster. I called Cindi, who dropped by once the kids were at camp. She opened up defensively, her hands flailing in the air: "This was not my doing, so don't start on me. I don't want him in the news any more than you do."

"It never ends with this guy. Turner probably took the picture with his Batphone and sent it off to the *Packet*."

"This photo?" Cindi said, examining the newspaper. "No."

"Why not?"

"This is a professional shot. It's very clean, a little artsy. Note the Christlike pose. You can't get something like this with a phone camera."

"Elena Molotov-Weinberg? Maybe to tease the *Major Player* article?"

"She doesn't shoot for the *Atlantic City Packet*, Jonah. Besides, she'd want credit. There's no credit listed here. This photo was sent in anonymously."

"Okay, another thing. Do you remember you sent me that KBRO interview with Bonita Chin?"

"Yes."

"When did that first run?"

"I don't know exactly. I can check my video files. Why?"

"I'm not sure yet. Do you know approximately?"

"Well, yeah, it ran after the crash when the press was trying to grab everybody tied to Bobby they could."

"Okay, let me know, would you?"

"Yes, Jonah, I'll let you know. By the way, I've got an intern over at KBRO who's been feeding me the latest from Nielsen on news ratings. Do you want the latest?"

"Hell, yeah."

Cindi opened up her laptop and logged on to her instant messenger. She explained that, unlike traditional e-mail, instant messages were nearly impossible to trace.

"SIN-D" typed: "Anything new from Nielsen?"

The response from her intern friend, MEDIAHOR: "Hold on a sec."

About thirty seconds later, the following message came back from MEDIAHOR: "Bobby coverage is down. Seems to be more interest in another 'bloid story."

> **SIN-D:** "Which one?
>
> **MEDIAHOR:** "Stand by . . . Kaylee Hopewell. Know anything about her?"
>
> **SIN-D:** "Just what I see on news."
>
> **MEDIAHOR:** "Journos going batshit they can't find much on her. Ratings going thru roof. More ad rev = bigger Christmas bonus."
>
> **SIN-D:** "Good 4 you. Thanks for help."
>
> **MEDIAHOR:** "Bye."

The Boys from Piney Spring

"They never learn."

I went for a run after Cindi left. I began to have another of my Tony Soprano brain-melting dreams despite the fact that it was daylight and I wasn't asleep. The Cohn of Silence made a cameo appearance. A facsimile of his comment about never having met a simple man in the entertainment business crept into my consciousness. I couldn't help feeling sorry for Lonesome Jake. Here Jake was working for a psychotic entertainer and a couple of scumbags, and all of a sudden this nonentity with a camera finds himself being judged.

There's a Hollywood morality tale in here somewhere. Still, Cindi's observation about the high-quality photo of Bobby and who could have been in the position to take it warranted a look. Or a break-in.

I visited with Chief Willie, who paced around his house for a few minutes, burly arms folded, thinking.

"Do you think the picture in the paper is a message?" he asked.

"What would that message be?"

"Don't know. Is it possible that that Lonesome fellow is angry you didn't find the smoking gun on the music library theory?"

"I don't know."

"Or that someone wants you to know they can get close to Bobby and make mischief?"

"No clue."

Chief Willie grilled me about Bobby's suite and the habits of his crew. It took about forty minutes for him to pinpoint the soft underbelly: Bobby's water consumption. He drank a lot of Piney Spring Water, which had to be replenished with regular deliveries from the company.

Cindi had arranged for Bobby to take an impromptu tour of the Atlantic City Convention Center, where the Miss America Pageant is held. This was to be a "dark" appearance, that is, Bobby would be adored by pageant planners, who were getting ready for the big event next month, but the adoration would be closed to outside media. Miss New Jersey, a striking Latino woman from Bergen County, was his ostensible tour guide. The Maggots were on hand, and Lonesome Jake shadowed Bobby with his appendage/recording device.

As Bobby's motorcade (a Hummer, ten motorcycles, a van, a Suburban, and a generic police car) pulled out of the Golden Prospect's garage, the Piney Spring Water delivery truck pulled in. At the wheel was Sheik Abu Heinous (Vinnie Santafurio). In the passenger seat was Chief Willie. Behind the Chief was Dorkus. All of them wore the coveted uniform of the Piney Spring Water deliveryman.

With a pushcart carrying several large containers and several boxes of individualized water bottles, the boys got on the freight elevator and rode up to the penthouse. The logistics weren't difficult. Chief Willie, who made his core living hunting down casino cheats, had a long-standing relationship with the hotel's security people.

Chief Willie opened the hotel door with a passkey and remained by the door with the fidgety Dorkus. Sheik Abu Heinous went room to room in the suite to make certain no one was there. It was clear.

"There's a bedroom down there to the left that has a laptop, a desktop, and some camera equipment," the Sheik said. "That must be it."

"I'll stay by the door. You guys carry a box of water bottles down there just in case."

Sheik Abu Heinous picked up a box of water bottles and proceeded toward Lonesome Jake's bedroom. Dorkus tried to lift one up, but failed. "Grab a few singles, for Crissakes," Chief Willie said.

The Sheik and Dorkus entered Lonesome Jake's room. Dorkus tapped the laptop and it came to life. It had been on, just hibernating. The Sheik inspected the room while Dorkus combed through Lonesome Jake's hard drive. Dorkus searched the hard drive by date of original entry. He highlighted a handful of items around the key dates and double-clicked. Dorkus laughed. "They never learn," he said. He pulled a small, flat, elliptical tube from his pocket, and attached it to a data port behind the laptop.

"C'mon, bud," Sheik Abu Heinous said.

The little tube began to flicker like a tiny Frankenstein that had been kissed by lightning. A notice on the screen read, "Transferring."

Chief Willie's loud voice from the other room said, "Load 'em up, we gotta drop some off down at the business office."

"C'mon, dammit!" said the Sheik. "Somebody's coming in."

"It'll take a few more seconds," Dorkus said.

"Dammit!"

The door to the suite opened. It was one of Kadaborah's linen-clad Flagellants. The Flagellant turned on the stereo. One of Bobby's CDs was on. Bobby belted out something like, *"Whoa there, turkey lips!"*

"Howya doin' there, Bud," Chief Willie said to the Flagellant, noting something on his clipboard. "What's Bobby saying on that song? *'Whoa there, turkey lips'*?"

"Um, no," said the Flagellant. "He's saying, 'Hope our love's turning up.' Who are you?" the Flagellant asked.

"Ah, we're from Piney. Now, you wanted ten of the big mommas and some individual water bottles, that right?"

"I don't know. I thought we had plenty."

"Look, Bud, all's I know is I got my ass chewed off 'cause we didn't leave enough last time, so I got my boys putting in the R-970 cooler containers in the main kitchen dispenser there and loading up the rooms with the nine-fluid-ounce bottles, which I guess is what the man likes. Hey, you boys done draggin' your asses?" Chief Willie shouted deep into the suite. "We got the customer back here. I don't need my ass chewed off again. You wanna sign off on this, bud?"

"I don't know that I can sign," the Flagellant said nervously.

"Just need your initials."

"I better not. They're real funny about who authorizes what. They'll all be back soon, they're in the garage."

"Well, no hurry, my man. You wanna check out the shipment and make sure we brought the right stuff? Don't wanna let Bobby down. The Piney people want our homegrown stars to be happy."

Dorkus and Sheik Abu Heinous emerged from the suite. The Sheik wiped his forehead and said in his best workman's voice, "All right, Bernie, we dropped the big units off and put a few consumer bottles in eacha the rooms."

"That's fine," Chief Willie said. He turned to the Flagellant. "All right, bud, you just whistle and we'll come get the bottles and bring you back some more. Just ask for Bernie."

"Okay."

Dorkus opened the door and the Sheik and Chief Willie/Bernie pushed the lightened water cart down the hall. Fast.

A Few Questions at the Irish Pub

"Thousands of law-abiding citizens rallied behind a Mafia boss."

Kadaborah called to meet with me. This was rare. Actually, it was unprecedented. He didn't say what he wanted to talk about, but I had a theory about that. I think he wanted to keep an eye on me because my little Mossad just might be getting close to something in our investigation. On the other hand, perhaps Kadaborah just wanted me to *think* we were getting close. When I factored in my search for a Plausible Alternative Scenario, our spadework into Bobby's business dealings, the Plush debacle, my Boardwalk punchout, my two anticlimatic kidnappings, the Lonesome Jake tip, and, of course, the not-too-subtle penetration of Bobby's suite by the delivery boys from Piney Spring, there were very good potential reasons to want to take a close look at me.

No problem. I wanted to keep an eye on Kadaborah, too.

We met at the Irish Pub in Atlantic City, a beloved century-old tavern on St. James Place that belonged more in James Joyce's Dublin than the millennial Jersey Shore. Its heavy olde-world architecture and historical memorabilia served as a reminder to the glittering casinos nearby that the gambling colossus hadn't annexed every last remnant of Atlantic City's soul. The lights of the great corporate hotels felt like beady neon eyes daring the little Irish pub to remain open.

It was here that AFL-CIO founder Samuel Gompers held meetings that would serve as the foundation for the American labor movement. And it was beside the great downstairs bar that Mickey once told me he had met with his Chicago partner, Al Capone, in 1930 to disclose his construction of a hidden railroad in the Pine Barrens that would hasten the shipping of booze from the wilderness to Philadelphia and points west.

When I walked into the dimly lit bar, I was greeted by . . . myself. I was looking into a small mirror—a restored antique from prehistoric times reading "Ladies' Dining Room in Rear." I thought I looked good in it. I found a table. I was early, Kadaborah was late. He did not apologize. Waiting for guys like him was the mission of guys like me. Kadaborah wore his sage white linens and that stupid-ass fez. One of Turner's shaven-headed lugs skulked a few yards away, looking grave in a Nation of Islam kind of way.

Kadaborah sat, asking me how I thought we were progressing.

"Bobby's free," I answered. "That's something, Your Flatulence."

Kadaborah squinted, trying to assess whether or not he heard what he thought he heard.

"He doesn't think so."

"I'm sure he doesn't."

"I talked to Mr. Cohn. I asked him why you're asking questions about Bobby's music library. I didn't get a straight answer."

"There's not much to it, Reverend. One of the people our investigators spoke to mentioned something about someone taking over Bobby's entertainment library. It never came to anything."

"Why didn't you just ask me?"

"You're not an easy man to meet with."

"Is it that, or that you don't trust me?"

"You don't want me around my own client. Why would I trust you?"

"I hired you. I sign off on payment."

"So I should just play ball, right?"

"I'm not asking you to look the other way on anything, Jonah. I'm not even asking you to approve of me. I'm asking you to ask me questions if you have them—touch base, rather than go on these wild-goose chases."

"I'm happy to comply. We're doing things this way for a reason. This is a legal investigation. I am part of a legal team. That means something very specific in the judicial system. If we run around updating everyone on everything, the discussions may not be privileged."

"I'm your client."

"Bobby is the defendant. He is the client."

"You're not an attorney, Jonah—"

"But I was raised by a criminal. A very good one, too."

Kadaborah sat back to process his options. I stood a better chance of maintaining my contract if I pushed back at him rather than sniveled. By keeping him wondering what I had on him, I was ensuring short-term job preservation.

In a liquid move, the seat beside me slid back, and Detective Galen of the ACPD sat down. "I see we've got a meeting of SPECTRE," he said.

"Good morning, Detective," I said.

Kadaborah nodded cautiously.

"Do you mind if I join you two choirboys for lunch?" Galen picked up a menu. He opened and shut it within seconds. He waved the waitress over, and told her he'd have the Poor Richard Special (soup and sandwich) and a Coke. "Did you guys order?"

"No," Kadaborah said.

"Hell, I'm sorry, what'll you be having?"

I ordered the same thing as Galen. Kadaborah ordered bottled water.

"I just have a few quick questions," Galen said, "and then we can talk about the Phillies or something. You don't mind," he said, not asked. Hearing no audible objections, he fired away. "So, Rev, how'd you get to A.C. on this trip?"

"I flew."

"Flew how?"

"Private jet?"

"Where'd you land?"

"Atlantic City."

"Pomona? Bader Field?"

"I don't pay attention to such things."

"A big picture man, huh?"

"Am I suspected of something, Detective?" Kadaborah asked.

"Hell, yeah. Everything. When did you fly in?"

"I don't remember the date."

"Was it before or after Bobby's plane crashed?"

"I found out about it on the news in the hotel. I guess it was the same day or the day before."

"You guess?"

"Yes, I guess."

"Around the time your meal ticket's plane goes down, you don't remember when you came to town?"

"It's a blur."

"I bet it is. You've been very helpful, Reverend." Galen rubbed his temples. "Do you know what I always wondered about Bobby's song, 'New Day'?"

"What, Detective?"

"What's he saying? That line: *'Gay morons have penis envy.'* What does that mean?"

"You misheard it," Kadaborah said. "Bobby's singing, 'Good morning, Mrs. Peterson.' She's the neighbor in 'New Day.'"

"I'm an idiot, I guess," Galen surrendered. "Now, Jonah," the cop turned to me. "Do you mind if I call you Jonah?"

"I prefer 'Commodore.'"

"Were you in the Navy?"

"No. I just like being called Commodore."

"Being a smartass won't help you, Eastman."

"Yes, sir," I responded with a salute.

"What kind of shit have you been crawling around in?"

"Lots of shit, sir!"

"We may need to hire you."

"Who?" I asked, caught off-guard.

"ACPD."

"Why?"

"Image problem. We're under fire. We can't crack Christian's disappearance. We can't crack this Kaylee Hopewell case. We can't seem to do anything right. Maybe you can come in and save the day."

"I couldn't help you, Detective. It would be a conflict with my Bobby work."

"How about Kaylee Hopewell? Could you help with that?"

"I don't know much about it. Just what I see on the news."

"I didn't ask you what you knew about it, Eastman. I asked if you could help us out."

"If I weren't going up against the ACPD for Bobby, I'd love to help you."

"I'll keep that in mind." Galen scratched his temple and then studied his nails. "You knew Mario Vanni, didn't you?"

"Yes."

Galen turned to Kadaborah and loudly whispered, "Mafia," adding (to me) "You worked with him a while back?"

"I did."

"One thing I always wondered," Galen said, staring me down, "was what you did for Vanni."

A hundred semiclever comebacks circled my brain, but none landed. Say nothing, Jonah, he wants you to hang yourself with your rhetoric.

I shrugged.

"I'm a cop. I'm not great with words," Galen said. "That's my friend Jonah's job. I guess what I'm saying is that it's not just criminals who have patterns. A guy gets a big client. Some other drama begins playing out."

I couldn't stay silent here.

"I'm not a chip off the old block, Detective. I know all you guys believe Mickey ran the galaxy. He didn't in his time, and I don't in mine. It's a tiresome theory. You guys have always been more interested in heat than light."

"That was poetic, Eastman."

"Thanks, Detective."

"I'm a romantic myself. In fact, I'm gonna spend this weekend staring up at the heavens from a lovely campsite in Lebanon State Forest. You ever been there, Reverend?"

"Leb—I can't say that I have?"

"That's too bad. Oh, look, our lunch is here," Galen said. He snapped up one of my potato chips even though he had plenty of his own on his plate.

Radical J

"Where'd you bury him?"

I calibrate my life against the backdrop of Bruce Springsteen's career milestones, but the depressing thing is that so do a lot of other people. It's another blow to my fantasy of uniqueness, but I'm not totally crazy for making the link, despite the liberal license I take in matching up the dates:

Dad dies—*Greetings From Asbury Park* released, Winter 1973
Mom dies—*The Wild, the Innocent and the E Street Shuffle* released, Summer 1973
Flee the country, Mickey's indictment—*Born to Run* released, October 1975
Atlantic City casinos open, Mickey sends me a prostitute to "get that outta the way"—*Darkness on the Edge of Town* released, June 1978
Off to Dartmouth—*The River* released, Fall 1980
Graduate Dartmouth—*Born in the U.S.A.* released, Summer 1984
Mickey dies (1999), I meet Edie—E Street Band reunites, Summer 2000

When Bobby called me on my mobile phone with a request to "rage," I felt as if I were on the verge of another Springsteen milestone, which really scared me. And excited me.

"Do you wanna rage with the Dude?" he asked.

"Rage?"

"Yeah."

"I'm sorry, but what's 'rage'?"

"It's when you go and do mindfucks."

"On who?"

"The regular people."

The kids were at camp, Edie and Irene had gone to an exercise class. I was in a sit-tight mode while my black-ops guys analyzed where things stood. As much as I self-dramatize my career, it's astonishing how much time I spend sitting around, waiting. I decided a little client face-to-face might be wise.

There was something peculiar about the Golden Prospect that I couldn't quite place. It felt calmer today. The crowds were thinner. Actually, no, that wasn't it at all. It was the absence of police. I was able to get up to the penthouse without going through security. I didn't see any reporters, either.

When I got to Bobby's floor, there was a lone buck-toothed policewoman pacing by the elevators. A couple of kindergartners could have overpowered her.

"Where's everybody, Officer?" I asked.

"Dunno. All pulled off. Lookin' for that girl, I think."

When I arrived at Bobby's suite, one of the Virgins stood beside a sliding-glass door holding a silver tray filled with water balloons in her high-tension arms. I observed in my periphery that Turner had already installed a camera on the top of his laptop, presumably for Bobby to entertain himself with narcotic fancies of World Wide Web exposure.

"C'mon, Jonah," Bobby said from the balcony.

I was the new Jonah, thrower of caution to the wind. I christened myself with the rap name "Radical J." *I wuz zup in Bobby's crib gettin' loose.*

Here's the thing: I never had my Frank Sinatra years. I was never into casual sex. I have never been drunk or high. I have never smoked a joint, which people can't believe. I don't drink alcohol. I went to a nightclub only once, and left after ten minutes. When my high school friends were feeling each other up to the space-age syncopation of Electric Light Orchestra, I was a *de facto* fugitive attached to my grandfather the criminal. When my college friends were backpacking across Europe, I got a low-end political job. With the exception of a lingering curiosity about casual sex, I really don't want these other things, but I have a gnawing conviction that I was robbed of my Sinatra years, that they're roaming on the prairie like an ornery appaloosa waiting to be broken. I probably deserve a kick in the ass for marinating in my adolescent fantasies, but it is what it is.

I proceeded out to the balcony, grabbed a red balloon, and hurled it over the side. I watched the angry little sphere careen to earth, and shatter on a metal strip of Boardwalk. A middle-aged couple stopped in their tracks, and looked up. Bobby was laughing hysterically. I backed up against the wall, afraid I would be spotted. Bobby's laughter, however, had a pandemic quality, so the Virgin and I caught the laughter, too.

The ubiquitous Tic Turner emerged from the kitchen with a plastic grin soldered to his face. Bobby grabbed another balloon and winged it over the balcony. All of us watched as it slammed onto the roof of a roller chair, mercilessly splashing the elderly black man who was pushing it. The poor old roller chair pusher shouted up at us. We ducked urgently back into the suite.

"C'mon, Jonah, let's rage," Bobby said, making for the door.

"Whoa, where are you going, Bobby?" Tic Turner asked.

"Me and Jonah are going out for a few minutes."

"Hold on—"

"No. No holding on, Tic! Stay here and Google yourself or something, we'll be back in a little bit. C'mon, Jonah," Bobby demanded.

Bobby was dressed in all black. He wore a black Sopranos baseball cap on his head. Big black wraparound sunglasses further obscured his features.

We got off at the mezzanine, which was busy, but only with tourists.

"There!" Bobby pointed. "See that guy there?"

A sixtyish man in a green polyester suit and wide tie entered the men's room. He wore a white belt and white loafers. I vaguely recall this ensemble being called a "Full Cleveland." I didn't know who he was, but perhaps that was the point. I followed Bobby into the bathroom.

Mr. Cleveland stood at the urinal farthest to the left. Bobby took the one next to him, immediately to the man's right. Bobby waived me toward the urinal next to him. Yours truly, Radical J, followed him.

Bobby began to crane his head so that he was visibly glancing over the marble divider between his urinal and Mr. Cleveland's. Bobby conjured up an expression of approving curiosity at the man's crotch. I pressed my lips together to contain an erupting volcano of laughter. I tried to think of unspeakable horrors, like plagues, in an effort to defuse my hysteria.

Now Bobby was nodding slowly at Mr. Cleveland, straining his head further downward over the divider. *"Niiiiice pecker!"* Bobby said suggestively.

That did it. I roared. Poor old Mr. Cleveland backed away hurriedly from the urinal, threw his hands under the faucet, and waddled like Papa Smurf out into the blinging casino.

Bobby wanted to leave the hotel. This was probably wise, given the balloon and Cleveland episodes. We went down to the garage. A few people studied Bobby quizzically, their tentative expressions querying, *"Is that . . . ?"*

The elevator took us down a few levels. A man coming in from the garage held the glass door for us. Without meeting the man's eyes, Bobby simply proceeded through, as if the man had been assigned by God to hold the door for him. I nodded thanks. I hadn't had any indication that he recognized Bobby until the door began its slow, whiny close and he said, "Where'd you bury him?"

Bobby swung around. The man walked into the elevator. With surprising speed, Bobby was inside the vestibule and then in the elevator.

"Bobby!" I shouted, chasing after him.

"What'd you say, asshole?" Bobby frothed at his tormentor, a thirtyish, neatly groomed professional. The heckler's lower jaw was now extended in a manner suggesting he had not planned for retaliation. As I set foot inside the elevator, the self-styled tough guy had a choice: Retract or confront? A retraction would have engendered the very thing men hate most, a certification of weakness in the great struggle for primacy. A confrontation, however, could lead to violence.

The elevator door closed, and the car jerked upward.

"C'mon, Bobby, it's not worth it," I said. Not profound, but succinct.

"I wanna know what he said. What'd you say?"

The heckler tilted his head to the side and stuffed his tongue into his cheek. He opted for bravery: "I said, 'Where'd you bury him?'"

Bobby lunged, slamming the heckler's head against the back of the elevator. I bear-hugged Bobby to try to prevent him from going at the man again.

"Get off me, Jonah!" Bobby shouted.

A small miracle graced us. The elevator door opened at the mezzanine, and the heckler got off. I waited until he was safely out of sight before I let Bobby go.

"What the fuck are you doing?" Bobby asked.

"Bobby, enough! You can't go around jumping people you don't like."

"Did you hear what he said?"

The elevator door closed. I pushed the button for the lobby.

"Yes, I heard—"

"I thought we were gonna rage," Bobby said.

"We can't. It's not safe. It was my mistake, Bobby. We can't take you out with everything going on. No way," I said, with force that surprised me.

I decided to personally escort Bobby all the way up to his penthouse for genuine fear of the consequences of leaving him alone. I was exhausted, but my enervation was tied more to my psychic sense of a terrible discovery versus anything physically taxing. The combination of the reckless way I had just spent the last thirty minutes and Bobby's hair-trigger reaction to the parking lot affront led me to a claustrophobic crawl space in my brain. Wounded inner child or not, this was a man capable of reckless violence. The slightest provocation set him off. He needed constant supervision, not like a five-year-old, but a one-year-old. You never knew what he'd try to shove in his mouth. Or somebody else's. Bobby had the impulse control of a baby, the physical power of an adult, and the real-world leverage of a king.

As I stood dazed against the elevator wall, I recalled Chief Willie's citation of Rudyard Kipling: "Power without responsibility—the prerogative of the harlot throughout the ages."

"What did you say?" Bobby asked.

I blinked to life. "What?"

"What did you just say?"

"I didn't think I said anything."

"You didn't *think* you said anything? I just fucking heard you. You said something about a harlot."

"I said that out loud?"

"Yeah, you said it out loud."

I couldn't believe it, but I must have.

"Oh, uh, it, uh, must have been some quote I was thinking about. I'm writing . . . a speech for a political thing—"

"You're such a goddamned liar," Bobby said. *Yes, I thought, but I do it all for you.* "You and Cindi both. You're supposed to help me turn this thing around and get good publicity, and all I see every time I turn on the news is goddamned Kaylee Bagwell, or whatever the slut's name is."

The elevator door opened at the penthouse.

"Hopewell. Her last name is Hopewell. Look, Bobby, this is a criminal investigation, it's not about good publicity."

"No, Jonah. It's about you not knowing how to do your job."

Bobby stepped out of the elevator. I followed until he swung around and jammed his palm into my chest. "Don't follow me."

Stunned and stung, I stood back in the elevator absorbing Bobby's rejection. I momentarily understood—not morally, but emotionally— why the Maggots lived in perpetual terror of being iced out of Bobby's life. I felt cold, physically, as if my parents had returned from the dead just to tell me they hated me. No more Mr. Clevelands, no more hurtling balloons off the balcony. Radical J shot dead like Tupac Shakur.

As the elevator door began to close, Bobby put a fist through the gap, which triggered it to reopen.

"Hey, Jonah," Bobby said playfully. A pinprick light of hope. "Did you know that Kaylee trick? You seem to be so worried about her and all."

"No. I didn't know her."

"That's too bad. She looks like my kind of spinner. She's a little *thang*—set her on up top of the Dude, and let her spin around the mechanical bull." He made a pumping gesture with his hips and arms, topping it off with a sneer.

The elevator door closed. It took me a minute to realize that I was not moving, and needed to push a button before it would take me back down to ground level.

The Apology Cometh

"Spin is never having to mean you're sorry."

On my TV that evening, my nightmares about what Bobby was capable of doing to Kaylee Hopewell were aggravated by a new report reinforcing her vulnerability. Newsman Freddy Zane passed between low wooden classroom desks, which appeared to part like an obedient sea. Standing beside him was Ruth McChoat, Kaylee's sixth-grade teacher. She had fluffy red helmet hair whipped up high atop her head like cherry-flavored butter, and grand red glasses that gave her the appearance of a friendly cartoon owl. There was a theatrical zaniness about her that conveyed a familiar but reassuring stereotype—the teacher everyone loves and returns to visit.

The camera showed a profile of Freddy Zane and Ruth McChoat. "What do you remember most about Kaylee, Mrs. McChoat?"

The schoolteacher brushed a rogue curl of hair from her forehead. "Kaylee came back to me in her junior year in high school. She wanted a recommendation for college, and I said, 'Kaylee, I was your sixth-grade teacher, for heaven's sake, those big colleges don't want to hear from me.' But Kaylee insisted. She felt like any college worth its salt would want to hear from her sixth-grade teacher.

"So I wrote the recommendation, and I'll be darned if she didn't get in. Kaylee always came back. One time, she brought a child she was babysitting. She loved babysitting. No matter how old or how smart or how pretty she got, she always . . . came back. I pray she comes back now."

Walking down the school's corridor at the conclusion of his interview, Freddy Zane signed off, "And the search continues, out on the streets and in the forests and in the hearts of those who love her . . . for the answer to the question: Kaylee Hopewell, where are you? This is Freddy Zane in Salem."

The following morning, the ACPD's Chief Desmond caved to the unceasing onslaught of protests. In a statement released to the press, he said of his "hinky" characterization of Kaylee's disappearance, "I want to take this opportunity to apologize to those in the community who may have misinterpreted or have been offended by remarks I made that some perceived to be insensitive. I didn't mean to imply that we aren't taking the investigation into Kaylee's disappearance very seriously. What I meant to convey is frustration over the fact that some things don't quite add up in this case, which happens from time to time in police work. The community should rest assured that we are doing all we can to return Kaylee Hopewell to her family and bring those responsible for her disappearance to justice."

And there they were, the codes of postmodern acceptance—the impotent apology and the invocation of "sensitivity." Hold on to your ass, chief D.

The spin wizards were all over cable TV soon after Desmond's statement hit. What was their verdict on his apology? "Too little too late," the pundits cried in tandem. Oh, Chiefie, don't you know, *Spin is never having to mean you're sorry?*

Thumb Drive

"This changes everything."

The brain trust gathered at Peace Pipe Asset Retrieval Worldwide's headquarters, meaning the Cohn of Silence and I were sitting across the kitchen table from Chief Willie, who was wearing an Oxford cloth shirt and khakis. Apparently he was sane enough not to slip into Injun character in front of Mr. Cohn. A laptop sat at the foot of the table beside Chief Willie.

The Chief began by putting a small cylinder—a flattened-out version of a tube of lip balm—onto the table.

"Do you know what this is?" Chief Willie asked sagaciously, and without his Indian patter. I had the distinct feeling that he hadn't known what this device was either until a certain geekoid/mutual friend told him.

The Cohn of Silence nodded "no." Seeing a metallic insertion port inside a translucent section of the device, I said, "It looks high-tech."

Chief Willie nodded. "They call it a thumb drive. You stick it in the side of a computer and you can save files on it, just like a hundred floppy disks."

"Files on *that?*" the Cohn of Silence asked.

Chief Willie nodded. The Chief was a man of many skills, but technology wasn't one of them. I knew that once I saw the device that he had taken Dorkus inside Bobby's suite with him. It was best, however, not to share this with the Cohn of Silence because he would lecture us about how more players meant greater exposure. It was not, after all, legal to break into someone's hotel suite and steal their property.

Chief Willie stuck the little device into his laptop.

"We found some interesting things. For one, the computer logs show that somebody looked for directions to Lebanon State Forest on Mapquest on the night the sculptor disappeared." Chief Willie nodded at me. He had shared this with me when Dorkus first combed through the files. "Of great interest now are two movies I'm going to show you," he said.

"Movies?" the Cohn of Silence asked.

"Movies. Films. Videos. Moving pictures. Recorded scenes."

"On that little thing?"

"Yes. Lonesome Jake records digitally. That means on a computer chip, not film or videotape. It can be stored and edited on a computer. We've been cleaning it up, making sure we had what we thought we did."

The Chief fired up the first footage, which lasted for about a minute. We silently watched. When it was over, the Cohn of Silence shook his head. His owlish self-confidence gave way to the passive despair of a proud man who wanted to say he had seen everything, but who just realized that he hadn't.

"Whatever happened to discretion?" he asked the laptop. "Whatever happened to basic fucking intelligence? What kind of jackass keeps a tape with a crime he helped cover up?" the Cohn of Silence asked himself. "The kind of jackass who's using the footage to blackmail a bigger jackass," he answered.

I had never heard the Cohn of Silence drop the F-bomb before.

"What do you think?" I asked.

"I didn't see evidence of a crime. Yet," Mr. Cohn said, backing off his earlier rumination. "But it suggests a certain frame of mind on somebody's part, perhaps a motive. It could poison a jury, I'll tell you that much. Chief, do you have any reason to believe that a crime was recorded? A crime by anyone, even if it's not our friend?"

"We didn't have enough time or enough memory on our transfer device to look at everything or clean out the whole computer, but we didn't see anything quite like what you're suggesting."

"You said 'quite.' I am nonplussed by that," Mr. Cohn said.

"I'll show you another preview."

"Enchanting," the Cohn of Silence said, visibly wondering what *Star Trek* episode he had found himself on.

The Chief fired up the second feature. This one lasted about two minutes. The camera was wobbly and it was hard to watch, so Chief Willie slowed it down on the second go-round.

"Is that what—who I think it is in the background?" I asked. "The guy with the hat?"

Chief Willie pressed a key that greatly magnified the frame. "That's Billy all right," Chief Willie said.

"You mean Bobby," Mr. Cohn said.

"No," the Chief said. "We know this one over here is Bobby. But him, way back here—that's Billy."

"Well," I said. "This changes everything."

book four

BLACK HOLE

Son, someday you're going to "find yourself"—
and be very disappointed.

—JACK E. LEONARD

His Honor

" 'Down the road' was now."

After going underground for a while, the Golden Prospect's pilot, Bucky Calhoun, wanted to meet me at the Cherry Hill Library. He didn't want to talk over the phone. I took this as a sign that he was either going to kill me like everybody else seemed inclined to do, or he had something. He had something.

I checked my e-mail on my laptop as I waited for him. There was a note from Cindi: "I checked the video file. KBRO interview with Bonita Chin ran at 10:02 near top of news cycle. Same night as Christian disappeared. Mean anything? Cin."

Mean anything? It meant that the interview with Bonita Chin had run about the same time that I had left Bobby's suite and Christian showed up.

As I noodled with the scenario, Bucky Calhoun showed up at my table, and unraveled a scroll of drawings of a Gulfstream V. The thing about guys who are scientifically competent is they don't understand how incompetent the rest of us truly are. It took me about twenty-five minutes to force Calhoun (who must have thought I was brain-damaged) to get past the science and give me a real-world conclusion about WHAT HAPPENED. Once we set aside the nuts, the bolts, the velocities, and the physics, I got what I needed: it was eminently possible for Turnpike Bobby Chin to have safely bailed out of a Gulf-stream V before it took its final dive in the Pines.

I showed Bucky Calhoun on my laptop the digital footage I had seen for myself the first time shortly before. I magnified a particular frame. Calhoun pointed at the laptop. "That there's Billy," he said.

M ayor Gary Simmons of Hopkins Pond was younger than me, late thirties, in other words, not old enough to hold a responsible job like mayor (somehow, I couldn't shake the notion I was still sixteen). A Dan Quayle–type Haddonfield lawyer with a palpable aura of impatience with his small-town status (destiny evidently awaited), Simmons had made promises to his community of simultaneous revenue growth and environmental purity. These two goals are usually incompatible. Nevertheless, politicians are in the business of promise pronouncement, not promise fulfillment, so Simmons plied his trade very well. When my polling failed to find a magical "message" to make his community feel good about the disposal of medical waste from its booming Lenape Hospital, he found himself in a quandary, the resolution of which was firing his consultant. That was me.

None of us want to think of ourselves as being vindictive any more than we want to think of ourselves as being bigots—even when hateful prejudices may dwell in our minds when some poor soul reinforces a stereotype. As a boy, I saw what happened when "uncles" failed to differentiate between what was business and what was personal: They'd disappear. "He shoulda bought one of those girlie books," I heard Mickey say once about a man named Sonny who vanished. It took me years to know what he meant. All I knew was that it was something with a woman.

As I grew older, I had lost my flexibility about getting stiffed in business. In lockstep, I lost my fear of burning bridges. It used to be that I'd put up with a certain amount of abuse on the grounds that I might need a contact down the road. What I was finding more and more, however, was that "down the road" never came. "Down the road" was now.

What was about to befall Mayor Simmons was not pure vindictiveness, I convinced myself. It was debt restructuring, asset protection, and reputation management—three grown-up terms that even smelled like stock certificates and other crackling emblems of financial weight.

Gibbsboro at rush hour was a twenty-minute drive from the Cherry Hill Library. I had seen the town's name hundreds of times over the years but had never been here. It was a hidden bucolic place that made me think of Lake Tahoe, where I had never been. The Chophouse restaurant was new. Situated on a lake, it had the feel of a ski lodge. Chief Willie assured me everything was in place.

The Chophouse food was excellent, which was too bad because I didn't eat much. I was too engaged in my deception, which required a disarming display of puppy dog regret to a disgruntled client.

"Well, Mayor—"

"Gary, please."

"Gary, again, I'm sorry you weren't happy with how the poll turned out, but I couldn't find a good way to position a medical waste dump."

"It would be a *post-implement relocation facility.*"

Dear Lord. Yeah, that'll fool everybody.

"Right. Still, it's not an easy challenge, but I don't want to burn a bridge with you long-term—who knows, if you're president, I could be Secretary of State, *heh*—so I'll cut down the invoice, but I've got vendors to pay, and I can't make it vanish."

"I understand that, but you have to understand my position, Jonah. I've been promising to cut budgets. Then I went and hired you. We didn't come up with a better way to site this post-implement relocation facility, and I had to present an eighty-three-thousand-dollar bill without anything to show for it."

"Mine is an intangible service. It's hard to show anything either way in my field. You don't stiff the doctor just because you're still sick."

"Of course, but there will be any number of opportunities coming down the pike, so to speak, and I'd ask you not to lose sight of that."

"And I won't. I owe poor Hank Stanford about twenty grand. He just sued me for payment, so not only do I have to pay him, I have to pay legal fees."

"Well, I'm sorry it came to that."

He was not remotely sorry it came to this.

"I can knock it back about twenty percent to sixty-five grand. I still lose a lot, but I'm willing to do that. For the future."

"I appreciate that, Jonah, but I don't think I can swing that."

"You have check-signing authority, right?"

"Right, but there's the politics of it."

"What do you think you could swing, Mayor?"

"Gary."

"Gary."

"No more than twenty thousand. I'm sorry."

I put my face in my hands. I counted to fifteen, which seemed like a good number. "With twenty, I pay Hank, then I'm left with nothing. Then I'll have to pay my lawyer. I'll eat seventy grand. That's a lot for a one-man band."

"Think of it as being for the future."

"What choice do I have?"

Mayor Gary Simmons of Hopkins Pond then bit his upper lip, a Clintonian expression vulcanized to convey empathy when it really conveyed *Get me the hell out of here because a man with my potential doesn't need to be wasting time with some washed-up pollster/grandson-of-a-dead-crime-lord who can't do a damned thing to advance my Destiny (but I couldn't blow him off totally because his pathetic ass agreed to a compromise).*

We walked to our cars and shook hands. The mayor drove a BMW sedan. He headed west back toward Hopkins Pond. I followed him at some distance down a two-lane road. It was sparse enough for imps to be hiding in shadows, but not so sparse that if someone were to drive by and, say, see something untoward, it wouldn't be a big fucking problem for somebody. Cicadas were screeching their chronic warning at a high pitch.

Simmons's BMW disappeared over a rise, and I heard a hideous shredding of metal, followed by a very loud crash. I sped up the hill and saw an old pickup truck in the opposite lane. Shattered glass had fallen all around. Beside the pickup, in my lane, was the proud rear end of Mayor Simmons's BMW. The vehicles were about two feet apart. I pulled up behind Simmons, who had been sideswiped. Because I was concerned and wanted to help.

Chief Willie Thundercloud ambled out of the truck dressed like a local farmer in overalls and a straw hat. "You okay, boss?" he said, moving toward the BMW. The trunk of the BMW had opened from the impact of the crash.

Simmons climbed out of the car. He appeared to be unhurt. "Why the hell did you try to pass me on a no-pass road?" he asked.

"You was goin' slow," Chief Willie said. "I don't know why in tarnation you were drivin' so slow."

"I was going the speed limit, for Christ's sake."

"You was crawlin'. I figured you was an old lady or somebody who didn't want to git noticed." Chief Willie said. He was southern all of a sudden.

"Are you okay, Gary?" I asked.

"I'm fine," he said. "Did you see this?"

"Yeah, uh, it's why I stopped," I said. "Geez."

A car slowed down on the side of the road where Chief Willie's truck was blocking traffic. Mayor Simmons glared at the driver, who

sped away. Simmons came back to the car. His earlier steps were as-
sertive, but when he beheld the breadth of Chief Willie's shoulders,
he eased off a little. Another car drove by and did its gawk.

"Looks like it's probably just body work," Chief Willie said. He
ran his fingers along the back of the trunk. He slipped a mini-crowbar
up his sleeve, the one he used to discreetly unhinge the trunk. "Yeah,
body work," he repeated.

Mayor Simmons lifted up the trunk. Standing off to the rear right
of the car, I'm pretty sure I saw it first. Saw *them* first. Three dead
women in the trunk, bloody as hell.

"Holy shit!" I said.

Simmons swung open the trunk. *"Oh my God!"* he cried, staring
in shock at the dead bodies.

"You got more than a car repair to concern yourself with, my
friend," Chief Willie said. "Them's *men*."

"What?"

"Men. Them's men dressed as girls. My my my," the Chief said.

Simmons stuck his head deeper into the trunk.

"I never saw nothin' like this before," Chief Willie said. "Wait 'til
Betty sees this!" He pulled out a camera and snapped a shot of Mayor
Simmons staring zombielike into the trunk with the bloody, dead
transvestites. The mayor turned and threw up his arms. "Are you
fucking nuts? I've never seen these girls in my life!"

"Them ain't girls, buckaroo. Look at the dark sheen around them
jawlines."

"Whoever the hell they are, I've never seen them in my life. Tell
him, Jonah. I had dinner with you."

Another car came by, this time on my side of the road. The
mayor shut the trunk and frantically waved the car onto the shoulder to pass. Yet another car came by. Mr. Helpful at the wheel asked
if everybody was okay. Could he call the police? Could he help?

"No, we're fine!" Simmons said frantically.

Mr. Helpful pulled away, appearing hurt.

"I think we should call the police," I suggested. I pulled out my phone.

"No!" Simmons insisted.

A light went on in a lonely farm-style house across the street. The front door opened. An elderly woman in a lime-green warmup suit waddled down a few concrete steps.

"Jesus Christ," Simmons gritted.

Two more cars pulled up in front of Chief Willie's. As I began to wave them around, I had to yell, "Ho!" because a beige Ford pulled up behind the pickup, right next to mine.

A light went on above the dashboard of the Ford. A police light. A tall, muscular authoritarian-looking man with a mustache pulled over, got out, and directed the two oncoming cars around his.

"I'm Panicola, Medford P.D. Off duty. You boys call this in?"

"No," Chief Willie said.

Simmons discretely closed his trunk further.

"Paul?" I said to Panicola.

"Jonah?"

"How are you?" I stepped forward to shake the cop's hand.

"Are you involved in this fender-bender, Jonah?" Panicola asked.

"I just had dinner with the mayor," I began.

"Mayor?"

"Mayor Gary Simmons of Hopkins Pond," I said, "Meet Paul Panicola, an old friend. He used to tail my grandfather around. Mickey had a retreat in the woods in Medford."

Mayor Simmons shook Panicola's hand and smiled tightly. In the streetlight, I saw beads of dense sweat creeping along his brow.

Chief Willie receded a few steps. Panicola took out his cell phone. "Nobody's hurt, are they?"

"No," Chief Willie, Simmons, and I said simultaneously. Simmons's eyes were pleading.

"Paul," I said. "These guys have already exchanged insurance information and that crap. Do we have to call it in?"

The busybody across the street turned around and waddled her sad self back inside her house.

"I don't have to file anything that's not in my jurisdiction, but it's kind of a courtesy cops do for each other," Panicola said.

"I totally understand," I said. "The mayor has to get over to Cherry Hill Hospital to see his mother-in-law. Can we spare the formalities? I'll owe you one, Paul."

Panicola laughed. "I know you, Jonah. That's your way of saying you won't sic one of your family's gangster buddies on me." He pinched my cheek.

"Aw, Paul, those gangsters are all gone now."

Panicola pointed to Chief Willie. "You all right?"

Chief Willie said he was fine, fixing his hat.

"You're okay, Mayor?" Panicola asked Simmons.

"A little frazzled, but okay."

"All right then," the cop concluded. "Let's call it a night. And Jonah, I'll call you on that favor. Good seeing you again."

"Thanks for your help, Paul."

As Panicola returned to his car, I cornered Mayor Simmons, who had begun to shake. "Gary, listen to me. Drive down the road. There's a Wawa shopping center. Pull in and leave your car in the back. Wait for me. I'll call some guys I know, friends of my grandfather's. They'll clean things up."

"I-I-I—"

"Do you understand me or not, Gary?"

"I'll go. I'll go. W-w-what about the farmer?" he asked, referring to Chief Willie.

"I'll get his address. You'll send him a check to fix his piece-of-shit truck, even though it wasn't your fault. He won't want to get involved in anything else. Just drive down to Wawa, and wait in the car."

"Uh–uh–uh–okay."

Simmons pulled away slowly. I approached Chief Willie/Farmer Brown.

"Nice work, Farmer Brown," I said.

"Farmer Brown say, 'You're welcome.' "

"You'll clean out the trunk for our friend?"

"No sweat. I'll drive our sexually confused buddies back down the shore and get 'em cleaned up."

"Are they all right back there?"

"I put 'em in when you guys got up to leave the Chophouse. They haven't been in there that long. They'll catch their breath and blow their fee, so to speak, at Caesar's."

"Good. Thank the Sheik for me. He makes a good cop."

I drove the half-mile down to the Wawa where Mayor Simmons was sitting on a bench outside nursing a beer.

"Did you touch anything?" I asked.

"I swear . . . I swear, I didn't, I-I-I—"

"I'll drive you home, Gary. Don't worry."

Ong's Hat

"Bobby's on the move."

The evening after my Chophouse adventure, I had dinner at home. Irene Grant was a superb cook. She had made a thin-crusted pizza that we all loved. Midbite into my first piece, Edie said, "Oh, Jonah, a guy from Commerce Bank, Joe Diamond or something, called. He wanted to confirm that eighty-three thousand dollars was wired into your account."

"Wow!" Ricky said.

"Is that the payment you've been chasing?" Edie asked.

"How about that?" I said archly.

"How did you finally get him to pay?"

Me, deadpan: "I promised the mayor I'd get rid of the three dead transvestites in the trunk of his car if he paid."

Irene and Edie laughed. "No, really," Edie asked.

"I'm serious," I said, thinking how strange it was to tell the truth and have the people I loved most laugh.

Seeing the women laugh, Lily said, "Daddy is silly."

I tucked the kids into bed and headed downstairs to join Edie and Irene, who were watching a Hugh Grant movie. I didn't have much feeling about Hugh one way or the other, but Irene's running joke was that she was married to him, given their shared surname. I was so tired that I would have happily watched reruns of *Love American Style.* Just let me sit in front of a screen and drool.

The ongoing conspiracy against my relaxation, however, had been hatched. Whether its provenance lay with the devil or God I couldn't be sure, but there was a force larger than I was that abhorred the very idea of me sitting on my ass.

I tried to keep my mobile phone on vibrate when I was in the house. Edie got really annoyed when it rang, so when I felt my pants rumble—and not in the good way—I'd walk out to the porch and take the call.

"Bobby's on the move," Chief Willie said.

"Do we know where?"

"Moving west. There's some activity in Ong's Hat. Douchebags with Jaguars seem to be pulling up to the cabin. You said you wanted to see what went on—"

"I know. Can you pick me up?"

"Gimme ten. Wear dark, brother."

I broke the news of my departure for Godknowswhere to Edie. She took it pretty well, probably because she and Irene were lost in their movie. Edie rolled her doe eyes when she saw me come downstairs after changing into a black T-shirt, dark green chinos, and a night-blue windbreaker. Her eyes said, *Woo, go get 'em, secret agent man.* Like my grandmother, Edie either had no idea what her husband was into, or had couriered her worries away into the mental equivalent of cold storage. Radical J was on the move.

Chief Willie drove an older Jeep that I hadn't seen before. He had a small screen set up on the armrest between the two front seats, which showed a red dot moving through the mapped-out streets in western Jersey. This was the signal from the beacon he had rigged on Bobby's motorcade.

"That's our boy," Chief Willie said. "It's Ong's Hat all the way. You wanna see once and for all what that freakazoid's up to at that proctologist's paradise?"

"What's the risk?"

"A hostile colonic. Not sure what else. We can pull into the woods pretty easily, but I'm not sure how close we can get."

"Let's try."

The roads to Ong's Hat were narrow and heavily wooded. When one considered the legends of the Jersey Devil and Blind Paul (a giant who had a thing for hatcheting sleeping campers), and the reality of the Pine Barrens as a final resting place for gangland rejects, these woods could make anybody anxious.

The blinking red dot on Chief Willie's monitor indeed stopped in Ong's Hat about ten minutes into our ride. Thirty minutes later, driving at an illegal speed, we made it there.

Not that I could tell where we were. The road was nameless and unlit. Moonlight was intermittent because of cloud cover. Chief Willie backed into the pines between two sleeping trees. He clearly wanted to be able to pull out fast. I was not comforted by this.

"Are you carrying?" he asked.

"Yeah. Are we near the Flagellants' place?"

"Uh-huh. Quarter-mile down. We'll parallel the road through the woods."

"How are we going to get over there? I can't see anything. Do you have flashlights?"

The Chief reached behind him and grabbed something I couldn't quite determine. He turned the dashboard light on. "No flashlights. Night vision goggles. We don't want them to see us coming."

Chief Willie showed me how to put the goggles on. It was a strange feeling. The world pitched toward me in grades of light green.

The dark background actually came in the brightest shade, to the point where I had to squint. The most peculiar sensation was not my sight within the oculus, but my total lack of peripheral vision. Then there was the high-pitched hum of the unit, which did not diminish. It made my head vibrate. So much for my delusion about joining the Special Forces. I just wanted to go home.

The Chief handed me a key to his Jeep. "Just in case, don't wait for me. Just go." I gulped, taking the key. He then reached for a square device, which he stuffed into a thick fanny pack.

"What's that?" I asked.

"My surveillance camcorder. Everybody else films this nut job, so we're gonna, too."

We trudged through the abandoned woods for about fifteen minutes. I held my hands a few feet away from my ears to protect me from the things that I could not see. Chief Willie, a master of the night, proceeded normally, stopping every few minutes to look around. There were lights at the front entrance to the lodge, which was set back a few hundred yards from the road. The Chief had been right: the dirt lot was filled with glowing luxury vehicles. There were no windows on the side or rear of the building. There was, however, a door at the rear. A wraparound porch hugged the simple knotted pine structure.

"That's a helluva big place for a colonic," Chief Willie said. "It's like a Colonoseum. Heh. Maybe they've got an assembly line. How much can you clean out of an intestine?"

"Colon," I corrected.

"Same friggin' thing."

"Right. I don't see how the hell we can get in the lodge," I said, revealing the kind of bravery that would surrender America to its enemies within moments of an initial threat. Every war hawk should find himself out in the Pine Barrens in the middle of the night facing down a band of rabid cultists and a megalomaniacal proctologist. See how much they like danger. I had a newfound respect for the men and women who protect the country. They actually took all the risks I glamorized, but could not take myself. Thank God for them. And get me home. My arteries raided my organs for fresh blood.

We moved closer to the Colonoseum. The crackle of dried pines beneath my feet startled me. Chief Willie shushed me, as if I didn't know that being quiet was the prudent move when one was spying on cult freaks in the woods.

The Chief stopped me. I heard my heart beating. It was a swishing sound mixed with a thumping—this on top of the whine from the goggles. I heard footsteps against the boards in the front of the structure. Chief Willie pointed toward the rear of the building.

As we moved, the Chief noted the sloped roof. "Do you see that?" he whispered so directly into my ear that it was loud.

"No," I said.

"Sections of the roof are glowing."

"So?"

"Skylights. We have to get up there."

"On the roof? You're shitting me."

"Chief Willie shit you not."

I followed him to the rear of the porch. The Chief grabbed a wooden beam with his right hand and hoisted himself onto the railing with surprising agility. Then, to my horror, he shimmied up the pole with considerably less grace, and grabbed onto the gutter.

"Mongoose," he whispered. "Push my feet up. Just hold them steady."

I palmed the Chief's shoes as he pulled himself onto the roof. There was an audible creaking, which echoed through the woods. With Chief Willie safely on another plane, I felt like the devil's bull's-eye. With my lack of peripheral vision fueling my fear, I grabbed onto the beam, brought myself to the railing, and clasped the gutter. As I pulled myself up, a Herculean force yanked me up from my armpits and onto the roof. I kept reminding myself that Chief Willie had once made his living hurling three-hundred pound steroid-hopped mutants into crowds. To him, I was weightless, which made me feel momentarily sleek, the way a spy should be. *Pretend you're Mossad,* I told myself.

We inched along the roof slowly. The creaking wasn't too bad. Once over the point of the roof, there were moths flitting around three skylights that were spaced evenly across its width.

As the scene below us came into view, I could make out a small cluster of people huddled around a central stained-glass light. They were all wearing white linen. Kadaborah stood at the front of the group and spoke to a woman kneeling on the ground before him. I vaguely recognized her as one of Bobby's Virgins. Chief Willie removed his goggles slowly. He took out his camcorder and began filming.

I took off my goggles. Kadaborah was saying something to the Virgin, quite sternly from his expression. The Virgin wept. Kadaborah handed her a cat-o'-nine-tails. She began to strike herself over her shoulders so that the leather straps streaked across her fragile back.

"Motherf——," Chief Willie said.

"The shower!" I said.

"What?" the Chief asked.

"Bobby had marks on him when I first met him. He was in the shower."

Kadaborah scolded the woman again. She whipped herself harder. Her back was reddening in streaks. It was blood.

Bobby stood at the front of the huddle. The roof vibrated. The Flagellants were shouting now at the woman, pointing to her. She struck herself again and again to the chorus of taunts.

"Well, Mongoose, I think we know what they do here now," Chief Willie said, shutting down his camcorder and stuffing it into his fanny pack.

"Yeah, they smack themselves senseless. Let's go."

We put our goggles back on and walked hunched down the back slope of the roof. I got flat against the shingles, gripped the gutter, and swung myself outward to the ground. Chief Willie copied my approach with one significant difference. His density was too much for the gutter, and he brought the thing crashing down and fell beside me with a thud.

There was stirring across the floorboards. "Let's haul ass!" Chief Willie said full-voiced. I throttled into a sprint through the woods. To my horror, the Chief was slow as sludge. *What the hell would I do if he got caught?* Screw it, just run.

A gaggle of voices rose from the night in the distance behind me. A new set of footsteps—fast ones—were coming upon us, as was a beam of light breaking like a strobe through the woods. Whoever he was, he didn't have night vision. "I got you, asshole!" the voice said. I tried to run and glance behind me at the same time. I saw Chief Willie's freighter of a body huffing through the woods. A slimmer figure, pantherlike, came at him from his right. I ran, I glanced back, I ran, I glanced back.

To my horror, Chief Willie veered off toward a collision course with our pursuer. I thought about shouting something to my partner, but choked down the impulse. Our pursuer didn't necessarily know how many of us there were, or the Chief's actual position. The catlike man only had a flashlight, which broke up his vision as he ran through the night.

Chief Willie's course appeared deliberate. I turned around to watch, quickly walking backward now. Chief Willie raised his ham-hock arm in the darkness. His thick hand held something flat. The pursuer also raised his arm—a heavy-duty flashlight. As the flashlight went up, the man lost his vision. Chief Willie did not. With a vicious growl, the Chief brought his arm down on the head of his pursuer, who groaned and fell hard. He then resumed full speed and hurtled his meteoric form in my direction. I resumed my sprint to the Jeep, pulling out the key Chief Willie had given me. I fired up the car and rolled down the passenger window. "Go! Go! Go," he shouted. I pulled out slowly as the Chief thunked closer to me. He opened up the door as the wheels reached the dark asphalt. With a dive bomb into the passenger seat, he shouted, "Haul ass, baby!"

For the first time in my life, I floored a gas pedal, and breathed rubber deep into my lungs as if it were oxygen.

You're the Man

"I'm not Mega Boy!"

About four miles out of Ong's Hat, Chief Willie turned on his little TV monitor. "This is screwy," he said as I tore down the rural road going eighty.

"What is?"

"The dots are split."

"What dots?"

"The beacons on the vehicle Kadaborah and Bobby travel in aren't moving, but Lonesome Jake is going northeast."

"What do you make of that?"

"I'm not sure. It's near Lebanon State Forest. Whitesbog, that area."

"Lebanon? That's the woods we talked about. You and me, Detective Galen and me. I bet that's where Christian is. Did you bring a shovel?"

"No, but Chief Willie say, 'He who use shovel to bury sculptor in first place use shovel to dig him up.' Turn around, Mongoose."

I slowed down and made a U-turn. When I picked up speed, I pulled out my mobile phone and made a call. When the voice answered, I said: "I'm going to be very brief. Do you know Whitesbog? No? You may want to pinch a helicopter and a map and get there very fast."

Chief Willie pulled out a map of his own and began to direct me in accordance with what his surveillance monitor was showing. The red dot representing Lonesome Jake's vehicle had stopped sliding along the monitor. He had pulled over.

"Head down here about a mile and a half," Chief Willie said. I drove on, slower. "Shut the lights and pull into the woods. Let's get our goodies and track 'em."

We got out, and revisited our earlier ritual with the night goggles. The Chief grabbed his camcorder and stuffed it in his ever-present pouch.

About a third of a mile into the woods, we saw a light and heard the hum of an engine. "Bastard has his engine on and lights pointed at something. Can you see how many there are?"

"No. I don't see anybody," I said.

We advanced a few hundred yards.

"It's him. It's Lonesome Jake," I said.

Chief Willie reached into his fanny pack and withdrew his camcorder. "Stay over to the left of the light. We don't want those beams hitting us."

As we drew closer, it became harder to differentiate the sounds. I could distinguish the engine of Lonesome Jake's truck. Then I heard the sound of a shovel hitting hard dirt. "He's digging," Chief Willie mouthed.

"I hear something else," I whispered.

It was the sound of muffled sobbing, dampened by the drone of the engine and the whine of the desperate few cicadas that had survived the summer. I tried to see Lonesome Jake's face, but couldn't make out individual features. I recognized him by his build, his ponytail, and his distinct critter movements. I saw none of the physical accompaniments of crying, no heaving shoulders, no wiping of tears.

The headlights from Lonesome Jake's truck hit something glitter-

ing in the earth, beneath a log. I squinted, trying to identify the odd-
ity that had come into my vision. Maggots. Not Bobby's Maggots,
Death's maggots. There were thousands of them crawling, giving the
impression of rolling tundra. Then I saw the smile, the broad grin of
eternity. The sculptor. I waited for myself to retch, but I didn't. Chief
Willie held his camcorder steady.

Lonesome Jake groaned. He turned his head and muffled his nose
in the crook of his arm. The sobs in the background grew more intense, broken by a loud choking sound. The crying figure, who must
have been seated on the ground, rose. It was a puking Turnpike Bobby
Chin moving into the weak moonlight.

"What the hell are you crying about, asshole?" Lonesome Jake
said. Chief Willie threw me a momentary sideways glance.

"Well, help me pull him out!" Lonesome Jake insisted.

"Why should I? You and Mom get all the money I pay you."

Mom?

"You pay me to take your picture lookin' all like Jesus and sneak it
to the press whenever you feel blue, you spoiled freak. Least you could
do is show some respect for your family. Besides, I didn't kill the guy."

"It was an accident. That bitch was trashing me on TV."

"Listen to"—*lissen-a*—"how you talk about your mother. You
crushed her soul."

"No, Jake, you crushed it because you were born, you no-talent
load."

"No, Mega Boy, you fucked it up. It was all about you the minute
you hatched. Nothing's ever your fault, is it, Bobby?"

Lonesome Jake bent over and pulled the body from its grave by the
feet. It was still clothed. Christian's hands and face were mostly skeletal; only red and white sinews remained. Chief Willie whispered to
me, "Bobby'll kill, but he won't dig." There was something poetic
about the observation. I had been thinking something similar, but had
yet to articulate it even in my own mind.

"Just keep him down there!" Bobby said.

"We can't. The cops know he's around here. I can't lug all your bloody fuckups out in a laundry bin down the service elevator, Mega Boy. Now, come on and help me get him in the car."

"I'm not Mega Boy!" Bobby cried. He sprinted to Lonesome Jake's SUV.

"Where the hell are you going, dammit?"

Bobby grabbed something from the passenger side of the car and staggered toward Lonesome Jake. I felt a rumbling beneath my feet. Chief Willie felt it, too, and muttered, "What the—?"

A beam of light, both broad and intense, suddenly cut through the pines from above. It was a helicopter.

Bobby raised his hand and screamed something indecipherable. The storm of light from above rendered my night vision goggles a nuisance, and I pulled them off.

"Jesus, Bobby has a gun," I said.

"DROP THE GUN, BOBBY, DROP IT NOW!" a cold voice from the sky shouted through a speaker. Galen, ACPD. I had called him.

Bobby looked up, covering his eyes but maintaining the incompetent trajectory of his gun. Lonesome Jake's ponytail blew wildly in the rush of the helicopter's blades, but he was frozen, stunned by the sudden sensory assault.

"I can't just let him kill somebody else," I said to Chief Willie, stepping forward.

"Stay the hell back here, Mongoose!" Chief Willie said.

I stepped forward into the collision of light. "Bobby, it's me, Jonah," I shouted. "Please, no more hurting anybody."

"Jonah?" Bobby said softly.

Lonesome Jake cursed under his breath, his head darting around in search of escape.

"Please, Bobby, it's got to stop," I said.

Chief Willie emerged. He had set his camcorder down, and used his home appliance of a body to block one of Lonesome Jake's potential escape routes. While I knew he was armed, Chief Willie's weapon was not visible. He either didn't want to aggravate Bobby's meltdown, or he didn't want a shooting on his docket with the cops watching from above.

Lonesome Jake burst out into laughter. "Look at Mega Boy now. Even with a gun, he can't do nothin' but shiver."

Chief Willie shook his head angrily at Lonesome Jake for baiting Bobby, who was indeed shaking. I thought again of Mickey watching the rollerblading man career over the Boardwalk. *Things usually end up going where they're headed.*

I motioned to Bobby to put the gun down. Galen repeated his command from the hovering black spider above us.

I saw Lonesome Jake collapse on top of Christian's body before I heard the shots. Traumas don't happen in the right order, at least not in the human mind. Bobby dropped his gun all right, but after he fired three rounds into Lonesome Jake from ten feet away. He didn't need to be an expert shot from that distance to connect with all three. He stepped back against the tire of Lonesome Jake's SUV and shook even more violently.

Chief Willie and I ran toward Lonesome Jake and pulled him off the unearthed corpse. I screamed one of those primal screams one sees in films, but can never imagine having cause to do oneself. The helicopter peeled away to set down someplace. Lonesome Jake's breath was shallow against the ground, until he had no breath at all.

Swords of narrow light danced through the woods, giving the strobelike syncopation of a jungle discothèque. "Jesus Christ," Detective Galen said, taking in the carnage. "Step away from him, Jonah," he ordered. I complied. Galen withdrew his gun and pointed it at Bobby.

"Put your hands above your head, Bobby. You are under arrest for the murders of these men."

Not surprisingly, Bobby didn't listen.

Chief Willie closed his camcorder. He popped out the chip containing the footage of Bobby's confession and argument with Lonesome Jake, not to mention the ritual at Ong's Hat. He put it in Galen's unarmed hand. "You know our motto, Detective: 'We're slow, but we're sloppy.'"

Galen laughed.

"It's all yours, Detective," I said. "The Chief and I don't exist. You're the man."

Galen sheathed his gun and mouthed "thanks." He handed me a sheet of crumpled paper, which I stuffed into my pocket.

Chief Willie popped his camcorder closed. Bobby glanced up at the familiar pop of the receptacle. He stopped shaking as he removed his St. Jude medallion. "Here you go, Jonah," Bobby said, handing the medallion to me. "Did you get it, Jonah? Did you get it?"

"I have it right here, Bobby."

"No. No. The Dude with the gun," Bobby laughed, his eyes miles away. "The Dude was cool with the gun. Did the camera work in the dark?"

"I'm not sure, Bobby."

"But you got it all, right?"

"We got it, Bobby."

Just One More Thing

"This has been masterful police work on the part of the ACPD."

TURNPIKE BOBBY CHIN BUSTED
FOR DOUBLE MURDER
A. C. POLICE CAPTURE ROCK STAR
IN PINE BARRENS SHOOTOUT

This was the headline that ran later that morning in the *Atlantic City Packet*. The best part of the story was the closing quotation from New Jersey Governor Chris Myers declaring, "This has been masterful police work on the part of the ACPD." Just what I wanted: A happy Detective Galen getting all the credit.

Lonesome Jake was identified in news reports as Bobby's half-brother, Jason Leeds, who had been born to Bonita out of wedlock during what she perceived to be her singing heyday. Jake's birth aborted Bonita's career, or at least served as a justification of her failure. Bonita's hopes for a narcissistic bailout fell to Mega Boy. Bastard Jake had grown up in the Chin household, but was emotionally abandoned, evolving into more of a babysitter for Bobby once his acting and eventual singing career took off. Our search of media databases had never turned up even one reference to Jake's existence, which could have only fueled his bitterness.

Witnessing the macabre may put some men to sleep, but not me. I still had a puzzle to complete.

The Arts & Entertainment channel was running the last episode of "*Columbo* Week." Peter Falk's Lt. Columbo nailed Jack Cassidy's magician/escaped-Nazi character because Cassidy hadn't realized that a typewriter ribbon of a certain era, if unraveled, could reveal what had been typed. What was being typed just prior to the murder was a letter to the authorities, which gave the unctuous Cassidy a motive for killing the whistleblower. I was mesmerized by Columbo, his Machiavellian absentmindedness, his meddling often sprinkled with "Just one more thing . . ." Feeling certain of my case, but creatively tapped, I decided to plagiarize the good lieutenant's essence.

I entered Bobby's suite at the Golden Prospect the following morning for brunch. The mood was somber. Bobby was in jail, Lonesome Jake was dead, the Virgins and other overhead were gone. A Piney Spring Water deliveryman was taking out the remaining bottles. Tic Turner's laptop was the only relic of the Maggots' management reign. Kadaborah and Turner sat in a corner of the living room. I joined them mournfully.

"I never would have suspected Lonesome Jake, I have to admit that." I scratched my head like the disheveled Columbo.

"Yes, Jonah, we were the most plausible villains, weren't we?" Kadaborah said. "A mysterious and greedy cult," he added, with a flittering of his fingers suggesting diabolical doings.

"When I'm wrong, I say I'm wrong."

"Just out of curiosity, what had been your operating hunch?" Kadaborah asked.

"I'm too embarrassed to even tell you." Sir Jonah, Eater of Crow.

"Tell us," Turner insisted.

"I thought you guys were interested in Bobby's music library."

"All that doo-wop music?" Kadaborah said. "I bet it's worth a fortune. It was a good hunch, but the catalogue belongs to Bobby."

"I know it. I was pretty pleased with myself there for a while."

"Every man is allowed his folly," Kadaborah said sympathetically. We retreated to a cozy sitting area with spinach crêpes. Souvenir decks of Golden Prospect playing cards were set out on a granite table. "I remember when I was your age, Jonah—it wasn't that long ago—I was looking to experiment with a new life, a new identity. Your foray into detective work is as good a folly as any."

As each Maggot popped a crêpe into his mouth, I said, as if sweeping off a crumb from my own lips, "I found Lonesome Jake's cinematography."

They began chewing a little slower. "Bobby saw his mom on TV and went nuts. He grabbled the mini-statue off the table. Christian was sitting, and Bobby hit him in the head. Then the camera went off. A person who wasn't trying to blackmail Bobby wouldn't have recorded even that, but you know . . ."

Guilty minds are not paranoid, they are rightly worried. I said nothing more, just found another crêpe and ate it. "These are so good," I said with a mouthful.

"I can only imagine what else that man must have filmed," Kadaborah, anxious now, said, feigning cool.

"You knew Jake was Bobby's half-brother, I take it?"

"Certainly," Kadaborah said. "He had it in for Bobby from the time they were boys."

"It would have been nice to know this at the beginning."

"Yes, well—"

"There are certain people it's best not to piss off, is that it?"

"We all have to make accommodations out of respect to family."

This line of inquiry wasn't getting me anywhere. Get back on track, Jonah. "It wasn't film Jake used, incidentally," I said. "It was digital. It's amazing, you can keep all that stuff organized on a computer like financial records or something. Point and click." I popped another crêpe. "I love these."

Turner had had enough. "Did it actually show what happened with that sculptor?" he said, knowing that Christian's killing at Bobby's hand was now safe territory, public information.

"Lonesome Jake recorded Bobby killing Christian, and then tried to blackmail him. Bobby saw the KBRO interview of his mother, and went nuts. Poor Christian was unlucky enough to have been there when Bobby flipped out. The lousy sculpture didn't help.

"Don't worry, gents, you guys weren't in the footage, but you probably weren't too far away . . . And with all Bobby did for him over the years . . . ," I said.

Relieved, Kadaborah said, "Nobody appreciates anything. That's what you learn in this business."

"Just one more thing," I said to the Maggots. "I didn't know Bobby skydived."

"What makes you think he did?" Kadaborah asked.

"Lonesome Jake recorded the jump from the plane," I said. "Oh, yeah, it was all laid out on Jake's computer. There was Bobby . . . and you, Tic. I guess it was Jake holding the camera. Bobby could never be without the camera."

I grabbed another crêpe. I wasn't hungry anymore. In fact, I was stuffed, but I liked the casual effect of eating while I cracked the case.

"So, it's affirmative, we went skydiving," Turner said to Kadaborah's intense displeasure.

"The recording shows a Gulfstream Five. Who jumps out of a G-Five?" I asked.

"Jets can slow down," Turner said cautiously.

"The G-Five cabin door opens outward—," I said.

"So what?"

"You're a pilot, Tic, aren't you? You'd know that an outward-opening door would be ripped off at any flying speed. You can't open it, jump, and close it again. You'd have to be opening it knowing full well that door is history, that it could have smashed against the wing or into the left engine—something that would be unwise unless you were jumping out to begin with. If, by some chance, the door missed the wing and the engine and you landed without it, there would be a lot of explaining to do on the ground. Unless, of course, you planned to crash it, and the plane would be expected to be in pieces. The door was found near Medford Lakes. The rest of the plane was scattered around Tabernacle, suggesting you jumped around Medford Lakes, not so far away from Ong's Hat that you couldn't have been picked up and hidden out at the lodge."

"Look, Jonah, Bobby liked to skydive, he liked to take risks. You don't know when Jake took that footage. It could have been from any number of dives."

"It could have, but it wasn't. We saw Billy in the background."

"Billy?"

"William Penn. The statue on the top of City Hall. Billy wears a hat."

People from Philadelphia and South Jersey cited Billy Penn's hat as a synonym for the Philadelphia skyline. Even though the skyline had vastly changed over the decades, lifelong residents often referenced their proximity to Philadelphia with an affectionate reference to "seeing Billy." The observation was to be taken figuratively.

"You and your guys stole Jake's laptop or downloaded his files!" Turner said. "That's a felony."

This was true, of course. The Piney Spring boys had cleaned out Lonesome Jake's computer files.

"I don't know what you're talking about. Jake carried backup disks in his vest in case somebody stole or tried to erase his hard drive. You probably checked yourself, but figured it was better not to piss Jake off. The police found everything."

"It still doesn't mean a thing," Kadaborah said. "They found burned bodies in the wreckage. Tic and Bobby sound like they were alive in the little film you saw." Kadaborah was smug now.

"It wasn't film. It was digital."

"What's the damned difference?"

"The damned difference is the accuracy of computer records . . . such as the lyrics to the song 'Flameout.'"

"So what?" Kadaborah said. "Bobby wrote a song after the crash."

"Then why was it recorded in the computer on June 25, about a week *before* the crash?" I said.

"That wasn't on Jake's computer, it—"

"It *what,* Tic? It was on yours? Interesting. No matter, it looks like Bobby wrote the song about an airplane flameout before it actually occurred. Bobby must have been psychic, among his other gifts."

Turner froze at the mention of his computer. Kadaborah held up his hand to keep Turner calm: "Come now, Jonah, what motive could Bobby have had to crash his own plane? Tell me."

"He couldn't fill the Golden Prospect's little theater. Nobody wanted to come to Bobby's comeback concert because he wasn't coming back. When Bobby's feelings are hurt, he does naughty things. He makes a scene, like a child. What better tantrum could he possibly throw than to fake his own death, punish the grown-ups? He'd get news coverage and then . . . resurrect. Which would get even more. At least in his twisted mind."

"Oh, I see. And what about Tic and me? What motive could we possibly have to stage such histrionics? You've already admitted we had no claim on the catalogue, that this was all between Jake and Bobby."

"It was a bust-out."

"Excuse me?"

"A bust-out. Like when the mob takes over a business on its way down and bleeds it dry. They order inventory they can't pay for, steal the goods. Bobby was that business, and you were that mob. You guys would indulge any fantasy Bobby had, including a psycho death-fake publicity stunt."

I had stated my hunch to Dorkus and Chief Willie weeks ago: Given that Turner had some say in the payment of the DEVIUS invoice, the Maggots may have had a deeper reach into Bobby's finances. I suggested that knowing more could help us develop a Plausible Alternative Scenario for what happened to Christian. Additional records might be on Turner's laptop, I theorized, which he appeared to use a lot.

Dorkus listened in his big-headed insect way and proposed the following: He could hack on to Turner's laptop. The laptop needed to be "live," meaning that Turner would have to have an online connection. The connection would be optimized if Turner's computer was communicating directly with mine, thus the need to have him e-mail me the photo of Bobby and me, which was a Trojan Horse. As I kept Turner online by having him demonstrate all of the ways he could load Bobby's picture onto the Internet, Dorkus cleaned out his hard drive remotely, from Chief Willie's place in Margate.

This disc Dorkus made—essentially a copy of Turner's hard drive—contained an astonishing amount of information about the Maggots and their various enterprises, the upshot of which was a collection of small businesses that existed to service the lifestyle of Turnpike Bobby Chin. There was a security service that provided bodyguards and vehicle maintenance at a cost of roughly two hundred thousand dollars per month. In addition to the telltale Web site design service that had hosed Bobby for three quarters of a million dollars, there was a web marketing ad agency that had racked up annual billings of about three million. Outside of a few lame ads, we could never find much else that qualified as marketing.

The disc contained financial records of a catering business that billed Bobby about thirty thousand a month; dry cleaners at three grand; a travel agency retainer was twenty thousand per month. Bobby tithed to the Ong's Hat Flagellants about nine hundred thousand a year. There was an escort service that got a half million the prior year. Then there were categories I couldn't begin to understand. Lonesome Jake had been paid approximately one million dollars a year for the service of filming Bobby's antics (and not releasing his work to the world). It was a gig old Jake didn't want to lose, especially when one factored in the psychic value of pillaging his baby brother.

I explained to the Maggots how the bust-out worked.

Bobby was billed obscene rates for every service imaginable. All of these lucky vendors just happened to be entities owned and operated by the Maggots. Kadaborah had Bobby's proxy to authorize payments to these vendors. While this proxy was legally granted, the law looked harshly upon those who abused the privilege and funneled cash into their own pockets.

I handed over a small article from the *Los Angeles Beacon* from last June headlined "Two Cadavers Missing from U.C.L.A. Med School." This was one of the papers that Detective Galen had handed me when he arrested Bobby. I did not share with the Maggots a notation Galen had scrawled on another piece of paper that a former adult film actor (who had appeared with Tic Turner in the X-rated *The Talented Mr. Nippley*) was being questioned by the authorities in Los Angeles, as was an airport security officer who had vanished. As best as I could figure, Galen's operating hunch was that Turner had presented false pilot credentials (using D'Amico's and Harwood's names) at the airport in Los Angeles, and had loaded the plane with two cadavers courtesy of an old porn buddy to "pose" as the dead pilots and/or Bobby at the crash site.

The Maggots ignored my handout. "May I remind you, Jonah, that there's nothing illegal about having lucrative contracts to manage a celebrity's complex affairs," Kadaborah said. Another admission. Beautiful.

"You got me there, Reverend. But it sure doesn't look good."

"*Look good?* Do you think those stunts you've been pulling for us look good?"

The counterthreat. Don't flinch.

"I just give advice on public opinion," I said. "I don't know anything about stunts. If I were you, I'd be thinking about documented proof, things that can be traced, verified—things that might justify, say, helping to cover up a murder, or crashing a fifty-million-dollar aircraft loaded with stolen cadavers in the woods."

"And who, other than you, has been doing all of this tracing and verifying?"

"Derek Plush. *Major Player.* And he's the one person in the world who would believe that Bobby would crash his own plane. He knows everything. He's running with it. I understand you posed for pictures, too. He said you look great. Tic, you've got that Hollywood player look, the all-black mystery-man thing. The way you kept Bobby doubting himself, smacking himself with those whips—"

"Bobby was free to choose his spiritual commitments," Kabarorah said.

"Free? I don't know. If Bobby knew you could unleash goons—kind of like the ones you sent to roll me on the Boardwalk that time—it doesn't sound too free."

"They said you didn't fight back for shit, Mr. Gangster," Secret Agent Turner said, adding, "By the way, you ever heard of libel?"

"Suing about a story you placed? I don't think so, boys. See, there's something you need to understand about investigative reporters. Every assignment begins and ends with a question: Who do I screw? Looks like you make the better screw. Besides, our little discussion here has been captured, digitally, of course."

Kadaborah scanned the room impotently for eavesdropping devices. "This is an invasion of privacy!"

"No, it's not. Tic's laptop on the table over there, the one with the camera and audio chip you acquired to keep Bobby happy? You bugged yourself, boys." I did not add that Dorkus was operating the apparatus remotely, an added dividend of our earlier hacking.

"We said nothing here that we wouldn't tell the world," Kadaborah said.

Ah, the false disclosure, the proclamation of openness that will never be fulfilled. Never has the current state of public relations been so beautifully encapsulated. Like Congressman Gary Condit, who, when confronted about his affair with the missing (and murdered) intern Chandra Levy, declared, "Ask me anything!" and proceeded to answer nothing, like a cold, dead mackerel.

"Looks like you'll get that chance."

What I did not share with the Maggots was just how much Derek Plush had to work with. It's best to see that kind of thing for the first time in print.

Gorgeous Lives

"Human behavior expands in accordance with what
one expects to get away with."

There is a set of makeshift stands that sits beneath the tusk of Lucy the Elephant in Margate. Derek Plush was sitting on them, following Lucy's gaze out over the Atlantic. Here was my Big Theory on fame chroniclers: What masquerades as moral outrage is really envy. They long for the stardom they so savagely criticize. Those who are obsessed enough with fame to devote their careers to chronicling it go through life with a pulsating voice that says, "It should be me," or, conversely, "Why him?" Failing to achieve this fame, the reporter enables the downfall he will ultimately chronicle, which, of course, leads to a derivative of the stardom he himself aches for. There are legitimate objections to excesses and violations, but implicit in these objections is the belief that if "I" were famous, "I" wouldn't blow up like Marlon Brando. Human behavior expands in accordance with what one expects to get away with.

Plush knew his market was huge because those born after the inauguration of John F. Kennedy were taught that their covenant with God was Iconhood. In exchange for that visibility, what our generation owed God was, well, just us being us. There was to be no debt at our end. We were only to grace the Almighty with our intrinsic specialness.

It wasn't that renown as a concept was new, it was its pervasive intimacy in our lives. There was a show on MTV called *Cribs,* in which one was invited into the celebrity's home, and could actually see the toilet where the star voided his or her bowels beside a neatly displayed magazine rack stocked with the latest periodicals (which often featured, go figure, the *Cribs* guest star). Was this the new Xanadu, the Divine Trifecta—being filmed on the can while reading a cover story about oneself? Whereas Ralph Lauren sold style, Martha Stewart sold perfection, and Jenny Craig sold hope, Derek Plush peddled resentment—a craftily worded affirmation that a fluke had befallen us, short-circuiting the Fame Covenant. Why *him?* Why *her?* We seethed as we read about how well things were going for Julia Roberts.

I sat beside Plush and handed him a midsized envelope containing the CD-ROM that Dorkus had pulled from my laptop the day Bobby pressured Turner to e-mail me the photo of us.

"If what you told me is on here, Jonah, is on here, this'll be a blockbuster. I'm still dumbfounded that these Maggots, as you call them, didn't snag Bobby's music library, that it was just a garden-variety grift."

"No, Derek, they didn't have the brains to go after the jackpot. They're really just schnorrers—mooches, leeches. Getting that library would have been a world-class twist."

"Are you sure you don't want to be quoted in some way? I usually throw my sources a valentine of some kind."

"I like to stay offstage."

"Tell me, Jonah, what motivates you to vindicate the indefensible—offstage? Mafia bosses. Reptilian politicians. Rock stars turned black holes. Is it spite against humanity? I can't tell if you love it or hate it." He stretched out the word *loooove.* "And don't tell me it's just a living. A man like you has options."

"Some people climb Mount Everest despite the risk. I climb icons. They repulse me but define me. They define me the way that a terrible mountain defines the lunatics who climb it. I suppose I find out who I am by scaring myself while I explore who I am not. And, occasionally, I get paid."

"Enchanting, really."

"My candor ends here. Now yours."

"Do you know of Marshall McLuhan, Jonah?" Plush didn't await my response. He knew I knew "of" McLuhan. It was my business to know the great media thinkers. "McLuhan once said that the bad news of reality gives way to the good news of advertising. Journalism is gone. It's just advertising now. These gorgeous lives I chronicle, these characters who've got the big secret that makes life one sustained orgasm—everybody else's life but yours?" Plush appeared as if he might cry. "Well, Jonah, I like pissing on that fantasy, pure and simple. Shining light on the rot gives me joy, it's a public service, an antidote to our American longing, the ceaseless wanting of more, more, more. My magazine's job is to make its readers feel like you've botched your life, and the only way you'll ever get it right is to keep reading, waiting in line outside our door for an invitation. Then, when you return to our pages yet again, you'll find yourself barred again, but you keep coming back with hope to this party you think we've invited you to attend. But you weren't invited to attend, you were invited to *watch*. And the cycle goes on. Like you, I know that some of what I do is wrong. I go overboard and whatnot. But I want everyone to know what I know: *There are no gorgeous lives.*"

I left Plush feeling more frightened by stardust than I ever was by my grandfather's old gang. At least with the racket boys, their menace was on the table and you knew the rules: Don't steal their money, don't poach their women, don't insult their fragile dignity, and don't impede their red-blooded American right to steal. With the celebrity crowd, it's hard to raise your fight-or-flight defenses in the company of a starfucking proctologist, but you should.

Just Like Everybody Else

"Hoffa was a suicide."

Bobby had been despondent during police questioning. His new trial lawyer, a competent South Jersey camera whore named Yale Mink, insisted that Bobby remain silent. He listened.

Yale Mink also insisted that Bobby remain isolated from the rest of the inmates. The cops complied until after Mink left and Bobby began barking orders, as if the Atlantic City Jail was room service at the Fontainbleu. The on duty ACPD captain, resentful of Bobby's antics throughout the summer, insisted that he be thrown into the holding tank "just like everybody else."

Bobby lasted four minutes, according to an ex-con sailor who had been in a barroom fight earlier that evening. The sailor was to recount his story in a whirlwind media tour in the weeks and months ahead.

The holding cell was vomit green. The paint was chipped in some places. In others, the August heat caused it to bubble up in the corners. There were now six men in the twelve-by-twelve cell, which consisted of three walls and one row of stubby floor-to-ceiling bars that paralleled a forlorn basement hallway.

The dominant primate was a thug in his fifties who had a clunky prosthetic arm that had been fabricated prior to the advancement of lightweight polymers. The men had been in various stages of sitting and standing. There were no magazines, clocks, windows, or other distractions. Strangely, there wasn't even graffiti to read.

Then Bobby came in wearing skintight jeans, straw Western hat, boots, and a chamois shirt. The imprisoned men just stared with quizzical grins when the guard opened the barred door, unlocked Bobby's handcuffs, and left.

Contrary to the prison clichés, there were no catcalls. No kissy noises, no threats of sodomy. There was no talking. The other men just studied Bobby, the first object of curiosity they had probably had in a very long time. Bobby, for his part, was curious, too. He studied his cellmates in return.

Until he had something to say. Bobby heard something that bothered him. He traced it to the wrist of the man with the prosthetic arm. Lead-arm wore a cheap watch that loudly ticked.

"Would you take that off?"

Lead-arm was stunned, a sentiment he expressed by surveying the eyes of the others in the holding tank. Some of the other men smiled like the damned.

The sailor-witness, for his part, didn't smile. He looked away.

The rage of a hundred lifetimes erupted in Lead-arm, who said, "Repeat that, Mega Boy?"

"Your watch," Bobby said. "It's annoying. Give it to the guard until I leave."

"When are you leaving, Mega Boy?"

"I'm not Mega Boy! And I'm leaving in a few minutes."

Lead-arm slammed Bobby across the temple. Bobby fell and hit the back of his head against a giant steel bolt that fastened the wall of prison bars to the concrete floor. Bobby, delirious, laughed a little, as if he were befuddled as opposed to scared, and coughed out, "Waste your summer prayin' in vain for a savior to rise from these streets," a verse from Springsteen's "Thunder Road."

Interpreting Bobby's burst into song as an emasculating taunt, Lead-arm bent down, grabbed Bobby by his ears, and slammed his head against the floor bolt one more time.

When the guards got to the holding tank, there was blood and laughter and life hissing away. Lead-arm, who was being held for transfer for the fatal bludgeoning of a prostitute, hadn't had a damned thing to lose. In fact, taking out Turnpike Bobby Chin was a step up. He'd be in all the papers and live on forever in the Age of Notorious.

I found out about Bobby later that morning from the Cohn of Silence. The moment I hung up the phone, Edie and Irene knew something bad had happened. They set down Irene's luggage in the entryway; Edie was about to drive her to the airport. I checked to make sure the kids were out of earshot.

"Well, Irene, you struck again—in a sprint to the finish," I said, referring to how her visits correlated with celebrity deaths. "Bobby."

Edie and Irene exchanged expressions of shock. While they had no affection for Bobby, sad was sad, and they had grown up on his reruns.

Even though I was exhausted, I wanted to be with my kids. They were watching *SpongeBob* on the couch. I lay down, resting my head on Ricky's lap while Lily pulled at my hair. My thoughts about Bobby melted into a long-buried memory of my grandfather.

In Mickey's world, there were questions one didn't ask. One such question was, "Who killed Jimmy Hoffa?" One time, though, I did ask him what he thought of the Hoffa legend.

"Hoffa was a suicide," Mickey said, immediately and, ostensibly, frankly. "The guys who did it liked him. They told him to retire, he could have all the dough he wanted."

"Then why did he try to get his old job back?" I asked, stunned by this epic dialogue.

"Because," Mickey said, "being Jimmy was all he knew."

That was all Mickey said, and we never discussed it again. It didn't make sense to me at the time. In fact, I thought Mickey might be playing with me. Now it made sense. Men of great abilities are also men of limited abilities. All Hoffa knew was running the Teamsters. Telling him to retire was like explaining quantum physics to a Yorkshire terrier. All Bobby knew was how to be Bobby, a creature who had never learned to negotiate a contract with life. This incapacity was glorious in the short-term, but fatal in the long run. If one's first experience with life's compromises occurs at middle age, it's too late. He had been stripping men of their watches for decades. Why would he expect a one-armed psychopath to be any different?

The Monte Carlo Teardrop

"You manufactured the perfect relationship."

The outpouring and vigils for Turnpike Bobby Chin were spontaneous, but muted. Anticlimax was in the air, a sense that we had just done this. I had a horrible thought: Bobby had gotten his death right the first time. Sure, it was a fraud, but it was also fresh, surprising, the way we consumers liked it. Like many entertainers, he had screwed up his encore by not knowing when to leave. Very few entertainers can stay onstage forever. Springsteen is one of them. He keeps playing, and nobody leaves. When the crowds dwindle, he'll do shore clubs again, and he'll be all right with it because what he really loves is the music.

Turnpike Bobby songs were unavoidable on the radio. His lyrics were analyzed like Biblical verse, drowning out the chitchat about the fate of Kaylee Hopewell. The most mordant interpretations of Bobby's music were permitted. One verse from a song on the *Turnpike Immortal* album always sounded to me like, *"I gotta heed Saul Bellow's nostrils."* An authority on pop culture music believed the words were actually "I'm gonna be all fellows' nightmare." Nevertheless, a stoner called in and argued that Bobby was really "imploring us to heed Saul Bellow's nostrils," that this meant something of profound gravity. I'd have to read *Herzog* once and for all.

I shuddered when one Philadelphia radio station announced that the song Bobby had sung for me, "Flameout," had been recorded, and was going to be released by an outfit called South Street Records. When had Bobby recorded this? And South Street? That was Doo-Wop territory. *Nah,* I thought, Doo-Wop had made a whole point of conveying his lack of involvement with Bobby. Haunted, I called the Cohn of Silence. No answer.

The Celebrity Motel was buzzing with out-of-shape families from the hinterlands. On my way up the steps to Mustang Sally's I passed a young married couple. The husband appeared to be walking on eggshells. The wife wore a facial expression that suggested having stepped in something coagulating. *"Here?"* her demeanor conveyed, "We're staying *here?*" I mouthed a prayer, thanking God I was not married to her.

I knocked on Mustang's door.

"Just a second," she said.

The door opened. An attractive but hard-looking woman stepped out, clutching a few prescriptions. She didn't meet my eye, the way one doesn't when one visits a doctor for an embarrassing ailment, or buys porn.

"Notice anything?" Mustang said.

I instinctively bore in on her chest.

"Let me guess: Thirty-four C."

"You got it, doll. I went with the Monte Carlo Teardrop."

"Intrepid."

"See how they taper down, naturally, very contoured?"

"Oh, yes."

"With the teardrop, you avoid looking like Buckminster Fuller set up shop under your neck. No geodesic domes here, babe."

"Ample yet tasteful. Protuberant yet not pendulous."

"Bless your heart."

"What should I get done, Stang? My hair's thinning, for one thing."

"You've got the hairline of a man your age, but you're still built like a college kid. It's a good combo. Keep it up, that's your assignment. Men who get hair work done are concealing a deeper tragedy."

"I don't want to walk around looking like a human toothbrush anyhow."

"Good for you. How are you dealing with the *dénouement?* Loony Boy got what he wanted—went out at the center of a drama."

"I guess we predicted how it would end. Just didn't have the details."

"I bet a lot of grotesque stuff is going to come out, huh, babes?"

My mind was still locked in on how a record label was going to release "Flameout." South Street? I had a bad feeling.

"Yoo-hoo, Jonah—"

"Sorry. I watched a woman flagellate herself bloody. That's what Bobby did to get those marks he had on him."

"Kept him as sane as possible. That's how cults snag big shots. They give them a God, something to keep them in line."

"You make it sound routine."

"It is. It's why gorgeous women go for brutes, like we discussed. People need there to be a force in their lives to keep them in line. Everybody in the head racket knocks religion. Not me. You won't hear me knocking a higher order. How are things going with the nightmares, the au pair, all that mind garbage?"

"I'm okay."

"You have a strange way of playing out these affairs."

"What do you mean?"

"You know exactly what I mean. Middle age. That longing men have. Most men cheat. You, Jonah—you created yourself a virgin, a fresh new life, a utopia, a receptacle for all that repressed energy. You manufactured the perfect relationship—a woman who doesn't exist.

What could possibly go wrong? Actually, knowing you, you'll miss her, too. You men . . . no matter how old you get, you never give up hope that you may still turn into a superhero. I'd like to shrink down to the size of a molecule and go spelunking around in that head of yours."

"Who knows, I may be back to talk some more."

"Say what you will about your grandfather, he left you with something that is growing extinct in American Jewish men."

"I'm afraid to hear what this legacy is."

"Simple. You have your doubts, but you don't wear that desperation to be loved like a medallion. You're not like Spielberg."

"Spielberg? What's wrong with Spielberg?"

"All that success and he still flies around the world collecting awards. He's got that needy, yearning, sensitive face like the tailor Motel Kamzoil in *Fiddler on the Roof. Love me, for Christ's sake, I'm so very good!"*

"But he *is* good, Stang."

"Yeah, well, he should fucking know that by now. You know you're good, Jonah, even with your dramas. No doubt you'll be back, though. Me and my two friends will be waiting for you."

The Diversion

"An empty room was original sin."

indi stirred her coffee and sucked the excess liquid from the straw. Ozzie's in Longport was quiet, save for a cop at the counter working on a scone.

"Did Bobby record a song while he was here?" I asked.

"Well, that's a warm greeting."

"Sorry, I'm preoccupied. I just heard something about a record label releasing a new song Bobby played for me."

"What label?"

"South Street."

"That's not Bobby's label. His label is Sun World. South Street sounds local."

"That's what's bothering me. It makes me wonder if somebody slipped us a red herring."

Cindi lost interest in my latest preoccupation. "Well, bud, we had ourselves a successful failure," Cindi said. "In the end, your mendacity failed."

"But at least my heart was in the wrong place. You have to give me that. I never saw the Jake connection, that's for sure."

"You're a pollster, not a psychic. Somebody somewhere along the line tried to sell you on your own supernatural powers."

"Maybe. I'll just keep trying to figure out the lesson here, Cin."

"The lesson is we ought to get out of this business, Jonah."

"You more than me," I said.

"Oh, really? Why's that?"

"Why wouldn't you just tell me about the goose egg attendance for Bobby's concert, Cin?"

She sighed. "You did advance work for President Reagan, right?"

"Yes, right."

"What's an advance man's greatest crime, Jonah?"

Now I sighed. "An empty room."

"Right. An empty room. I couldn't fill it, Jonah. I was giving away free tickets, and people laughed. I never told Bobby the gory details, just that I couldn't fill it."

You didn't have to be in the publicity racket to understand Cindi was being utterly serious. An empty room was original sin, the crime from which all other crimes flowed.

"Failing to fill a room doesn't rise to the level of murder, destruction of a plane—"

"Thank you, Mr. Brady, that was a very helpful lesson for all us kids," Cindi huffed. She brushed aside a tear. "I think it may have triggered everything. I told Bobby about the attendance a week before the crash."

I thought of something Mustang Sally had told me at the outset: how the modus operandi of those around the icon is to "delay the tantrum." That's what Cindi had been trying to do. She failed, and the ultimate tantrum had come in the form of the plane crash, two murders, and God knows what else.

As Cindi contemplated her straw, a willow of a man vamped to our table. Unrepentantly effeminate, he kissed Cindi and said in a perfect Streisand, "Hello, gorgeous." He held out his hand to me and said, "If it's not my adorable Machiavelli with the dimples. I see you've got the rugged Ralph Lauren thing going, Jonah."

I stroked my face, unsure of what he meant. Machiavelli and Ralph Lauren in one sentence were a lot to process.

"Do you mean that I didn't shave, Freddy?" I asked.

"Of course. Do you use one of those special stubble razors for that, or do you just let it go nuts?" Freddy asked. Cindi was laughing.

"There's a razor that gives you stubble?"

Sitting down, Freddy said, "Would you listen to this breeder, Cindi? Of course there's an electric razor that leaves you with two days of stubble. Not like the close shave my friends and I needed in the trunk of that poor mayor's car."

"You did great."

"You betcha, by golly. What do you say you and me go out shopping for one of those razors? I'll get you all set up, real metro, my Jonah of Arc."

"I always thought razors were supposed to shave close. I just skipped a day," I said.

"So little time, so much knowledge to impart, peanut." Freddy said, adding, "so, campers, did you just *loovvve* your summertime Freddypalooza, or WHAT?"

As Freddy O'Shea, aka Freddy Zane, aka Teapot Freddy, Atlantic City's greatest casino shill and con man, unwound before us in all of his burlesque glory, my mind became a splicing room in which I connected this summer's optical farce.

There had never been a Kaylee Hopewell, only the idea of her. I dreamed her up after establishing the need to divert the ACPD, and after I saw that au pair on the beach in July. She moved me for all the reasons men at middle age are moved by Kaylees. Those reasons are a collision of hormones and hope, enzymes that need to propagate the species with someone richly deserving of a little propagation.

Kaylee was the personification of my Big Theory on Men, Women, and Power: It's eventually a man's world, but first, it's a young, beautiful woman's world. Her leverage is absolute and non-negotiable because it cannot be attacked on any rational or strategic basis. Like the eternal Middle East/Isaac and Ishmael struggle, Her power is rooted in something primal—that ache to possess, to be declared the Chosen One, who will never definitively be chosen (which only immortalizes the ache).

Mustang Sally had been right: I had to find a nonlethal way to play out the affair, so I orchestrated a fling between the public and the nonperson I had named Kaylee. The name sounded innocent and impossible. It was also in the top fifty names given to newborn girls in the early 2000s. As for the surname Hopewell, this was the name of the New Jersey town where the Lindbergh baby was kidnapped.

What I failed to tell Mustang was how protective I had become of this imaginary woman. I had became outraged when Bobby, who had never been told about the diversion, had made his devouring remarks about her. My outrage turned inward when I realized that his jealousy of Kaylee rendered Bobby capable of hurting her. I don't know what was sicker, my fear of what Bobby might do to Kaylee or my obsessive worry over a woman who I had dreamed up.

One of Chief Willie's wrestling buddies, the one known as the Viking, had made a trip to Denmark. His job was to "cast" Kaylee. Smitten with my favorite au pair, I provided a general description.

I wanted the photo of Kaylee to be in black and white because it lent her an aura of otherworldliness. One wouldn't need evidence to know she was gone, the photo would say it. In an age of infinite color, when we can pinpoint the contours in polyps and the exact moment when warbling sluts lost their virginities, Kaylee's defining characteristics were the things we didn't know about her.

I was nervous when the first cycle of Kaylee news dried up. When Chief Desmond of the ACPD expressed skepticism about the Kaylee case, we didn't retreat, we just hit him harder. Audacity was the answer. Tragedies, after all, will always be portrayed as being somebody's fault in Perpetual News America.

When the Viking was in Denmark, he had been tasked with procuring two visuals: the black-and-white photo of Kaylee and the grainy footage of her being shoved into the black SUV.

Teapot Freddy played a crucial role when Kaylee began to go stale. Disguised in his thespian best as a nicely baritoned newsman, Freddy became the star of a handful of "video news releases," known in the public relations world as "VNRs."

In an age of packaged news, all you need to gain notoriety is a resonant story concept, the players to execute it, and the technological means to convey it. The VNR was our technology. VNRs were, quite literally, press releases created in broadcast form for a paying client. Footage was transmitted by satellite to newsrooms all over the country. Those newsrooms could take bits and pieces of the VNR and use them as they wished. The key was to have short enough segments that contained footage that people wanted to see. This summer, everybody wanted to see more of Kaylee Hopewell.

Every time we released a VNR via satellite, the New Jersey authorities began searching for leads in Franklin, Riverside, Salem, and Springfield, the towns from where Freddy Zane had claimed to be broadcasting. They found nothing in these towns because there was nothing. Because Freddy Zane had not specified the *state*, the police eventually began to wonder if these towns might be outside New Jersey. They expanded their investigations into other states. The problem then became that most states in the United States had Franklins, Riversides, Salems, and Springfields. Jersey girl Kaylee Hopewell could have been from anywhere and everywhere.

By the time the authorities began to suspect they might be chasing ghosts, everyone who had appeared—thickly disguised and falsely identified—on camera had long vanished. None of the players ever knew each other's real names.

There was no kidnapper, Wayne Hatfield, either. Every year, the humorist Dave Barry does a rundown on criminals named Wayne. There are lots of naughty Waynes, apparently. That's the joke, of course—that being named Wayne destines a child to a life of violent crime. The surname Hatfield? Pure redneck. The Viking had found a Copenhagen chef who wanted to make a little extra money doing a crime prevention film. All the chef had to do was put on a dark wig, wear one of those cheap mesh baseball caps Americans wear, and stuff our damsel in distress into a black SUV outside the nondescript store rear.

Evelyn Wallace of Hammonton, after a lifetime of suing people and institutions that had done her wrong, had given up. Our litigation database research revealed a woman who furiously awaited Destiny, and wasn't picky about whatever form it came in. For twenty-five grand in cash, there wasn't much she wouldn't allege. She did a great job following our talking points on the kidnapper and his vehicle.

Autumn would land with a rude thunk, and the police and the media, having nothing new in L'affaire Kaylee, would begin to question Evelyn Wallace. For four summer weeks, Evelyn was the only game in town. By that point, she would have embraced her star status and stopped at nothing to retain it. She would become a diva, not unlike Turnpike Bobby Chin, her arm's-length employer. Evelyn was a potential savior to the desperate police, who escorted her to and from stations around the region as if she were a visiting dignitary. To the press, she was the ultimate "get."

There was always a chance she might break and confess. What would she say? That a great big red-headed Indian emerged from the Pine Barrens with a bundle of cash and made her say she witnessed the kidnapping?

Kaylee sightings might continue, but where would the authorities look? Some women, searching for their own destiny, might even claim to be the Kaylee in the picture. Fine. What were the chances that a beat cop in Jersey would have an epiphany and conclude that there was a pretty waitress in Copenhagen looking for a few extra bucks who decided to be Kaylee for about a half-hour?

Everything else was accomplished anonymously. The video and the Kaylee photo were e-mailed from walk-in photo shops in Trenton. We phoned in the initial media and police tips (including the one "identifying" Wayne Hatfield), but public hysteria took care of the rest. The campers who claimed to see the black SUV leaving the Pine Barrens field that night were, for all we knew, reporting something they actually saw. America was filled with black SUVs leaving campsites.

The firestorms that followed each morsel of "news" about Kaylee delivered the hounds of hell to the doorstep of the ACPD. We put so much pressure on them that the cops could not properly investigate what had or had not happened to Christian Josi. During the time that the authorities were diverted from the hunting of Turnpike Bobby Chin, we solved Christian's murder and unraveled the unholy apparatus surrounding him.

Detective Galen's confrontation of Kadaborah and I in Lou's restaurant had been a ruse. I wanted Kadaborah to be nervous, and to believe the two of us were equally suspect in the eyes of the authorities. After Dorkus determined that Lonesome Jake had searched for directions to Lebanon State Forest on his computer on the night of the murder, I fudged the truth and told Galen I had heard Jake "talking about" Lebanon. The objective of Galen's interrogation had been to hint to Kadaborah that he knew Christian might have been buried there. While I didn't know this for sure at the time, it seemed like the kind of thing that might rattle Kadaborah's cage and pressure him to have Lonesome Jake move the body. This would make a nice opportunity to catch him at work. Judging from Lonesome Jake's actions on the night he was killed, Kadaborah must have told him about Galen's mentioning of Lebanon.

Turnpike Bobby Chin was constitutionally incapable of doing

anything but squandering our ill-gotten opportunity. Bobby provoked the law, the news media, and the gods at every turn. By being shielded from life's frictions and workaday indignities, he came to believe that aerodynamics was for others. All the king's horses and all the king's men can't do anything for a lunatic egg hell-bent on diving from very high walls.

My cell phone rang. I excused myself to Cindi and Freddy. The wily voice spoke: "I understand you've been looking for me, *boychik?*"

The Music

"So much of who a person is comes down to where they put their passions."

The Cohn of Silence's ice cream truck jingled into our driveway. Ricky and Lily, as expected, had a volcanic reaction. They ran outside, jumping up and down like pogo sticks until the window slid open and the bullfrog mouth of Mr. Cohn's brother, Izzy, appeared. I slapped a five-dollar bill on the ledge and insisted on paying. Both kids chose a Popsicle that mimicked a red, white, and blue rocket ship. I patted them on their behinds, and they ran back inside. I anticipated finding a patriotic trail of water ice on the carpet soon enough.

The Cohn of Silence stepped from the truck. "It's the Sabbath. Good *yontif.*"

"*Ich bin ein Berliner.*"

"Excellent point. Well, it's over," he said, gesturing for me to walk.

"How's by you, Mr. Cohn?"

"I'm having my prostate removed next week."

"Are you?"

"Yes. My philosophy is, throw out what you don't use."

"Makes sense. . . . Well, it ended like you thought it would, Mr. Cohn."

"I can usually predict the result. The method becomes academic."

"Were you as stunned as I was that Lonesome Jake was Bobby's brother?"

"In retrospect, it makes sense. I don't know, son, with these things, there's always an X factor, some variable that you should have seen, but didn't."

"You knew he was dirty, though."

"I knew there were no virgins in show business, only whores."

The Cohn of Silence reached into his pocket and handed me a large check. "This should cover you and your rapscallions."

"It's nice when people pay."

"Why, is somebody not paying you?"

"I had a problem recently, but it's okay now."

"*Mazel tov.* I hope nobody got hurt."

"He'll be fine."

"Good. I'm sure your methods of enlightenment were most noble. You probably inherited your grandfather's debt collection techniques."

"Do you know any of them?"

The Cohn of Silence gazed heavenward. "Mickey was always very gentle at first, very patient. What bothered him was all the creativity people put into not paying. He used to say that if people put as much industry into working as they do malingering, we would be a productive society. But that's not people, I suppose. It's easier to build Potemkin villages to cover your failures than it is to go about the boring business of working to improve things. Cover up. Cover up. It's what people do. It goes back to Adam and Eve. What's the first thing they did when they got pinched on the apple thing? They covered up, and so do we. So much of who a person is comes down to where they put their passions."

"Something to think about. I've got lots of stuff to think about, like a man I met this summer called Doo-Wop. He didn't look old enough to have been a big player when that doo-wop music was big."

Cohn laughed. "Ah, Doo-Wop. I heard you met. Back then, Doo-Wop was a teenager. He loved the music, so your grandfather kept him close to the action because nobody ever suspects a kid of anything. Doo-Wop kept his eyes on the acts, reported back to Mick and whatnot. As he got older, Mick gave him responsibility, and finally Doo-Wop had his own thing."

"But he worked for Mickey, right?"

"As a kid, yes. The thing about your grandfather that everybody got wrong was this: Mick didn't have to control everything. That was his genius. He knew you couldn't control everything, that it was futile. He had tried that during Prohibition, and it didn't work. So Mick just took a taste. When you try to dominate everything is when the trouble starts. The FBI and the press"—Cohn laughed—"they were always looking for an organization. That's what they got wrong. There wasn't one, just independent operators who made deals on the fly. Then, when Mick died, people asked, 'Who inherited the big empire?' It was all personality driven: Guy #1 trusts another Guy #2 on a given Tuesday. When Guy #1 dies or goes to prison, it's not like you train another guy in that life to replace him like in a dental practice, because it's all driven by personality, skills, contacts, and how these things come together at a particular time. Doo-Wop's his own man. And your grandfather? He lived to be almost a hundred, unlike the other *vilda chayas* in his world."

As we approached the seawall, I spied a familiar figure sitting with his buttery woven loafers against the concrete. Doo-Wop?

I looked to the Cohn of Silence for a justification of this serendipity. "Now, son, I want you to hear something from us before you hear it on the grapevine. You with me?"

An invisible toad began jumping around my digestive tract. A surge of something that felt ambiguously hot and cold fell through me. Mr. Cohn's preamble, combined with Doo-Wop's sudden appearance, was reminiscent of:

*J*onah, honey, Daddy got very, very sick last night . . ."

 Jonah, sweetheart, Mommy found a little bump and went to see the doctor . . ."

"Now listen, kid, those goddamned Nazis in the FBI are stirring up all kinds of trouble for us. A van's gonna pick you up at school. You go out the back door . . ."

All of those introductions resulted in death, orphanhood, and fugitive life. Oh, and the alleged strengthening of my character, which had been doing fine prior to God's hatred of my family becoming self-evident. *Et tu, Doo-Wop?*

Doo-Wop rose from the seawall and shook my hand. His smile was warm, his lyrical eyes appearing reticent. I was not going to be gunned down here and now. Something else was coming.

As the three of us took positions on the seawall, an autumnal breeze whipping through our linens, the Cohn of Silence continued his verbal journey: "People always made your grandfather's world into a corporation like Procter & Gamble, a business that grinds out soap day in and day out. All bullshit. It was always about opportunities grabbed today—"

"Usually based on someone else's foolishness," Doo-Wop interjected.

"Jonah," the Cohn of Silence said, "I was the one who told Doo-Wop that he should talk to you. I told him that we—you and I—were looking around on Bobby's behalf, and that some of our looking might carry in his direction."

"My head began spinning with opportunity," Doo-Wop said. "I wanted to get a feel for you and make sure you were your grandfather's grandson in the noodles department."

"Am I?" I asked.

"Same wattage," Doo-Wop said, "different kind of bulb. Mickey had a head for figures. You've got the poet in you."

The Cohn of Silence continued: "I spent some time with Bobby. I saw where things were headed. I had your little friend Cindi hook the press up with Bobby's sister-in-law, additional interviews with his pain-in-the-ass mother. So Bobby got so angry, he changed his will to make sure they were aced out of his estate."

"So, who gets the music library, all of his assets?" I asked.

"That's where things get interesting," the Cohn of Silence said. "These Maggots really bled him—just schnorrers. Your intelligence on that account was spot-on, very valuable, although I didn't realize how many old movies were in the collection until we dug into it. With all these satellites and cables and whatnot, they've got to fill it with something. Anyhow, they bled him so badly, Bobby needed cash to survive."

"We negotiated a fire-sale price for his library," Doo-Wop said. "I paid about twenty cents on the dollar for it."

"You own Bobby's library now?" I asked. Master of the Obvious.

"South Street Music, to be accurate," Doo-Wop said.

"So somebody wanted the music library all along?" I said.

"Incorrect," Mr. Cohn said. "Not until Lonesome Jake pulled the idea out of his dirty boxers, and you ferried it to me. Of course, the Maggots are partners in South Street Music. We made them feel they were getting a piece of the library for a steal. Unfortunately, as you know, adverse publicity is about to befall them thanks to you, Jonah, as is a criminal investigation thanks to certain ambitious individuals within law enforcement you need not concern yourself with. The banks that financed the Maggots' part ownership will call the loan. Fortunately, Doo-Wop will be there to buy out their share. After all, they will need to pay for attorneys and whatnot."

"We apologize for using you in this manner," Doo-Wop said with ostensible sincerity, adding, "But an opportunity is an opportunity."

"What do you think the library would fetch on the open market?" I asked, feeling oddly fatalistic. After all, how can a manipulator justify his outrage at having been manipulated?

"Now that Bobby's gone, probably between fifty and a hundred million. It includes his own music, the films, which will now be seen as classics of some kind," Doo-Wop said, adding, "You'll receive a delivery in currency of two hundred thousand dollars. Does that seem fair?"

"As a finder's fee? Sure."

"It's not a finder's fee," Mr. Cohn corrected. "Nobody found anything. It's just foolish arithmetic."

I nodded in agreement.

Doo-Wop and the Cohn of Silence ambled down the steps of the seawall toward the ice cream truck. "You probably heard that I listened to 'Gravity Outlaw,' " Doo-Wop said. "What with all the news about the new release."

"And?"

"I liked it."

The Neon of Aborted Renewal

"In the Age of Notorious, there is no discretion. There is only footage."

Derek Plush sent me a hot-off-the-press edition of *Major Player*, which featured his ten-thousand-word cover story on Bobby. The cover photo was of Bobby on the Boardwalk draped in pale linens, gazing peacefully into the sun. Behind him, faceless fans milled about in soft-focus. There was something shamefully evangelical about the pose, a cirrus cloud, almost certainly airbrushed, floated above Bobby's scalp aping a halo.

The opening paragraphs follow:

THE BUST-OUT OF TURNPIKE BOBBY CHIN
By Derek Plush
Exclusive to *Major Player*

My story of the rise and fall of Robert Barton Chin is a whodunit. It is a murder mystery set in coastal New Jersey where there is more than one killer and more than one victim. To complicate matters, some of the victims will prove to be the killers and some of the killers will turn out to be the victims. If you're confused, you should be.

The recent death of Bobby Chin was not "tragic," despite the enormous media predilection for deploying that word. The real tragedy was Bobby's life. If you are looking for a eulogy, stop reading. If you want to know about what catastrophic success did to Bobby Chin, read on.

The first thing you need to know is that Bobby Chin was not a nice guy. Bobby's self-depiction was riddled with references to "sharing" and "giving"—the watchwords of New Age sensitivity— but when pressed for specifics of sacrifice, he was unable to point to a single thing that validated this portrait other than his solipsistic belief in his own martyrdom. To the contrary, all evidence suggests that Bobby Chin's generosity was uniquely bestowed upon none other than Bobby Chin. A more charitable analysis of Bobby's life, however, might lead with the conclusion that Bobby was generous in the end because his antics provided the public with titillation, which we value for better or worse. Bobby lived and died for our amusement.

His musical talent was marginal, his self-inflicted rivalry with that other New Jersey rocker, Bruce Springsteen, laughable. Bobby's showmanship, however, was prescient—pop culture history may well remember him as a pioneer in the merchandising of personality as opposed to talent. Bobby Chin beat the boy bands, J. Lo and the never-ending circus of teen tarts to the store shelves by two decades at least, no small achievement.

For all of his pathological self-indulgence, like Springsteen's mythological Johnny 99, Bobby's palpable guilt cannot be judged without considering the human landscape in which his crimes took place. That crime scene was South Jersey, a rugged wilderness with America's cradle, Philadelphia, at one end, and the neon of aborted renewal, Atlantic City, at the other.

Bobby Chin the boy and Bobby Chin the man had been pillaged by a pack of predators throughout his life, beginning with his immediate family and ending with his pseudoreligious management team, spearheaded by a disgraced South Jersey proctologist and his aide-de-camp, a minor porn star.

Unlike in the movies, most conspiracies are not hatched, they are improvised. Things already in motion due to nature, not guile, are built upon, coopted, and exploited on the go. Still, the whole debauched game rests on the weakness of the principal, in this case a soul who was once anointed "Mega Boy," and his unrelenting desperation for exposure.

A thirst for notoriety and rekindled fame, of course, is not new. What may be, however, are the multiple methods of self-display that are now available to the Turnpike Bobby Chins of the world, and how these media can be a vicious tiger that eats her rider when he finally falls. In prior eras, exposure came and went. Naughty agents did dirty deeds whispered in poorly lit restaurants, stars did what they did at the Château Marmont, unpleasantness was covered up, rumors were denied, and that was that.

What makes the rape and pillage of Bobby Chin especially disturbing is that it was all memorialized in a way that is indisputable and immortal. In the old days, smart meant discreet. In the Age of Notorious, there is no discretion. There is only footage.

Roll tape.

The remainder of Plush's narrative portrayed an intricate mosaic of Turnpike Bobby Chin's life as a collection of impulses that occasionally collided with external events. He was an entertainment phenomenon, short of musical talent, long on shtick. Plush pegged the death of Christian Josi as manslaughter on Bobby's part, but the killing of Lonesome Jake as aggravated homicide provoked by Jake's extortion. Both deaths were positioned as having derived from the waning of Bobby's fame and his suffering at the hands of the venal circle around him. Plush's harshest words were reserved for Kadaborah and Turner, who had pitched the story to *Major Player* in the first place. The Maggots came across as a mixture of greedy, clever, and stupid, the stupidity being a side effect of their own need to be in the story, which is where they really screwed up. Subscribers will surely believe, as I do, that they are reading a tragedy.

"Gravity Outlaw" was released by the South Street Records label in the only version it had been recorded, acoustic. Bobby's voice was raw and desperate, which was good. The lyrics were precisely as he had sung them for me. He had been right: I hadn't known anything about music. His verses contradicted themselves, but that was the point. Bobby had been delusional enough to mistake the G-forces he had been feeling for the rush of rocketing upward when, in fact, he had been crashing all along. That's what happens when a gyroscope fails. As Labor Day weekend approached, "Gravity Outlaw" was number one on most rock charts.

I had spent the summer as a tourist on that narrow plane where life's overdogs dwelled in all their freakishness, but I was just visiting that plane. This was something that I loved so much about Edie: despite her patrician bearing, she retained the earthbound soul of her Indian forbears. Edie stayed close to the wigwam. My greatest instinct is to stay on the reservation, too, but these middle years . . . the riptide must carry a man to strange places before he learns to love his home.

I used the occasion of Bobby's death to put the finishing touches on my Big Theory of success, which I accomplished during a run on the Boardwalk: the measure of a person is what he does after he peaks. Some people never get used to not being God, they remain outraged that they were not perpetually chosen. Nor can they accept that catastrophic success is nothing more than a cosmic collision between a desirable feature and the fragile moment in which that feature resonates.

I'm afraid of August. It's the devil's month. August is when young lovers correctly anticipate that it's all coming to an end, the fear of the end being the origin of their bond. In August, inland doctors pack their wives off for the shore while they meet young nurses at their one-bedroom suburban nests. In August, juvenile delinquents—

and some good kids, too—hammer cars with eggs in protest of impending restrictions. There is the plaintive hum of neighboring air conditioners, the elderly remaining cool indoors to contemplate winter.

Or maybe it's just me. My cortex is wired for overreflection, and I tend toward melancholy when I have too much August on my hands. I love watching my children engage the sea, but am attacked by pricks of sadness when waves wash over them, however swiftly. For those narrow seconds, I ask, "Where did they go?" I do better during the school year when there are schedules and tangible things to nail down.

I imagine the last twenty years of Turnpike Bobby's life to have been one protracted August, nothing to do but cook in his own exoskeleton. He was a dead planet suspended in space on gravity alone. Contrary to contemporary fantasies, living human beings are just not wired for protracted hibernation like the cicadas. And to think there is a part of me, of us, that covets that altitude above the commercial traffic, even though the air is too thin for life. The desire for this altitude isn't rational, but nothing is. Perhaps that's what Bobby, whose lyrics were critically dismissed as meaningless, meant after all—that what we want derives from what we feel, not what we reason.

My grandfather once told me that charming people are easily charmed. With this template, it's clear that media manipulators are easily manipulated. I had virtually invented Kaylee Hopewell and had fallen in love with my own snare. The affair was all about passion and faith, about what I badly needed to believe in at midlife. It wasn't because I was a tortured soul disappointed in his lot. I know I am blessed. Still, there's that clock ticking, and that ever-present crocodile reminding me that regardless of my blessings, everything is finite. Choice is choice.

August slides forward, the Atlantic throbs in, and the pulse of New

Jersey washes over the husks of the final few cicadas. I am wearing Bobby's St. Jude medallion as a reminder of lost causes. *Mega Boy* survives in reruns on a satellite tickling Venus. The spirits of Turnpike Bobby and Radical J prowl in a red Jaguar through neon to the Irish Pub to dope that ache for high altitudes, the applause of our mothers, and lost girls.

Acknowledgments

Norm Ornstein lent his name to the character Doo-Wop. Anyone who knows Norm knows that he is not really a music industry racketeer but a shadowy enforcer for the American Enterprise Institute who is not to be trifled with.

My friend Budd Schulberg's chronicles of fame, namely his 1957 film, *A Face in the Crowd,* have been critical touchstones. The Irish Pub's Cathy Burke imparted the history of her fine establishment.

Eric Smith, an airline pilot, indulged my fantasies about what nasty things might be done to a Gulfstream V if one were so inclined.

Christian Josi requested to be "brutally murdered" in a work of fiction. I am not certain why, but I was happy to oblige him. There were plenty of people I would rather have bludgeoned.

My thanks to Dr. Sally Satel for her psychiatric insights and for allowing me to borrow—and fabricate—some of her attributes in various sections of the book.

My wife, Donna, and children, Stuart and Eliza, have been supportive of my efforts to further besmirch the family name.

My colleagues John Weber, Malinda Waughtal, Maya Shackley, Marty Kramer, and the rest of the suspicious characters at Dezenhall Resources allow me to do what must be done.

My agents, Kris Dahl and Alan Rautbort at ICM, continue to be my champion, as does literary consigliere Bob Stein. Thanks also to Karen Robson.

My editor at Thomas Dunne Books, Sean Desmond, consistently provides insights that sharpen my work.

Nina Zucker, Craig Shirley, Kevin McVicker, Diana Banister, Sandi Mendelson, and Judy Hilsinger have been central to the shameless self-promotion that is essential to selling my books.